GALACTIC WAR

"Sirius is conducting successful espionage and we can't stop them," said Conway.

"And I suppose that what you want me to do is go out to Jupiter Nine and see if I can learn something."

Conway nodded gloomily. "It's what I'm asking you to do. But one thing, David"—and it was only at moments of deep concern that he used Lucky's real name, the one by which the young councilman had been known all through childhood—"I want you to appreciate the importance of this. If we don't find out what the Sirians are doing, it means they are really ahead of us at last. And that means war can't be delayed much longer.

"War or peace hangs on this."

By Isaac Asimov

LUCKY STARR AND THE MOONS OF JUPITER

&

LUCKY STARR AND THE RINGS OF SATURN

ISAAC ASIMOV
writing as Paul French

BANTAM BOOKS

NEW YORK · TORONTO · LONDON · SYDNEY · AUCKLAND

All the characters in this book are fictitious, and any resemblance
to actual persons living or dead is purely coincidental.

This edition contains the complete text
of the original hardcover edition.
NOT ONE WORD HAS BEEN OMITTED.

LUCKY STARR, BOOK 3

A Bantam Spectra Book / by arrangement with Doubleday

PUBLISHING HISTORY

*Lucky Starr and the Moons of Jupiter copyright © 1957 by
Doubleday.*
*Lucky Starr and the Rings of Saturn copyright © 1958 by
Doubleday.*

Bantam edition / June 1993

ISBN 0-553-29682-5

Published simultaneously in the United States and Canada

PRINTED IN THE UNITED STATES OF AMERICA

RAD   0 9 8 7 6 5 4 3 2 1

Lucky Starr
and the
Moons of Jupiter

CONTENTS

Preface

Back in the 1950s, I wrote a series of six derring-do novels about David "Lucky" Starr and his battles against malefactors within the Solar System. Each of the six took place in a different region of the system and in each case I made use of the astronomical facts—as they were then known.

LUCKY STARR AND THE MOONS OF JUPITER was written in 1956. In late 1973, however, the Jupiter-probe, Pioneer X, passed by Jupiter and recorded an enormous magnetic field containing dense concentrations of charged particles. The large satellites of Jupiter are buried in that field and the intensity of radiation would certainly make it difficult or even impossible for manned ships to maneuver in their neighborhood.

Lucky's trip through the satellite system would have to be adjusted to take the intense radiation into account if I were writing the book today. And in 1974, a 13th satellite of Jupiter was discovered, a very small one only a few miles across, with an orbit quite similar to that of Jupiter-IX. I'd have mentioned it if I were doing the book now.

I hope my Gentle Readers enjoy the book anyway, as

an adventure story, but please don't forget that the advance of science can outdate even the most conscientious science-fiction writer and that my astronomical descriptions are no longer accurate in all respects.

ISAAC ASIMOV

1

Trouble on Jupiter Nine

Jupiter was almost a perfect circle of creamy light, half the apparent diameter of the moon as seen from Earth, but only one seventh as brightly lit because of its great distance from the sun. Even so, it was a beautiful and impressive sight.

Lucky Starr gazed at it thoughtfully. The lights in the control room were out and Jupiter was centered on the visiplate, its dim light making Lucky and his companion something more than mere shadows. Lucky said, "If Jupiter were hollow, Bigman, you could dump thirteen hundred planets the size of Earth into it and still not quite fill it up. It weighs more than all the other planets put together."

John Bigman Jones, who allowed no one to call him anything but Bigman, and who was five feet two inches tall if he stretched a little, disapproved of anything that was big, except Lucky. He said, "And what good is all of it? No one can land on it. No one can come near it."

"We'll never land on it, perhaps," said Lucky, "but we'll be coming close to it once the Agrav ships are developed."

"With the Sirians on the job," said Bigman, scowling in the gloom, "it's going to take *us* to make sure that happens."

"Well, Bigman, we'll see."

Bigman pounded his small right fist into the open palm of his other hand. "Sands of Mars, Lucky, how long do we have to wait here?"

They were in Lucky's ship, the *Shooting Starr,* which was in an orbit about Jupiter, having matched velocities with Jupiter Nine, the giant planet's outermost satellite of any size.

That satellite hung stationary a thousand miles away. Officially, its name was Adrastea, but except for the largest and closest, Jupiter's satellites were more popularly known by numbers. Jupiter Nine was only eighty-nine miles in diameter, merely an asteroid, really, but it looked larger than distant Jupiter, fifteen million miles away. The satellite was a craggy rock, gray and forbidding in the sun's weak light, and scarcely worth interest. Both Lucky and Bigman had seen a hundred such sights in the asteroid belt.

In one way, however, it was different. Under its skin a thousand men and billions of dollars labored to produce ships that would be immune to the effects of gravity.

Nevertheless, Lucky preferred watching Jupiter. Even at its present distance from the ship (actually three fifths of the distance of Venus from Earth at their closest approach), Jupiter showed a disc large enough to reveal its colored zones to the naked eye. They showed in faint pink and greenish-blue, as though a child had dipped his fingers in a watery paint and trailed them across Jupiter's image.

Lucky almost forgot the deadliness of Jupiter in its beauty. Bigman had to repeat his question in a louder voice.

"Hey, Lucky, how long do we have to wait here?"

"You know the answer to that, Bigman. Until Commander Donahue comes to pick us up."

"I know that part. What I want to know is why we have to wait for him."

"Because he's asked us to."

"Oh, he has. Who does the cobber think he is?"

"The head of the Agrav project," Lucky said patiently.

"You don't have to do what he says, you know, even if he is."

Bigman had a sharp and deep realization of Lucky's powers. As full member of the Council of Science, that selfless and brilliant organization that fought the enemies of Earth within and without the solar system, Lucky Starr could write his own ticket even against the most high-ranking.

But Lucky was not quite ready to do that. Jupiter was a known danger, a planet of poison and unbearable gravity; but the situation on Jupiter Nine was more dangerous still because the exact points of danger were unknown— and until Lucky could know a bit more, he was picking his way forward carefully.

"Be patient, Bigman," he said.

Bigman grumbled and flipped the lights on. "We're not staring at Jupiter all day, are we?"

He walked over to the small Venusian creature bobbing up and down in its enclosed water-filled cage in the corner of the pilot room. He peered fondly down at it, his wide mouth grinning with pleasure. The V-frog always had that effect on Bigman, or indeed, on anyone.

The V-frog was a native of the Venusian oceans,* a tiny thing that seemed, at times, all eyes and feet. Its body was green and froglike and but six inches long. His two

* See *Lucky Starr and the Oceans of Venus.*

big eyes protruded like gleaming blackberries, and its
sharp, strongly curved beak opened and closed at irregu-
lar intervals. At the moment its six legs were retracted, so
that the V-frog hugged the bottom of its cage, but when
Bigman tapped the top cover, they unfolded like a carpen-
ter's rule and became stilts.

It was an ugly little thing but Bigman loved it when he
was near it. He couldn't help it. Anyone else would feel
the same. The V-frog saw to that.

Carefully Bigman checked the carbon-dioxide cylinder that kept the V-frog's water well saturated and health-
ful and made sure that the water temperature in the cage
was at ninety-five. (The warm oceans of Venus were
bathed by and saturated with an atmosphere of nitrogen
and carbon dioxide. Free oxygen, nonexistent on Venus
except in the man-made domed cities at the bottom of its
ocean shallows, would have been most uncomfortable for
the V-frog.)

Bigman said, "Do you think the weed supply is
enough?" and as though the V-frog heard the remark, its
beak snipped a green tendril off the native Venusian weed
that spread through the cage, and chewed slowly.

Lucky said, "It will hold till we land on Jupiter Nine,"
and then both men looked up sharply as the receiving
signal sounded its unmistakable rasp.

A stern, aging face was centered on the visiplate after
Lucky's fingers had quickly made the necessary adjustments.

"Donahue at this end," said a voice briskly.

"Yes, Commander," said Lucky. "We've been waiting
for you."

"Clear locks for tube attachment, then."

On the commander's face, written in an expression as
clear as though it consisted of letters the size of Class I
meteors, was worry—trouble and worry.

Lucky had grown accustomed to just that expression on men's faces in these past weeks. On Chief Councilman Hector Conway's for instance. To the chief councilman, Lucky was almost a son and the older man felt no need to assume any pretense of confidence.

Conway's rosy face, usually amiable and self-assured under its crown of pure white hair, was set in a troubled frown. "I've been waiting for a chance to talk to you for months."

"Trouble?" Lucky asked quietly. He had just returned from Mercury less than a month earlier, and the intervening time had been spent in his New York apartment. "I didn't get any calls from you."

"You earned your vacation," Conway said gruffly. "I wish I could afford to let it continue longer."

"Just what is it, Uncle Hector?"

The chief councilman's old eyes stared firmly into those of the tall, lithe youngster before him and seemed to find comfort in those calm, brown ones. "Sirius!" he said.

Lucky felt a stir of excitement within him. Was it the great enemy at last?

It had been centuries since the pioneering expeditions from Earth had colonized the planets of the nearer stars. New societies had grown up on those worlds outside the solar system. Independent societies that scarcely remembered their Earthly origin.

The Sirian planets formed the oldest and strongest of those societies. The society had grown up on new worlds where an advanced science was brought to bear on untapped resources. It was no secret that the Sirians, strong in the belief that they represented the best of mankind, looked forward to the time when they might rule all men everywhere; and that they considered Earth, the old mother world, their greatest enemy.

In the past they had done what they could to support

the enemies of Earth at home* but never yet had they felt
quite strong enough to risk open war.

But now?

"What's this about Sirius?" asked Lucky.

Conway leaned back. His fingers drummed lightly on
the table. He said, "Sirius grows stronger each year. We
know that. But their worlds are underpopulated; they
have only a few millions. We still have more human beings in our solar system than exist in all the galaxy besides. We have more ships and more scientists; we still
have the edge. But, by Space, we won't keep that edge if
things keep on as they've been going."

"In what way?"

"The Sirians are finding out things. The Council has
definite evidence that Sirius is completely up-to-date on
our Agrav research."

"What!" Lucky was startled. There were few things
more top-secret than the Agrav project. One of the reasons actual construction had been confined to one of the
outer satellites of Jupiter had been for the sake of better
security. "Great Galaxy, how has that happened?"

Conway smiled bitterly. "That is indeed the question.
How has that happened? All sorts of material are leaking
out to them, and we don't know how. The Agrav data is
most critical. We've tried to stop it. There isn't a man on
the project that hasn't been thoroughly checked for loyalty. There isn't a precaution we haven't taken. Yet material still leaks. We've planted false data and that's gone
out. We know it has from our own Intelligence information. We've planted data in such ways that it *couldn't* go
out, and yet it has."

"How do you mean *couldn't* go out?"

"We scattered it so that no one man—in fact, no half

---

* See *Lucky Starr and the Pirates of the Asteroids.*

dozen men—could possibly be aware of it all. Yet it went. It would mean that a number of men would have to be co-operating in espionage and that's just unbelievable."

"Or that some one man has access everywhere," said Lucky.

"Which is just as impossible. It must be something new, Lucky. Do you see the implication? If Sirius has learned a new way of picking our brains, we're no longer safe. We could never organize a defense against them. We could never make plans against them."

"Hold it, Uncle Hector. Great Galaxy, give yourself a minute. What do you mean when you say they're picking our brains?" Lucky fixed his glance keenly on the older man.

The chief councilman flushed. "Space, Lucky, I'm getting desperate. I can't see how else this can be done. The Sirians must have developed some form of mind reading, of telepathy."

"Why be embarrassed at suggesting that? I suppose it's possible. We know of one practical means of telepathy at least. The Venusian V-frogs."

"All right," said Conway. "I've thought of that, too, but they don't have Venusian V-frogs. I know what's been going on in V-frog research. It takes thousands of them working in combination to make telepathy possible. To keep thousands of them anywhere but on Venus would be awfully difficult, and easily detectable, too. And without V-frogs, there is no way of managing telepathy."

"No way we've worked out," Lucky said softly, "so far. It is possible that the Sirians are ahead of us in telepathy research."

"Without V-frogs?"

"Even without V-frogs."

"I don't believe it," Conway cried violently. "I can't

believe that the Sirians can have solved any problem that has left the Council of Science so completely helpless."

Lucky almost smiled at the older man's pride in the organization, but had to admit that there was something more than merely pride there. The Council of Science represented the greatest collection of intellect the galaxy had ever seen, and for a century not one sizable piece of scientific advance anywhere in the Galaxy had come anywhere but from the Council.

Nevertheless Lucky couldn't resist a small dig. He said, "They're ahead of us in robotics."

"Not really," snapped Conway. "Only in its applications. Earthmen invented the positronic brain that made the modern mechanical man possible. Don't forget that. Earth can take the credit for all the basic developments. It's just that Sirius builds more robots and," he hesitated, "has perfected some of the engineering details."

"So I found out on Mercury," Lucky said grimly.*

"Yes, I know, Lucky. That was dreadfully close."

"But it's over. Let's consider what's facing us now. The situation is this: Sirius is conducting successful espionage and we can't stop them."

"Yes."

"And the Agrav project is most seriously affected."

"Yes."

"And I suppose, Uncle Hector, that what you want me to do is to go out to Jupiter Nine and see if I can learn something about this."

Conway nodded gloomily. "It's what I'm asking you to do. It's unfair to you. I've gotten into the habit of thinking of you as my ace, my trump card, a man I can give any problem and be sure it will be solved. Yet what can you do here? There's nothing Council hasn't tried and we've lo-

---

* See *Lucky Starr and the Big Sun of Mercury.*

cated no spy and no method of espionage. What more can we expect of you?"

"Not of myself alone. I'll have help."

"Bigman?" The older man couldn't help smiling.

"Not Bigman alone. Let me ask you a question. To your knowledge, has any information concerning our V-frog research on Venus leaked out to the Sirians?"

"No," said Conway. "None has, to my knowledge."

"Then I'll ask to have a V-frog assigned to me."

"A V-frog! One V-frog?"

"That's right."

"But what good will that do you? The mental field of a single V-frog is terribly weak. You won't be able to read minds."

"True, but I might be able to catch whiffs of strong emotion."

Conway said thoughtfully, "You might do that. But what good would that do?"

"I'm not sure yet. Still, it will be an advantage previous investigators haven't had. An unexpected emotional surge on the part of someone there might help me, might give me grounds for suspicion, might point the direction for further investigation. Then, too—"

"Yes?"

"If someone possesses telepathic power, developed either naturally or by use of artificial aids, I might detect something much stronger than just a whiff of emotion. I might detect an actual thought, some distinct thought, before the individual learns enough from my mind to shield his thoughts. You see what I mean?"

"He could detect your emotions, too."

"Theoretically, yes, but I would be listening for emotion, so to speak. He would not."

Conway's eyes brightened. "It's a feeble hope, but, by Space, it's a hope! I'll get you your V-frog . . . But one thing, David," and it was only at moments of deep concern that he used Lucky's real name, the one by which the young councilman had been known all through childhood—"I want you to appreciate the importance of this. If we don't find out what the Sirians are doing, it means they are really ahead of us at last. And *that* means war can't be delayed much longer. War or peace hangs on this."

"I know," said Lucky softly.

2

The Commander Is Angry

And so it came about that Lucky Starr, Earthman, and his small friend, Bigman Jones, born and bred on Mars,* traveled beyond the asteroid belt and into the outer reaches of the solar system. And it was for this reason also that a native of Venus, not a man at all, but a small mind-reading and mind-influencing animal, accompanied them.

They hovered, now, a thousand miles above Jupiter Nine and waited as a flexible conveyer tube was made fast between the *Shooting Starr* and the commander's ship. The tube linked air lock to air lock and formed a passageway which men could use in going from one ship to the other without having to put on a space suit. The air of both ships mingled, and a man used to space, taking advantage of the absence of gravity, could shoot along the tube after a single initial push and guide himself along those places where the tube curved with the gentle adjusting force of a well-placed elbow.

* See *David Starr, Space Ranger.*

The commander's hands were the first part of him visible at the lock opening. They gripped the lip of the opening and pushed in such a way that the commander himself leapfrogged out and came down in the *Shooting Starr*'s localized artificial gravity field (or pseudo-grav field, as it was usually termed) with scarcely a stagger. It was neatly done, and Bigman, who had high standards indeed for all forms of spacemen's techniques, nodded in approval.

"Good day, Councilman Starr," said Donahue gruffly. It was always a matter of difficulty whether to say "good morning," "good afternoon," or "good evening" in space, where, strictly speaking, there was neither morning, afternoon, nor evening. "Good day" was the neutral term usually adopted by spacemen.

"Good day, Commander," said Lucky. "Are there any difficulties concerning our landing on Jupiter Nine that account for this delay?"

"Difficulties? Well, that's as you look at it." He looked about and sat down on one of the small pilot's stools. "I've been in touch with Council headquarters but they say I must treat with you directly, so I'm here."

Commander Donahue was a wiry man, with an air of tension about him. His face was deeply lined, his hair grayish but showing signs of having once been brown. His hands had prominent blue veins along their backs, and he spoke in an explosive fashion, rapping out his phrases in a quick succession of words.

"Treat with me about what, sir?" asked Lucky.

"Just this, Councilman. I want you to return to Earth."

"Why, sir?"

The commander did not look directly at Lucky as he spoke. "We have a morale problem. Our men have been investigated and investigated *and* investigated. They've all come through clear each time, and each time a new investigation is started. They don't like it and neither would you. They don't like being under continual suspicion. And I'm completely on their side. Our Agrav ship is almost ready and this is not the time for my men to be disturbed. They talk of going on strike."

Lucky said calmly, "Your men may have been cleared but there is still leakage of information."

Donahue shrugged. "Then it must come from elsewhere. It must . . ." He broke off and a sudden incongruous note of friendliness entered his voice. "What's that?"

Bigman followed his eyes and said at once, "That's our V-frog, Commander, I'm Bigman."

The commander did not acknowledge the introduction. He approached the V-frog instead, staring into the enclosed water-filled cage. "That's a Venus creature, isn't it?"

"That's right," said Bigman.

"I've heard of them. Never saw one, though. Cute little jigger, isn't it?"

Lucky felt a grim amusement. He did not find it strange that in the midst of a most serious discussion the commander should veer off into an absorbed admiration for a small water creature from Venus. The V-frog itself made that inevitable.

The small creature was looking back at Donahue now out of its black eyes, swaying on its extensible legs and clicking its parrot beak gently. In all the known universe its means of survival was unique. It had no defensive weapons, no armor of any sort. It had no claws or teeth or horns. Its beak might bite, but even that bite could do no harm to any creature larger than itself.

Yet it multiplied freely along the weed-covered surface of the Venusian ocean, and none of the fierce predators of the ocean's deeps disturbed it, simply because the V-frog could control emotion. They instinctively caused all other forms of life to like them, to feel friendly toward them, to have no wish whatever to hurt them. So they survived. They did more than that. They flourished.

Now this particular V-frog was filling Donahue, quite obviously, with a feeling of friendliness, so that the army man pointed a finger at it through the glass of its cage and laughed to see it cock its head and sink down along its collapsing legs, as Donahue moved his finger downward.

"You don't suppose we could get a few of these for Jupiter Nine, do you, Starr?" he asked. "We're great ones for pets here. An animal here and there makes for a breath of home."

"It's not very practical," said Lucky. "V-frogs are difficult to keep. They have to be maintained in a carbon-dioxide-saturated system, you know. Oxygen is mildly poisonous to them. That makes things complicated."

"You mean they can't be kept in an open fish-bowl?"

"They can be at times. They're kept so on Venus, where carbon dioxide is dirt cheap and where they can always be turned loose in the ocean if they seem to be unhappy. On a ship, though, or on an airless world, you don't want to bleed carbon dioxide continuously into the air, so a closed system is best."

"Oh." The commander looked a bit wistful.

"To return to our original subject of discussion," said Lucky briskly, "I must refuse your suggestion that I leave. I have an assignment and I must carry it through."

It seemed to take a few seconds for the commander to emerge from the spell cast by the V-frog. His face darkened. "I'm sure you don't understand the entire situation." He turned suddenly, looking down at Bigman. "Consider your associate, for instance."

The small Martian, with a stiffening of spine, began to redden. "I'm Bigman," he said. "I told you that before."

"Not very big a man, nevertheless," said the commander.

And though Lucky placed a soothing hand on the little fellow's shoulder at once, it didn't help. Bigman cried, "Bigness isn't on the outside, mister. My name is Bigman, and I'm a big man against you or anyone you want to name regardless of what the yardstick says. And if you don't believe it . . ." He was shrugging his left shoulder vigorously. "Let go of me, Lucky, will you? This cobber here . . ."

"Will you wait just one minute, Bigman?" Lucky urged. "Let's find out what the commander is trying to say."

Donahue had looked startled at Bigman's sudden verbal assault. He said, "I'm sure I meant no harm in my remark. If I've hurt your feelings, I'm sorry."

"My feelings hurt?" said Bigman, his voice squeaking. "Me? Listen, one thing about me, I never lose my temper and as long as you apologize, we'll forget about it." He hitched at his belt and brought the palms of his hands down with a smart slap against the knee-high orange and vermilion boots that were the heritage of his Martian farm-boy past and without which he would never be seen in public (unless he substituted others with an equally garish color scheme).

"I want to be very plain with you, Councilman," said Donahue, turning to Lucky once more. "I have almost a thousand men here at Jupiter Nine, and they're tough, all of them. They have to be. They're far from home. They do a hard job. They run great risks. They have their own outlook on life now and it's a rough one. For instance, they haze newcomers and not with a light hand, either. Sometimes newcomers can't stand it and go home. Sometimes they're hurt. If they come through, everything's fine."

Lucky said, "Is this officially permitted?"

"No. But it is permitted unofficially. The men have to be kept happy somehow, and we can't afford to alienate them by interfering with their horseplay. Good men are hard to replace out here. Not many people are willing to come to the moons of Jupiter, you know. Then, too, the initiation is helpful in weeding out the misfits. Those that don't pass would probably fail in other respects eventually. That is why I made mention of your friend."

The commander raised his hands hurriedly. "Now make no mistake. I agree that he is big on the inside and capable and anything else you want. But will he be a match for what lies ahead? Will you, Councilman?"

"You mean the hazing?"

"It will be rough, Councilman," said Donahue. "The men know you are coming. News gets around somehow."

"Yes, I know," murmured Lucky.

The commander scowled. "In any case, they know you are to investigate them and they will feel no kindness toward you. They are in an ugly mood and they will hurt you, Councilman Starr. I am asking you not to land on Jupiter Nine for the project's sake, for my men's sake, and for your own. There you have it as plainly as I can put it."

Bigman stared at the change that came over Lucky. His usual look of calm good nature was gone. His dark brown eyes turned hard, and the straight lines of his lean and handsome face were set in something that Bigman rarely saw there: bitter anger. Every muscle of Lucky's tall body seemed tense.

Lucky said ringingly, "Commander Donahue, I am a member of the Council of Science. I am responsible only to the head of the Council and to the President of the Solar Federation of Worlds. I outrank you and you will be bound by my decisions and orders.

"I consider the warning you have just given me to be evidence of your own incompetence. Don't say anything, please; hear me out. You are obviously not in control of your men and not fit to command men. Now hear this: I will land on Jupiter Nine and I will conduct my investigations. I will handle your men if you cannot."

He paused while the other gasped and vainly attempted to find his voice. He rapped out, "Do you understand, Commander?"

Commander Donahue, his face congested almost beyond recognition, managed to grind out, "I will take this up with the Council of Science. No arrogant young whipsnap can talk like that to me, councilman or no councilman. I will match my record as a leader of men against that of anyone in the service. Furthermore, my warning to you will be on record also and if you are hurt on Jupiter Nine, I will run the risk of court-martial gladly. I will do nothing for you. In fact, I hope—I hope they teach you manners, you . . ."

He was past speech once more. He turned on his heel, toward the open lock, connected still with the space tube to his own ship. He clambered in, missing a hand hold in his anger and stumbling badly.

Bigman watched with awe as the commander's heels disappeared down the tube. The other's anger had been so intense a thing that the little Martian had seemed to feel it in his own mind as though waves of heat were rolling in upon him.

Bigman said, "Wow, that cobber was really *going!* You had him rocking."

Lucky nodded. "He was angry. No doubt about it."

Bigman said, "Listen, maybe *he's* the spy. He'd know the most. He'd have the best chance."

"He'd also be the most thoroughly investigated, so your theory is doubtful. But at least he's helped us out in a little experiment, so when I see him next I will have to apologize."

"Apologize?" Bigman was horrified. It was his firm view that apologies were strictly something that other people had to do. "Why?"

"Come, Bigman, do you suppose I really meant those things I said?"

"You weren't angry?"

"Not really."

"It was an act?"

"You could call it that. I wanted to make him angry, really angry, and I succeeded. I could tell that firsthand."

"Firsthand?"

"Couldn't you? Couldn't you feel the anger just pouring out of him all over you?"

"Sands of Mars! The V-frog!"

"Of course. It received the commander's anger and rebroadcast it on to us. I had to know if one V-frog could do it. We tested it back on Earth, but until I tried it under actual field conditions, I wasn't sure. Now I am."

"It broadcast fine."

"I know. So at least it proves we have a weapon, one weapon, after all."

3

The Agrav Corridor

"**G**ood deal," said Bigman fiercely. "Then we're on our way."

"Hold it," said Lucky at once. "Hold everything, my friend. This is a non-specific weapon. We'll sense strong emotion but we may never sense one that will give us the key to the mystery. It's like having eyes. We may see, but we may not see the right thing, not ever."

"You will," said Bigman confidently.

Dropping down toward Jupiter Nine reminded Bigman very strongly of similar maneuvers in the asteroid belt. As Lucky had explained on the voyage outward, most astronomers considered Jupiter Nine to have been a true asteroid to begin with; a rather large one that had been captured by Jupiter's tremendous gravity field many millions of years previously.

In fact, Jupiter had captured so many asteroids that here, fifteen million miles from the giant planet, there was a kind of miniature asteroid belt belonging to Jupiter alone. The four largest of these asteroid satellites, each from forty to a hundred miles in diameter, were Jupiter

Twelve, Eleven, Eight, and Nine. In addition there were
at least a hundred additional satellites of more than a mile
in diameter, unnumbered and unregarded. Their orbits
had been plotted only in the last ten years when Jupiter
Nine was first put to use as an anti-gravity research center, and the necessity of traveling to and from it had made
the population of surrounding space important.

The approaching satellite swallowed the sky and became a rough world of peaks and rocky channels, un-
softened by any touch of air in the billions of years of its
history. Bigman, still thoughtful, said, "Lucky, why in
Space do they call this Jupiter Nine, anyway? It isn't the
ninth one out from Jupiter according to the Atlas. Jupiter
Twelve is a lot closer."

Lucky smiled. "The trouble with you, Bigman, is that
you're spoiled. Just because you were born on Mars, you
think mankind has been cutting through space ever since
creation. Look boy, it's only a matter of a thousand years
since mankind invented the first spaceship."

"I know that," said Bigman indignantly. "I'm not ignorant. I've had schooling. Don't go shoving your big brain
all over the place."

Lucky's smile expanded, and he rapped Bigman's
skull with two knuckles. "Anybody home?"

Bigman's fist whipped toward Lucky's abdomen, but
Lucky caught it in midair and held the little fellow motionless.

"It's as simple as this, Bigman. Before space travel was
invented, men were restricted to Earth and all they knew
about Jupiter was what they could see in a telescope. The
satellites are numbered in the order they were discovered, see?"

"Oh," said Bigman, and yanked free. "Poor ancestors!"
He laughed, as he always did, at the thought of human

beings cooped up on one world, peering out longingly, even as he struggled to free himself from Lucky's grip.

Lucky went on. "The four big satellites of Jupiter are numbered One, Two, Three, and Four, of course, but the numbers are hardly ever used. The names Io, Europa, Ganymede, and Callisto are familiar names. The nearest satellite of all, a small one, is Jupiter Five, while the farther ones have numbers up to Twelve. The ones past Twelve weren't discovered till after space travel was invented and men had reached Mars and the asteroid belt . . . Watch out now. We've got to adjust for landing."

It was amazing, thought Lucky, how you could consider tiny a world eighty-nine miles in diameter as long as you were nowhere near it. Of course, such a world is tiny compared to Jupiter or even to Earth. Place it gently on Earth and its diameter is small enough to allow it to fit within the state of Connecticut without lapping over; and its surface area is less than that of Pennsylvania.

And yet, just the same, when you came to enter the small world, when you found your ship enclosed in a large lock and moved by gigantic grapples (working against a gravitational force of almost zero but against full inertia) into a large cavern capable of holding a hundred ships the size of the *Shooting Starr*, it no longer seemed so small.

And then when you came across a map of Jupiter Nine on the wall of an office and studied the network of underground caverns and corridors within which a complicated program was being carried out, it began to seem actually large. Both horizontal and vertical projections of the work volume of Jupiter Nine were shown on the map, and though only a small portion of the satellite was being used, Lucky could see that some of the corridors penetrated as much as two miles beneath the surface and that others spread out just under the surface for nearly a hundred miles.

"A tremendous job," he said softly to the lieutenant at his side.

Lieutenant Augustus Nevsky nodded briefly. His uniform was spotless and gleaming. He had a stiff little blond mustache, and his wide-set blue eyes had a habit of staring straight ahead as though he were at perpetual attention.

He said with pride, "We're still growing."

He had introduced himself a quarter of an hour earlier, as Lucky and Bigman had stepped from the ship, as the personal guide assigned them by Commander Donahue.

Lucky said with some amusement, "Guide? Or guardian, Lieutenant? You are armed."

Any trace of feeling was carefully washed out of the other's face. "My arms are regulation for officers on duty, Councilman. You will find you will need a guide here."

But he seemed to relax, and there was ordinary human feeling about him as he listened to the visitors' awed praise of the project. He said, "Of course the absence of any significant gravitational field makes certain engineering tricks feasible that wouldn't work on Earth. Underground corridors require practically no support."

Lucky nodded, then said, "I understand that the first Agrav ship is about ready for take-off."

The lieutenant said nothing for a moment. His face blanked free, again, of emotion or feeling. Then he said stiffly, "I will show you your quarters first. It can be most easily reached by Agrav, if I can persuade you to use an Agrav cor—"

"Hey, Lucky," called Bigman in sudden excitement. "Look at this."

Lucky turned. It was only a half-grown cat, gray as smoke, with the look of solemn sadness that cats usually have, and a back that arched readily against Bigman's curved fingers. She was purring.

Lucky said, "The commander said they went for pets here. Is this one yours, Lieutenant?"

The officer flushed. "We all have shares in it. There are a few other cats around, too. They come on the supply ships sometimes. We've got some canaries, a parakeet, white mice, goldfish. Things like that. Nothing like your whatever-it-is, though." And his eyes, as they looked quickly at the V-frog's bowl tucked under Lucky's arm, contained a spark of envy.

But Bigman was concentrating on the cat. There was no native animal life on Mars and the furry pets of Earth always had the charm of novelty to him.

"He likes me, Lucky."

"It's a she," said the lieutenant, but Bigman paid no attention. The cat, tail hoisted into a stiff vertical with only the tip drooping, walked past him, doubling sharply so as to present first one side, then the other, to Bigman's gentle stroking.

And then the purring stopped, and through Bigman's mind stabbed one pure touch of fevered and hungry desire.

It startled him for a moment, and then he noticed that the cat had stopped purring and was squatting slightly in the tense hunting posture dictated by its millions-of-years-old instincts.

Her green slitted eyes stared directly at the V-frog.

But the emotion, so feline in its touch, was gone almost as soon as it had come. The cat padded softly over to the glass container Lucky was holding and stared in curiously, purring with contentment.

The cat, too, liked the V-frog. It had to.

Lucky said, "You were saying, Lieutenant, we would have to reach our quarters by Agrav. Were you going to explain what that means?"

The lieutenant, who had also been staring fondly at the V-frog, paused to gather his wits before answering. "Yes. It's simple enough. We have artificial gravity fields here on Jupiter Nine as on any asteroid or on any space ship for that matter. They are arranged at each of the main corridors, end to end, so that you can fall the length of them in either direction. It's like dropping straight down a hole on Earth."

Lucky nodded. "How fast do you drop?"

"Well, that's the point. Ordinarily, gravity pulls constantly and you fall faster and faster . . ."

"Which is why I ask my question," interposed Lucky dryly.

"But not under Agrav controls. Agrav is really A-grav: no gravity, you see. Agrav can be used to absorb gravitational energy or store it or transfer it. The point is you only fall so fast, you see, and no faster. With a gravitational field in the other direction, too, you can even slow down. An Agrav corridor with two pseudo-grav fields is very simple and it has been used as a steppingstone to an Agrav ship which works in a single gravitational field. Now Engineers' Quarters, which is where your rooms will be, is only a little over a mile from here and the most direct route is by Corridor A-2. Ready?"

"We will be once you explain how we're to work Agrav."

"That's hardly a problem." Lieutenant Nevsky presented each with a light harness, adjusting them over the shoulders and at the waist, talking rapidly about the controls.

And then he said, "If you'll follow me, gentlemen, the corridor is just a few yards in this direction."

Bigman hesitated at the opening of the corridor. He was not afraid of space in itself, or of drops in themselves. But all his life he had been used to bridging gaps under Martian gravity or less. This time the pseudo-grav field was at full Earth-normal, and under its influence the corridor was a brilliantly lighted hole, plummeting, apparently, straight downward, even though in actuality (Bigman's mind told him) it paralleled the satellite's surface closely.

The lieutenant said, "Now this is the lane for travel in the direction of Engineers' Quarters. If we were to approach from the other side, 'down' would appear to be in the other direction. Or we could make 'up' and 'down' change places by appropriate adjustments of our Agrav controls."

He looked at the expression on Bigman's face and said, "You'll get the idea as you go along. It becomes second nature after a while."

He stepped into the corridor and didn't drop an inch. It was as though he were standing on an invisible platform.

He said earnestly, "Have you set the dial at zero?"

Bigman did so, and instantly all sensation of gravity vanished. He stepped into the corridor.

Now the lieutenant's hand on the central knob of his own controls turned it sharply, and he sank, gathering speed. Lucky followed him, and Bigman, who would sooner have fallen the length of the corridor under double gravity and been smashed to pulp than fail to do anything Lucky did, took a deep breath and let himself fall.

"Turn back to zero," called the lieutenant, "and you'll be moving at constant velocity. Get the feel of it."

Periodically they approached and passed through luminous green letters that glowed KEEP TO THIS SIDE. Once there was the flash of a man passing (falling, really) in the other direction. He was moving much more rapidly than they were.

"Are there ever any collisions, Lieutenant?" asked Lucky.

"Not really," said the lieutenant. "The experienced dropper watches for people who might be overtaking him or whom he might be overtaking, and it's easy enough to slow down or speed up. Of course the boys will bump on purpose sometimes. It's a kind of rowdy fun that ends with a broken collarbone sometimes." He looked quickly at Lucky. "Our boys play rough."

Lucky said, "I understand. The commander warned me."

Bigman, who had been staring downward through the well-lit tunnel into which he was sinking, cried in sudden exhilaration, "Hey, Lucky, this is fun when you get used to it," and turned his controls into the positive region.

He sank faster, his head moving down to a level with Lucky's feet, then farther down at an increasing rate.

Lieutenant Nevsky cried out in instant alarm, "Stop that, you fool. Turn back into the negatives!"

Lucky called out an imperious, "Bigman, slow down!"

They caught up to him, the lieutenant angrily exclaiming. "Don't ever do that! There are all sorts of barriers and partitions along these corridors, and if you don't know your way, you'll be slamming into one just when you think you're safe."

"Here, Bigman," said Lucky. "Hold the V-frog. That will give you some responsibility and make you behave, perhaps."

"Aw, Lucky," said Bigman, abashed. "I was just kicking my heels a bit. Sands of Mars, Lucky . . ."

"All right," said Lucky. "No harm done," and Bigman brightened at once.

Bigman looked down again. Falling at a constant rate was not quite the same as free fall in space. In space, nothing seemed to move. A space ship might be traveling at a velocity of hundreds of thousands of miles an hour and there would still be the sensation of motionlessness all about. The distant stars never moved.

Here, though, the sense of motion was all about. The lights and openings and various attachments that lined the corridor walls flashed past.

In space, one expected that there would be no "up" and "down," but here there was none either and it seemed wrong. As long as he looked "down" past his feet, it seemed "down" and that was all right. When he looked "up," however, there would be a quick sensation that "up" was really "down," that he was standing head downward falling "up." He looked toward his feet again quickly to get rid of the sensation.

The lieutenant said, "Don't bend too far forward, Bigman. The Agrav works to keep you lined up in the direction of fall, but if you bend over too much, you'll start tumbling."

Bigman straightened.

The lieutenant said, "There's nothing fatal about tumbling. Anyone who's used to Agrav can straighten himself out again. Beginners would find it troublesome, however. We'll decelerate now. Move the dial into the negatives and keep it there. About minus five."

He was slowing as he spoke, moving above them. His feet dangled at Bigman's eye level.

Bigman moved the dial, trying desperately to line

himself up with the lieutenant. And as he slowed, "up"
and "down" became definite, and in the wrong way. He
was standing on his head.

He said, "Hey, the blood's rushing to my head."

The lieutenant said sharply, "There are footholds
along the sides of the corridor. Hook one with the toe of
your foot as you reach it and let go quickly."

He did so as he said this. His head swung outward,
and head and feet reversed position. He continued swinging and stopped himself with a quick hand tap against the
wall.

Lucky followed suit, and Bigman, flailing widely with
his short legs, managed to catch one of the footholds at
last. He whirled sharply and caught the wall with his elbow just a trifle too hard for comfort but managed to line
up properly.

At least he was head-up again. He wasn't falling any
more, but rising, as though he had been shot out of a
cannon and rising against gravity more and more slowly;
but at least he was head-up.

When they were moving at a slow crawl, Bigman,
looking uneasily toward his feet, thought: We're going to
be falling again. And suddenly the corridor looked like an
endlessly deep well and his stomach tightened.

But the lieutenant said, "Adjust to zero," and at once
they stopped slowing down. They just moved upward, as
though in a smooth, slow elevator, until they reached a
cross-level at which the lieutenant, seizing a foothold with
one toe, brought himself to a feathery stop.

"Engineers' Quarters, gentlemen," he said.

"And," added Lucky Starr gently, "a reception committee."

For men were waiting for them in the corridor now,
fifty of them at least.

Lucky said, "You said they liked to play rough, Lieu-tenant, and maybe they want to play now."

He stepped firmly out into the corridor. Bigman, nos-trils flaring with excitement and grateful to be on the firm pseudo-grav of a solid floor, clutched the V-frog's cage tightly and was at Lucky's heels, facing the waiting men of Jupiter Nine.

4

Initiation!

Lieutenant Nevsky tried to make his voice crackle with authority as he placed his hand on the butt of his blaster. "What are you men doing here?"

There was a small murmur from the men, but by and large they remained quiet. Eyes turned to the one of them who stood in front, as though they were waiting for him to speak.

The leader of the men was smiling, and his face was crinkled into an expression of apparent good will. His straight hair, parted in the middle, had a light-orange tint to it. His cheekbones were broad and he chewed gum. His clothing was of synthetic fiber, as was true of that of the others, but unlike the others', his shirt and trousers were ornamented with brass buttons that were large and bulky. Four on his shirt front, one each on the two shirt pockets, and four down the side of each pants leg: fourteen altogether. They seemed to serve no purpose; to be only for show.

"All right, Summers," said the lieutenant, turning to this man, "what are the men doing here?"

Summers spoke now in a soft, wheedling voice. "Well,

now, Lieutenant, we thought it would be nice to meet the new man. He'll be seeing a lot of us. He'll be asking questions. Why shouldn't we meet him now?"

He looked at Lucky Starr as he spoke, and for a moment there was a touch of ice in that glance that swallowed up all the show of softness.

The lieutenant said, "You men should be at work."

"Have a heart, Lieutenant," said Summers, chewing even more slowly and leisurely. "We've *been* working. Now we want to say hello."

The lieutenant was obviously uncertain as to his next move. He looked doubtfully at Lucky.

Lucky said, "Which rooms are to be ours, Lieutenant?"

"Rooms 2A and 2B, sir. To find them—"

"I'll find them. I'm sure one of these men will direct me. And now, Lieutenant Nevsky, that you've directed us to our quarters, I think your assignment is completed. I'll be seeing you again."

"I can't leave!" said Lieutenant Nevsky in a low, appalled whisper.

"I think you can."

"Sure you can, Lieutenant," said Summers, grinning more broadly than ever. "A simple hello won't hurt the boy." There was a snicker of laughter from the men behind him. "And besides, you've been asked to leave."

Bigman approached Lucky and muttered in an urgent whisper. "Lucky, let me give the V-frog to the lieutenant. I can't fight and hold it, too."

"You just hold it," said Lucky. "I want it exactly here. . . . Good day, Lieutenant. Dismissed!"

The lieutenant hesitated, and Lucky said in a tone that, for all its softness, bit like steel. "That's an order, Lieutenant."

Lieutenant Nevsky's face assumed a soldierly rigidity. He said sharply, "Yes, sir."

Then, surprisingly, he hesitated one further moment and glanced down at the V-frog in the crook of Bigman's arm, as it chewed idly at a fern frond. "Take care of that little thing." He turned and was in the Agrav corridor in two steps, disappearing almost at once in a rush of speed.

Lucky turned to face the men again. He was under no illusions. They were grim-faced and they meant business, but unless he could face them down and prove that he meant business as well, his mission would come to nothing against the rock of their hostility. He would have to win them over somehow.

Summers' smile had become the least bit wolfish. He said, "Well, now, friend, the uniform-boy is gone. We can talk. I'm Red Summers. What's your name?"

Lucky smiled in return. "My name is David Starr. My friend's name is Bigman."

"Seems to me I heard you called Lucky when all that whispering was going on a while back."

"I'm called Lucky by my friends."

"Isn't that nice. Do you want to stay lucky?"

"Do you know a good way?"

"Matter of fact, Lucky Starr, I do." Suddenly his face contorted itself into a bitter scowl. "Get off Jupiter Nine."

There was a hoarse roar of approval from the others, and a few voices took up the cry of "Get off! Get off!"

They crowded closer, but Lucky stood his ground. "I have important reasons to stay on Jupiter Nine."

"In that case, I'm afraid you aren't lucky," said Summers. "You're a greenhorn and you look soft, and soft greenhorns get hurt on Jupiter Nine. We worry about you."

"I think I won't get hurt."

"That's what you think, eh?" said Summers. "Armand, come here."

From the ranks behind him, a huge man stepped forward, round-faced, beefy of build, with large shoulders and a barrel chest. He topped Lucky's six feet one by half a head and looked down at the young councilman with a smile that showed yellowed, wide-spaced teeth.

The men were beginning to take seats on the floor. They shouted to one another with lighthearted cheer, as though they were about to watch a ball game.

One called out, "Hey, Armand, watch out you don't step on the kid!"

Bigman started, and glared furiously in the direction of the voice but could not identify the speaker.

Summers said, "You could still leave, Starr."

Lucky said, "I have no intention of doing so, particularly at a moment when you seem to be planning some sort of entertainment."

"Not for you," said Summers. "Now listen, Starr, we're ready for you. We've been ready since we got word that you were coming. We've had enough of you little tinhorns from Earth and we aren't taking any more. I've got men stationed on various levels. We'll know if the commander tries to interfere, and if he does, then by Jupiter, we're ready to go on strike. Am I right, men?"

"*Right!*" came back the multiple roar.

"And the commander knows it," said Summers, "and I don't think he'll interfere. So this gives us our chance to give you our initiation and after that I'll ask you again if you want to leave. If you're conscious, that is."

"You're going to a lot of trouble for nothing," said Lucky. "What harm am I doing you?"

"You won't be doing us any," said Summers. "I guarantee that."

Bigman said, in his tense, high-pitched voice, "Look,

you cobber, you're talking to a councilman. Have you
stopped to figure what happens if you fool with the Council of Science?"

Summers looked at him suddenly, put his fists on his
hips, and bent his head back to laugh. "Hey, men, it talks.
I was wondering what it was. It looks as though Lucky
Snoop has brought along his baby brother for protection."

Bigman went dead-white, but under the cover of the
laughter Lucky stooped and spoke through stiff lips. "Your
job is to hang on to the V-frog, Bigman. I'll take care of
Summers. And, Great Galaxy, Bigman, stop broadcasting
anger! I can't get a thing on the V-frog except that."

Bigman swallowed hard twice, three times.

Summers said softly, "Now, Councilman Snoop, can
you maneuver under Agrav?"

"I just have, Mr. Summers."

"Well, we'll just have to test you and make sure. We
can't have anyone around who hasn't learned all the Agrav
ropes. It's too dangerous. Right, men?"

"Right!" they roared again.

"Armand here," said Summers, and his hand rested on
one of Armand's huge shoulders, "is our best teacher.
You'll know all about Agrav maneuvering when you're
through with him. Or you will know if you stay out of his
way. I suggest you get out into the Agrav corridor now.
Armand will join you."

Lucky said, "If I choose not to go?"

"Then we'll throw you into the corridor anyway and
Armand goes after you."

Lucky nodded. "You seem determined. Are there any
rules to this lesson I'm going to get?"

There was wild laughter, but Summers held up his
arms. "Just keep out of Armand's way, Councilman. That's
the only rule you'll have to remember. We'll be at the lip
of the corridor watching. If you try to crawl out of Agrav

before you've completed your lesson, we'll throw you back in, and there are men stationed at other levels, watching, and they're ready to do the same."

Bigman cried, "Sands of Mars, your man outweighs Lucky by fifty pounds and he's an expert with Agrav!"

Summers turned on him in mock surprise. "*No!* I never thought of that. What a shame!" There was laughter from the men. "On your way, Starr. Get into the corridor, Armand. Drag him in if you have to."

"He won't have to," said Lucky. He turned and moved into the open space of the wide Agrav corridor. As his feet drifted out into empty air, his fingers caught gently at the wall, twisting him in a slow, turning motion that he stopped with another touch against the wall. He stood there in midair, facing the men.

There was some murmuring at Lucky's maneuver, and Armand nodded, speaking for the first time in a rolling appreciative bass. "Hey, mister, that's not bad."

Summers, lips suddenly set and with a frown newly creasing his forehead, struck Armand a sharp blow on the back. "Don't talk, you idiot! Get in after him and give it to him."

Armand moved forward slowly. He said, "Hey, Red, let's not make too much of this."

Summers' face contorted in fury. "Get in there! And you do what I said. I told you what he is. If we don't get rid of him, they'll be sending more." His words were a harsh whisper that didn't carry.

Armand stepped into the corridor and stood face to face with Lucky.

Lucky Starr waited in what was almost absence of mind. He was concentrating on the faint whiffs of emotion brought him by the V-frog. Some he could recognize without difficulty, both as to their nature and their owner.

Red Summers was easiest to detect: fear and niggling hate mixed with an undertone of anxious triumph. Armand loosed a small leak of tension. Occasionally there were sharp pinpoints of excitement from one or another, and sometimes Lucky could identify the owner because it coincided with a happy shout or a threatening one. All of it had to be sorted out from the steady trickle of Bigman's anger, of course.

But now he was staring into Armand's small eyes and he was aware that the other was bobbing up and down, a few inches either way. Armand's hand fingered his chest control.

Lucky was instantly alert. The other was alternating the gravitational direction, moving the controls this way and that. Was he expecting to confuse Lucky?

Lucky was sharply aware that for all his experience with space he was inexperienced in the type of weightlessness brought about by Agrav, for this was a weightlessness that wasn't absolute, as in space, but one that could be changed at will.

And suddenly Armand dropped as though he had stepped through a trap door—except that he dropped upward!

As Armand's large legs moved up past Lucky's head, they parted and came together as if to catch Lucky's head in a vise.

Automatically Lucky's head snapped back, but as it did so, his legs moved forward, his body swinging about its center of gravity, and for a moment, he was off balance and flailing helplessly. A roar of laughter arose from the watching men.

Lucky knew what was wrong. He should have dodged by gravity. If Armand moved up, Lucky should have adjusted controls to move up with him or to race down past him. And now it would take the pull of gravity to straighten him out. At gravity zero, he would tumble indefinitely.

But before his fingers could touch his controls, Armand was past the top of his rise and was gathering speed downward. As he dropped past Lucky once more, his elbow caught Lucky a sharp jab in the hip. He dropped farther and his thick fingers clutched at Lucky's ankles, carrying him down, down. Armand pulled strongly downward and reached up to seize Lucky's shoulders. His harsh breath stirred Lucky's hair. He said, "You need a lot of training, mister."

Lucky brought up his own arms head-high and broke the other's hold sharply.

Lucky dialed gravity up and helped his upward movement by bringing his foot sharply down on the other's shoulder, accelerating his own pace and slowing the other's. To his own senses it now seemed that he was falling head downward and there was a tenseness about that sensation that seemed to be slowing his reactions. Or was it his Agrav controls which were somewhat sluggish? He tested them and lacked the experience to be certain, yet felt that they were.

Armand was on him now, bellowing, thrusting against him, attempting to use his own greater mass of body to maneuver Lucky hard against the wall.

Lucky wriggled his hand toward the controls in order to reverse the direction of gravity. He readied his knees for an upward thrust to coincide and lurch Armand out of position.

But it was Armand's field that shifted first, and it was Lucky who was lurched out of position.

Armand's feet shot backward now, striking the wall of the corridor as it was flashing by and angling the pair, by recoil, against the opposite wall. Lucky struck bruisingly and skidded along it some feet before his ankle caught one of the metal railings and his body swung away and into the open corridor.

Armand whispered hotly in Lucky's ear, "Had enough, mister? Just tell Red you'll leave. I don't want to hurt you bad."

Lucky shook his head. Strange, he thought, that Armand's gravitational field had beaten his own to the shift. He had felt Armand's hand move to the controls and he was certain his own controls had moved first.

Twisting suddenly, Lucky placed his elbow sharply in the pit of Armand's stomach. Armand grunted, and in that split second Lucky got his legs between himself and the other's and straightened them. The two men flew apart and Lucky was free.

He shot away an instant before Armand returned, and then for the next few minutes Lucky concentrated only on staying away. He was learning the use of the controls and they *were* sluggish. It was only by skillful use of the footholds along the walls and lightning-like head-to-foot reversals that he managed to avoid Armand.

And then while he was drifting feather-fashion, allowing Armand to shoot past him, he turned his Agrav controls and found no response at all. There was no change in the gravitational field direction; no sudden sensation of accelerating one way or the other.

Instead, Armand was on him again, grunting, and Lucky found himself crashing with stunning force against the corridor wall.

5

Needle-Guns and Neighbors

Bigman felt fully confident of Lucky's ability to handle any overgrown mass of beef, and though he felt a sharp anger at the unsympathetic crowd, he felt no fear.

Summers had approached the lip of the corridor and so had another, a gangling, dark-complexioned fellow who barked out events as they occurred in a raucous voice, as though it were a flight-polo game on the subetherics.

There were cheers when Armand first slammed Lucky against the corridor wall. Bigman discounted those with contempt. Of course that shouting fool would try to make it look good for his own side. Wait till Lucky got the feel of the Agrav technique; he would cut that Armand guy into ribbons. Bigman was sure of it.

But then when the dark fellow yelled, "Armand has him now in a head lock. He's maneuvering for a second fall; feet against the wall; retract and extend and *there's the crash, a beauty!*" Bigman felt the beginnings of uneasiness.

He edged close to the corridor himself. No one paid any attention to him. It was one advantage of his small size. People who didn't know him tended to discount him as a possible danger, to ignore him.

Bigman looked down and saw Lucky pushing away from the wall, Armand drifting nearby, waiting.

"Lucky!" he yelled shrilly. "Stay away!"

His cry was lost in the hubbub, but the dark man's voice as it was lowered in a conversational aside to Red Summers was not. Bigman caught it.

The dark man said, "Give the snoop some power, Red. There won't be any excitement."

And Summers growled in response, "I don't want excitement. I want Armand to finish the job."

Bigman didn't get the significance of the short exchange for a moment, but only for a moment. And then his eyes darted sharply in the direction of Red Summers, whose hands, held closely against his chest, were manipulating some small object Bigman could not identify.

"Sands of Mars!" Bigman cried breathlessly. He sprang back. "You! Summers! You foul-fighting cobber!"

This was another one of those times when Bigman was glad he carried a needle-gun even in the face of Lucky's disapproval. Lucky considered it an unreliable weapon, as it was too hard to focus accurately, but Bigman would sooner doubt the fact that he was as tall as any six-footer as doubt his own skill.

When Summers didn't turn at Bigman's shout, Bigman clenched his fist about the weapon (of which only half-inch of snout, narrowing to a needlepoint, showed between the second and third fingers of his right hand) and squeezed just tightly enough to activate it.

Simultaneously there was a flash of light six inches in front of Summers' nose, and a slight pop. It was not very impressive. Only air molecules were being ionized. Summers jumped, however, and panic, transmitted by the V-frog, rose sharply.

"Everybody," called Bigman. "Freeze! *Freeze!* You split-head, underlipped miseries." Another needle-gun discharge popped the air, this time over Summers' head where all could see it plainly.

Few people might have handled needle-guns, which were expensive and hard to get licenses for, but everybody knew what a needle-gun discharge looked like, if only from subetheric programs, and everyone knew the damage it could do.

It was as though fifty men had stopped breathing.

Bigman was bathed in the cold drizzle of human fear from fifty frightened men. He backed against the wall.

He said, "Now listen, all of you. How many of you know that this cobber Summers is gimmicking my friend's Agrav controls? This fight is fixed!"

Summers said desperately, through clenched teeth, "You're wrong. You're wrong."

"Am I? You're a brave man, Summers, when you've got fifty against two. Let's see you stay brave against a needle-gun. They're hard to aim, of course, and I might miss."

He clenched his fist again, and this time the pop of the discharge was sharply ear-splitting and the flash dazzled all the spectators but Bigman, who, of them all, was the only one who knew exactly when to close his eyes for a moment.

Summers emitted a strangled yell. He was untouched except that the top button on his shirt was gone.

Bigman said, "Nice aiming if I do say so myself, but I suppose having a run of luck is too much to ask. I'd advise you not to move, Summers. Pretend you're stone, you cobber, because if you do move, I'll miss and feeling a chunk of your skin go will hurt you worse than just losing a button."

Summers closed his eyes. His forehead was glistening with perspiration. Bigman calculated the distance and clenched twice.

Pow! Smack! Two more buttons gone.

"Sands of Mars, my lucky day! Isn't it nice that you've arranged to have no one come around to interfere? Well, one more—for the road."

And this time Summers yelled in agony. There was a rent in the shirt and reddened skin showed.

"Aw," said Bigman, "not on the nose. Now I'm rattled and I'll probably miss the next by two inches . . . Unless you're ready to say something, Summers."

"All right," yelled the other. "I've fixed it."

Bigman said mildly, "Your man was heavier. Your man had experience and still you couldn't leave it a fair fight. You don't take *any* chances, do you? Drop what you're holding . . . Don't the rest of you move, though. From here on in, it's a fair fight in the corridor. No one's moving until someone climbs out of the corridor."

He paused and glared as his fist with the needle-gun moved slowly from side to side. "But if it's your ball of gristle that comes back, I'll just be a bit disappointed. And when I'm disappointed, there's no telling what I'll do. I just might be disappointed and mad enough to fire this needle-gun into the crowd, and there isn't a thing in the world any of you can do to stop me from clenching my fist ten times. So if there are ten of you bored with living, just hope that your boy beats Lucky Starr."

Bigman waited there desperately, his right hand holding the needle-gun, his left arm crooked over the V-frog in its container. He longed to order Summers to bring the two men back, to end the fight, but he dared not risk Lucky's anger. He knew Lucky well enough to know that the fight couldn't be allowed to end by default on Lucky's side.

A figure whizzed past the line of sight, then another. There was a crash as of a body hitting a wall, then a second and a third. Then silence.

A figure drifted back, with a second gripped firmly by one ankle.

The person in control came lightly out into the corridor; the person being held followed and dropped like a sack of sand.

Bigman let out a shout. The man standing was Lucky. His cheek was bruised and he limped, but it was Armand who was unconscious.

They brought Armand back to consciousness with some difficulty. He had a lump on his skull resembling a small grapefruit, and one eye was swollen closed. Though his lower lip was bleeding, he managed a painful smile and said, "By Jupiter, this kid's a wildcat."

He got to his feet and threw his arms about Lucky in a bear hug. "It was like tangling with ten men after he got his bearings. He's all right."

Surprisingly, the men were cheering wildly. The V-frog transmitted relief first, swallowed up at once by excitement.

Armand's smile widened, and he dabbed at the blood with the back of his hand. "This councilman is all right. Anyone who still doesn't like him has to fight me, too. Where's Red?"

But Red Summers was gone. So was the instrument he had dropped at Bigman's order.

Armand said, "Listen, Mr. Starr, I've got to tell you. This wasn't my idea, but Red said we had to get rid of you or you'd make trouble for all of us."

Lucky raised his hand. "That's a mistake. Listen, all of you. There'll be no trouble for any loyal Earthman. I guarantee it. This fight is off the record. It was a bit of excitement, but we can forget it. Next time we meet, we all meet fresh. Nothing's happened. Right?"

They cheered madly and there were shouts of "He's all right" and "Up the Council!"

Lucky was turning to go when Armand said, "Hey, wait." He drew in a vast breath and pointed a thick finger. "What's this?" He was pointing to the V-frog.

"A Venusian animal," said Lucky. "A pet of ours."

"It's cute." The giant simpered down at it. The others crowded close to stare at it and make appreciative comments, to seize Lucky's hand and assure him that they had been on his side all along.

Bigman, outraged at the shoving, finally yelled, "Let's get to quarters, Lucky, or I swear I'll kill a few of these guys."

There was an instant silence and men squeezed back to make a path for Lucky and Bigman.

Lucky winced as Bigman applied cold water to the bruised cheek in the privacy of their quarters.

He said, "Some of the men were saying something about needle-guns in that final crush, but in the confusion I didn't get the story straight. Suppose you tell me, Bigman."

Reluctantly Bigman explained the circumstances.

Lucky said thoughtfully, "I realized that my controls were off, but I assumed mechanical failure particularly since they came back after my second fall. I didn't know you and Red Summers were fighting it out over me."

Bigman grinned. "Space, Lucky, you didn't think I'd let that character pull a trick like that?"

"There might have been some way other than needle-guns."

"Nothing else would have frozen them so," said Bigman, aggrieved. "Did you want me to shake my finger at them and say, 'Naughty, naughty?' Besides, I *had* to scare the green bejeebies out of them."

"Why?" Lucky said sharply.

"Sands of Mars, Lucky, you spotted the other guy two falls when the fighting was fixed, and I didn't know if you had enough left to make out. I was going to make Summers call the fight off."

"That would have been bad, Bigman. We would have gained nothing. There would have been men convinced the cry of 'foul' was an unsportsmanlike fake."

"I knew you'd figure that, but I was nervous."

"No need to be. After my controls started responding properly, things went fairly well. Armand was certain he had me, and when he found there was still fight in me, the fight seemed to go out of him. That happens sometimes with people who have never had to lose. When they don't win at once, it confuses them, and they don't win at all."

"Yes, Lucky," said Bigman, grinning.

Lucky was silent for a minute or two, then he said, "I don't like that 'Yes, Lucky.' What did you do?"

"Well—" Bigman applied the final touch of flesh tint to hide the bruise and stepped back to consider his handiwork critically—"I couldn't help but hope that you'd win, now could I?"

"No, I suppose not."

"And I told everyone in that place that if Armand won, I would shoot as many of them as I could."

"You weren't serious."

"Maybe I was. Anyway, they thought I was; they were sure I was after they saw me needle four buttons off that cobber's shirt. So there were fifty guys there, even including Summers, who were sweating themselves blind hoping you would win and Armand lose."

Lucky said, "So that's it."

"Well, I couldn't help it if the V-frog was there and transmitted all those thoughts to you too, could I?"

"So all the fight went out of Armand because his mind

was blanketed with wishes he would lose." Lucky looked chagrined.

"Remember, Lucky. Two foul falls. It wasn't a fair fight."

"Yes, I know. Well, maybe I needed the help at that."

The door signal flashed at that moment, and Lucky raised his eyebrows. "Who's this, I wonder?" He pressed the button that retracted the door into its slot.

A chunky man, with thinning hair and china-blue eyes that stared at them unblinkingly, stood in the doorway. In one hand he held an oddly shaped piece of gleaming metal, which his limber fingers turned end for end. Occasionally the piece ducked between fingers, traveling from thumb to pinkie and back as though it had a life of its own. Bigman found himself watching it, fascinated.

The man said, "My name is Harry Norrich. I'm your next-door neighbor."

"Good day," said Lucky.

"You're Lucky Starr and Bigman Jones, aren't you? Would you care to come to my place a few minutes? Visit a bit, have a drink?"

"That's kind of you," said Lucky. "We'll be glad to join you."

Norrich turned somewhat stiffly and led the way down the corridor to the next door. One hand touched the corridor wall occasionally. Lucky and Bigman followed, the latter holding the V-frog.

"Won't you come in, gentlemen?" He stood aside to let them enter. "Please sit down. I've heard a great deal about you already."

"Like what?" asked Bigman.

"Like Lucky's fight with Big Armand and Bigman's marksmanship with a needle-gun. It's all over the place. I doubt there's anyone on Jupiter Nine who won't hear of it by morning. It's one of the reasons I asked you in. I wanted to talk to you about it."

He poured a reddish liquor carefully into two small glasses and offered them. For a moment Lucky put his hand some three inches to one side of the glass, waited without result, then reached over and took it from Norrich's hand. Lucky put the drink to one side.

"What's that on your worktable?" asked Bigman.

Norrich's room, in addition to the usual furnishings, had something that looked like a worktable running the length of one wall with a bench before it. On the worktable was a series of metal gimmicks spread out loosely, and in the center was an odd structure, six inches high and very uneven in outline.

"This thing?" Norrich's hand slid delicately along the surface of the table and came to rest on the structure. "It's a threedee."

"A what?"

"A three-dimensional jigsaw. The Japanese had them for thousands of years, but they've never caught on elsewhere. They're puzzles, made up of a number of pieces that fit together to form some sort of structure. This one, for instance, will be the model of an Agrav generator when it's finished. I designed and made this puzzle myself."

He lifted the piece of metal he was holding and placed it carefully in a little slot in the structure. The piece slid in smoothly and held in place.

"Now you take another piece." His left hand moved gently over the structure, while his right felt among the loose pieces, came up with one, and moved it into place.

Bigman, fascinated, moved forward, then jumped back at a sudden animal howl from beneath the table.

A dog came squirming out from beneath the table and

put its forefeet on the bench. It was a large German shepherd dog and it stood now looking mildly at Bigman.

Bigman said nervously, "Here, now, I stepped on it by accident."

"It's only Mutt," said Norrich. "He won't hurt anyone without better cause than being stepped on. He's my dog. He's my eyes."

"Your eyes?"

Lucky said softly, "Mr. Norrich is blind, Bigman."

6

Death Enters the Game

Bigman shrank back. "I'm sorry."

"No need to be sorry," Norrich said cheerfully. "I'm used to it and I can get along. I'm holding a master technician's rank and I'm in charge of constructing experimental jigs. I don't need anyone to help me, either, any more than I need help in my threedees."

"I imagine the threedees offer good exercise," said Lucky.

Bigman said, "You mean you can put those things together without even being able to see them? Sands of Mars!"

"It's not as hard as you might think. I've been practicing for years and I make them myself so I know the tricks of them. Here, Bigman, here's a simple one. It's just an egg shape. Can you take it apart?"

Bigman received the light-alloy ovoid and turned it in his hands, looking over the pieces that fit together smoothly and neatly.

"In fact," Norrich went on, "the only thing I really need Mutt for is to take me along the corridors." He leaned down to scratch the dog behind one ear, and the

dog permitted it, opening his mouth wide in a sleepy
yawn, showing large white fangs and a length of pink
lolling tongue. Lucky could feel the warm thickness of
Norrich's affection for the dog pour out via the V-frog.

"I can't use the Agrav corridors," Norrich said, "since
I'd have no way of telling when to decelerate, so I have to
walk through ordinary corridors and Mutt guides me. It
makes for the long way around, but it's good exercise, and
with all the walking Mutt and I know Jupiter Nine better
than anybody, don't we, Mutt? . . . Have you got it yet,
Bigman?"

"No," said Bigman. "It's all one piece."

"Not really. Here, give it to me."

Bigman handed it over, and Norrich's skillful fingers
flew over the surface. "See this little square bit here? You
push it and it goes in a bit. Grab the part that comes out
the other end, give it half a turn clockwise, and it pulls out
altogether. See? Now the rest comes apart easily. This,
then this, then this, and so on. Line up the pieces in order
as they come out; there are only eight of them; then put
them back in reverse order. Put the key piece in last, and
it will lock everything into place."

Bigman stared dubiously at the individual pieces and
bent close over them.

Lucky said, "I believe you wanted to discuss the re-
ception committee I met up with when I arrived, Mr.
Norrich. You said you wanted to talk about my fight with
Armand."

"Yes, Councilman, yes. I wanted you to understand.
I've been here on Jupiter Nine since Agrav project started
and I know the men. Some leave when their hitch is up,
some stay on, greenhorns join up; but they're all the same
in one way. They're very insecure."

"Why?"

"For several reasons. In the first place, there is danger

involved in the project. We've had dozens of accidents and lost hundreds of men. I lost my eyes five years ago and I was fortunate in a way. I might have died. Secondly, the men are isolated from friends and family while they're here. Really isolated."

Lucky said, "I imagine there are some people who enjoy the isolation."

He smiled grimly as he said that. It was no secret that men who in one way or another had gotten entangled with the law sometimes managed to find work on some of the pioneer worlds. People were always needed to work under domes in artificial atmospheres with pseudo-grav fields, and those who volunteered were usually not asked too many questions. Nor was there anything very wrong with that. Such volunteers aided Earth and its people under difficult conditions, and that, in a way, was a payment for misdeeds.

Norrich nodded at Lucky's words. "I see you're not naïve about it and I'm glad. Leaving the officers and the professional engineers to one side, I imagine a good half of the men here have criminal records on Earth, and most of the rest might have such records if the police knew everything. I doubt that one in five gives his real name. Anyway, you see where tension comes in when investigator after investigator arrives. You're all looking for Sirian spies; we know that; but each man thinks that maybe his own particular trouble will come out and he'll be dragged back to jail on Earth. They all want to go back to Earth, but they want to go back anonymously, not at the other end of a set of wrist locks. That's why Red Summers could rouse them so."

"And is Summers something special that he takes the lead? A particularly bad record on Earth?"

Bigman looked up briefly from his threedee to say bitterly, "Murder, maybe?"

"No," said Norrich with instant energy. "You've got to understand about Summers. He's had an unfortunate life: broken home, no real parents. He got into the wrong crowds. He's been in prison, yes, for being involved in some minor rackets. If he'd stayed on Earth, his life would have been one long waste. But he's come to Jupiter Nine. He's made a new life here. He came out as a common laborer and he educated himself. He's learned low-grav construction engineering, force-field mechanics, and Agrav techniques. He's been promoted to a responsible position and has done wonderful work. He's respectable, admired, well liked. He's found out what it is to have honor and position and he dreads nothing more than the thought of going back to Earth and his old life."

"Sure, he hates it so much," said Bigman, "that he tried to kill Lucky by gimmicking the fight."

"Yes," said Norrich, frowning, "I heard he was using a sub-phase oscillator to kill the councilman's control response. That was stupid of him, but he was in panic. Look, fundamentally the man is goodhearted. When my old Mutt died—"

"Your old Mutt?" asked Lucky.

"I had a Seeing Eye dog before this one which I also called Mutt. It died in a force-field short circuit that killed two men besides. He shouldn't have been there, but sometimes a dog will wander off on his own adventures. This one does, too, when I'm not using him, but he always comes back." He leaned down to slap his dog's flank lightly, and Mutt closed one eye and thumped his tail against the floor.

"Anyway, after old Mutt died, it looked for a while as though I mightn't get another and I would have to be sent home. I'm no use here without one. Seeing Eye dogs are in short supply; there are waiting lists. The administration here at Jupiter Nine didn't want to pull any strings because they weren't anxious to publicize the fact that they were employing a blind man as construction engineer. The economy bloc in Congress is always waiting for something like that to make bad publicity out of. So it was Summers who came through. He used some contacts he had on Earth and got me Mutt here. It wasn't exactly legal, it was even what you might call the black market, but Summers risked his position here to do a friend a favor and I owe him a great deal. I'm hoping you'll remember Summers can do and has done things like that and that you'll go easy on him for his actions earlier today."

Lucky said, "I'm not taking any action against him. I had no intention of doing so even before our conversation. Still, I'm sure that Summers' real name and record are known to the Council and I'll be checking on the facts."

Norrich flushed, "By all means, do so. You'll find he's not so bad."

"I hope so. But tell me something. Through all that has just taken place, there was no attempt on the part of the project administration to interfere. Do you find this strange?"

Norrich laughed shortly. "Not at all. I don't think Commander Donahue would have cared much if you'd been killed, except for the trouble it would have taken to hush it up. He's got bigger troubles on his mind than you or your investigation."

"Bigger troubles?"

"Sure. The head of this project is changed every year; army policy of rotation. Donahue is the sixth boss we've had and far and away the best. I've got to say that. He's cut through red tape and he hasn't tried to make an army camp out of the project. He's given the men leeway and let them raise a bit of cain now and then so he's gotten results. Now the first Agrav ship will be ready to take off any time. Some say it's a matter of days."

"That soon?"

"Could be. But the point is that Commander Donahue is due to be relieved in less than a month. A delay now could mean that the launching of the Agrav ship won't take place until Donahue's successor comes in. Donahue's successor would get to ride in it, have the fame, go down in the history books, and Donahue would miss out."

"No wonder he didn't want you on Jupiter Nine," Bigman said hotly. "No wonder he didn't want you, Lucky."

Lucky shrugged. "Don't waste temper, Bigman."

But Bigman said, "The dirty cobber! Sirius can gobble up Earth for all he cares as long as he can get to ride his miserable ship." He lifted a clenched fist, and there was a muted growl from Mutt.

Norrich said sharply, "What are you doing, Bigman?"

"What?" Bigman was genuinely astonished. "I'm not doing a thing."

"Are you making a threatening gesture?"

Bigman lowered his arm quickly. "Not really."

"You've got to be careful around Mutt. He's been trained to take care of me. . . . Look, I'll show you. Just step toward me and make believe you're going to throw a punch at me."

Lucky said, "That's not necessary. We understand—"

"Please," said Norrich. "There's no danger. I'll stop Mutt in time. As a matter of fact, it's good practice for him. Everyone on the project is so careful of me that I swear I don't know if he remembers his training. Go ahead, Bigman."

Bigman stepped forward and raised his arm half-heartedly. At once Mutt's ears flattened, his eyes slitted, his fangs stood sharply revealed, his leg muscles tensed for a spring, and a harsh growl issued from the recesses of his throat.

Bigman drew back hastily, and Norrich said, "Down, Mutt!" The dog subsided. Lucky could sense, clearly, the gathering and relaxation of tension in Bigman's mind and the fond triumph in Norrich's.

Norrich said, "How are you doing with the threedee egg, Bigman?"

The little Martian, in exasperation, said, "I've given up. I've got two pieces put together and that's all I can do."

Norrich laughed. "Just a matter of practice, that's all. Look."

He took the two pieces out of Bigman's hand and said, "No wonder. You've got these together wrong. He flipped one piece end for end, brought the two together again, added another piece and another until he held seven pieces in the shape of a loose ovoid with a hole through it. He picked up the eighth and key piece, slipped it in, gave it a half turn counterclockwise, pushed it the rest of the way, and said, "Finished."

He tossed the completed egg into the air and caught it, while Bigman watched in chagrin.

Lucky got to his feet. "Well, Mr. Norrich, we'll be seeing you again. I'll remember your remarks about Summers and the rest. Thank you for the drink." It still rested untouched on the desk.

"Nice to have met you," said Norrich, rising and shaking hands.

It was some time before Lucky could fall asleep. He lay in the darkness of his room hundreds of feet below the surface of Jupiter Nine, listening to Bigman's soft snoring in the adjoining room, and thought of the events of the day. Over and over them he went.

He was bothered! Something had happened that shouldn't have; or something had not happened that should have.

But he was weary and everything was a bit unreal and twisted in the half-world of half-sleep. Something hovered at the edge of awareness. He clutched at it, but it slipped away.

And when morning came there was nothing left of it.

Bigman called out to Lucky from his own room as Lucky was drying himself under the soft jets of warm air after his shower.

The little Martian yelled, "Hey, Lucky, I've recharged the V-frog's carbon-dioxide supply and dumped in more weed. You'll be taking it down to our meeting with that blasted commander, won't you?"

"We certainly will, Bigman."

"It's all set then. How about letting me tell the commander what I think of him?"

"Now, Bigman."

"Nuts! It's me for the shower now."

Like all men of the solar system brought up on planets other than Earth, Bigman reveled in water when he could get at it, and a shower for him was a leisurely, loving experience. Lucky braced himself for a session of the tenor caterwauling that Bigman called singing.

The intercom sounded after Bigman was well launched into some dubious fragment of melody that sounded piercingly off-key and just as Lucky completed dressing.

Lucky stepped to it and activated reception. "Starr speaking."

"Starr!" Commander Donahue's lined face showed in the visi-panel. His lips were narrow and compressed and his whole expression was one of antagonism as he gazed at

Lucky. "I have heard some story of a fight between yourself and one of our workers."

"Yes?"

"I see you have not been hurt."

Lucky smiled. "All's well."

"You'll remember I warned you."

"I am making no complaints."

"Since you aren't, and in the interest of the project, I
would like to ask if you plan on making any report concerning it."

"Unless it turns out to have some direct bearing on
the problem which concerns me here, the incident will
never be mentioned by me."

"Good!" Donahue looked suddenly relieved. "I wonder if I could extend that attitude to our meeting this
morning. Our meeting might be taped for confidential
records and I would prefer—"

"There will be no need to discuss the matter, Commander."

"Very good!" The commander relaxed into what was
almost cordiality. "I'll be seeing you in an hour then."

Lucky was dimly aware that Bigman's shower had
stopped and that his singing had subsided to a humming.
Now the humming stopped, too, and there was a moment
of silence.

Lucky said into the transmitter, "Yes, Commander,
good—" when Bigman exploded into a wild, near-
incoherent shout.

"*Lucky!*"

Lucky was on his feet with smooth speed and at the
door connecting the two rooms in two strides.

But Bigman was in the doorway before him, eyes big
with horror. "Lucky! The V-frog! It's dead! It's been
killed!"

7

A Robot Enters the Game

The V-frog's plastic cage was shattered and shriveled, and the floor was wet with its watery contents. The V-frog, half covered with the fronds it fed upon, was quite, quite dead.

Now that it was dead and unable to control emotion, Lucky could look at it without the enforced fondness that he, as well as all others that came within its radius of influence, had felt. He felt anger, however—mostly at himself for having allowed himself to be overreached.

Bigman, fresh from his shower, with only his shorts on, clenched and unclenched his fists. "It's my fault, Lucky. It's all my fault. I was yelling so loud in the shower I never heard anyone come in."

The phrase "come in" was not quite appropriate. The killer had not simply come in; he had burnt his way in. The lock controls were fused and melted away with what had obviously been an energy projector of fairly large caliber.

Lucky stepped back to the interphone. "Commander Donahue?"

"Yes, what happened? Is anything wrong?"

"I'll see you in an hour." He broke connections and returned to the grieving Bigman. He said somberly, "It's my fault, Bigman. Uncle Hector said the Sirians had not yet discovered the facts concerning the emotional powers of the V-frog, and I accepted that too thoroughly. If I had been a little less optimistic about Sirian ignorance, neither one of us would ever have left that little creature out of our sight for a second."

Lieutenant Nevsky called for them, standing at attention as Lucky and Bigman left their quarters.

He said in a low voice, "I am glad, sir, that you were unharmed in yesterday's encounter. I would not have left you, sir, had you not strictly ordered me to."

"Forget it, Lieutenant," Lucky said absently. His mind kept returning to that moment just before sleep the preceding night when, for a brief instant, a thought had hovered at the outskirts of consciousness, then vanished. But it would not come now, and finally Lucky's mind sped to other matters.

They had entered the Agrav corridor now, and this time it seemed crowded with men, streaming accurately and unconcernedly in both directions. There was a "beginning of the work day" atmosphere all about. Though men worked underground here and there was no day or night, yet the old twenty-four-hour schedule held. Mankind brought the familiar rotation of the Earth to all the worlds on which he lived. And though men might work in shifts the clock round, the largest number always worked on the "day shift" from nine to five, Solar Standard Time.

It was nearly nine now, and there was a bustle through the Agrav corridors as men traveled to the work posts. There was a feel of "morning" almost as strong as though there were a sun low in the eastern sky and dew on the grass.

• • •

Two men were sitting at the table when Lucky and Bigman entered the conference room. One was Commander Donahue, whose face bore the appearance of a carefully controlled tension. The commander rose and coldly introduced the other: James Panner, the chief engineer and civilian head of the project. Panner was a stocky man with a swarthy face, dark deep-set eyes, and a bull neck. He wore a dark shirt open at the collar and without insignia of any sort.

Lieutenant Nevsky saluted and retired. Commander Donahue watched the door close and said, "Since that leaves the four of us, let's get to business."

"The four of us and a cat," said Lucky, stroking a small creature that hitched its forepaws on the table and stared at him solemnly. "This isn't the same cat I saw yesterday, is it?"

The commander frowned. "Perhaps. Perhaps not. We have a number of cats on the satellite. However, I presume we're not here to discuss pets."

Lucky said, "On the contrary, Commander, I think it will do as a topic of conversation to begin with and I chose it deliberately. Do you remember my own pet, sir?"

"Your little Venusian creature?" said the commander with sudden warmth. "I remember it. It was—" He stopped in confusion as though wondering, in the V-frog's absence, what the reason for his enthusiasm concerning it might be.

"The little Venusian creature," said Lucky, "had peculiar abilities. It could detect emotion. It could transmit emotion. It could even impose emotion."

The commander's eyes opened wide, but Panner said in a husky voice, "I once heard a rumor to that effect, Councilman. I laughed."

"You needn't have. It is true. In fact, Commander

Donahue, my purpose in asking for this interview was to make arrangements to have every man on the project interviewed by me in the presence of the V-frog. I wanted an emotional analysis."

The commander still seemed half stunned. "What would that prove?"

"Perhaps nothing. Still, I meant to try it."

Panner intervened. "*Meant* to try it? You use the past tense, Councilman Starr."

Lucky stared solemnly at the two project officials. "My V-frog is dead."

Bigman said furiously, "Killed this morning."

The commander said, "Who killed it?"

"We don't know, Commander."

The commander sat back in his chair. "Then your little investigation is over, I suppose, till the animal can be replaced."

Lucky said, "There will be no waiting. The mere fact of the V-frog's death has told me a great deal, and the matter becomes much more serious."

"What do you mean?"

All stared. Even Bigman looked up at Lucky in profound surprise.

Lucky said, "I told you that the V-frog has the capacity to impose emotion. You yourself, Commander Donahue, experienced that. Do you recall your feelings when you saw the V-frog on my ship yesterday? You were under considerable strain, yet when you saw the V-frog— Do you remember your feelings, sir?"

"I was rather taken with the creature," the commander faltered.

"Can you think why, as you look back at the moment now?"

"No, come to think of it. Ugly creature."

"Yet you liked it. You couldn't help yourself. Could you have harmed it?"

"I suppose not."

"I'm certain you couldn't. No one with emotions could have. Yet someone did. Someone killed it."

Panner said, "Do you intend to explain the paradox?"

"Easily explained. No one *with emotions*. A robot, however, does *not* have emotions. Suppose that somewhere on Jupiter Nine there is a robot, a mechanical man, in the perfect form of a human being?"

"You mean a humanoid?" exploded Commander Donahue. "Impossible. Such things exist only in fairy tales."

Lucky said, "I think, Commander, you are not aware of how skillful the Sirians are in the manufacture of robots. I think they might be able to use some man on Jupiter Nine, some thoroughly loyal man, as model; build a robot in his shape and substitute it for him. Such a humanoid robot could have special senses that would enable it to be the perfect spy. It might, for instance, be able to see in the dark or sense things through thicknesses of matter. It would certainly be able to transmit information through the subether by some built-in device."

The commander shook his head. "Ridiculous. A man could easily have killed the V-frog. A desperate man frightened to an extreme might have overcome this—this mental influence the animal exerted. Have you thought of that?"

"Yes, I have," said Lucky. "But why should a man be so desperate, why so wild to kill a harmless V-frog? The most obvious reason is that the V-frog represented a desperate danger, that it was not harmless at all. The only danger a V-frog might have to the killer would involve the animal's capacity to detect and transmit the killer's emotions. Suppose those emotions would be an immediate giveaway to the fact that the killer was a spy?"

"How could it be?" Panner asked.

Lucky turned to look at him. "What if our killer had no emotions at all? Wouldn't a man without emotions be revealed at once as a robot? . . . Or take it another way altogether. Why kill only the V-frog? Having gotten into our rooms, having risked so much, having found one of us in the shower and one at the intercom and both unsuspecting and unready, why did not the killer kill *us* instead of the V-frog? For that matter, why not kill us *and* the V-frog?"

"No time, probably," said the commander.

"There's another and more plausible reason," said Lucky. "Do you know the Three Laws of Robotics, the rules of behavior that all robots are built to follow?"

"I know them generally," the commander said. "I can't quote them."

"I can," said Lucky, "and with your permission I will, so that I may make a point. The First Law is this: A robot may not injure a human being or, through inaction, allow a human being to come to harm. The Second Law is: A robot must obey the orders given it by human beings except where such orders would conflict with the First Law. The Third Law is: A robot must protect its own existence as long as such protection does not conflict with the First or Second Law."

Panner nodded. "All right, Councilman, what does that prove?"

"A robot can be ordered to kill the V-frog, which is an animal. It will risk its existence, since self-preservation is only Third Law, to obey orders, which is Second Law. But it cannot be ordered to kill Bigman or myself, since we are humans, and First Law takes precedence over all. A human spy would have killed us and the V-frog; a robot spy would have killed only the V-frog. It all points to the same thing, Commander."

The commander considered that for long minutes, sitting motionless, the lines on his tired face grooving deeper. Then he said, "What do you propose to do? X-ray every man on the project?"

"No," said Lucky at once. "It's not that simple. Successful espionage is going on elsewhere than here. If there is a humanoid robot here, there are probably others elsewhere. It would be well to catch as many of the humanoids as possible; all of them if we can. If we act too eagerly and openly to catch the one under our hands, the others may be snatched away for use at another time."

"Then what *do* you propose doing?"

"To work slowly. Once you suspect a robot, there are ways of making it give itself away without its being aware of it. And I don't start completely from scratch. For instance, Commander, I know you are not a robot, since I detected emotion in you yesterday. In fact, I deliberately induced anger in you to test my V-frog, and for that I ask your pardon."

Donahue's face had gone mauve. "I, a robot?"

"As I said, I used you only to test my V-frog."

Panner said dryly, "You have no reason to feel sure about me, Councilman. I never faced your V-frog."

"That is right," said Lucky. "You are not cleared yet. Remove your shirt."

"What!" cried Panner indignantly. "Why?"

Lucky said mildly, "You have just been cleared. A robot would have had to obey that order."

The commander's fist banged down on his desk. "*Stop it!* This ends right here. I will not have you testing or annoying my men in any way. I have a job to do on this satellite, Councilman Starr; I have an Agrav ship to get into space, and I'm getting it into space. My men have been investigated and they're clear. Your story about a robot is flimsy, and I'm not going along with it.

"I told you yesterday, Starr, that I didn't want you on this satellite disturbing my men and wrecking their morale. You saw fit yesterday to address me in insulting fashion. You say now it was just to test your animal, which makes it no less insulting. For that reason, I feel no need to co-operate with you and I am not doing so. Let me tell you exactly what I have done.

"I've cut off all communication with Earth. I've put Jupiter Nine under emergency orders. I have the powers of a military dictator now. Do you understand?"

Lucky's eyes narrowed a trifle. "As councilman of the Council of Science, I outrank you."

"How do you intend to enforce your rank? My men will obey me and they have their orders. You will be restrained forcibly if you try in any way, by word or deed, to interfere with my orders."

"And what are your orders?"

"Tomorrow," said Commander Donahue, "at 6 P.M., Solar Standard Time, the first functioning Agrav ship in existence will make its first flight from Jupiter Nine to Jupiter One, the satellite Io. After we're back—*after* we're back, Councilman Starr, and not one hour sooner—you may conduct your investigation. And if you then want to get in touch with Earth and arrange court-martial proceedings, I will be ready for you."

Commander Donahue stared firmly at Lucky Starr.

Lucky said to Panner, "Is the ship ready?"

Panner said, "I think so."

Donahue said scornfully. "We leave tomorrow. Well, Councilman Starr, do you go along with me or will I have to have you arrested?"

The silence that followed was a tense one. Bigman virtually held his breath. The commander's hands were clenching and unclenching, and his nose was white and pinched. Panner slowly fumbled a stick of gum out of his shirt pocket, stripped it of its plastofoil coating with one hand, and crumpled it into his mouth.

And then Lucky clasped his hands loosely, sat back in his chair, and said, "I'll be glad to co-operate with you, Commander."

8

Blindness

Bigman was at once outraged. "Lucky! Are you going to let him stop the investigation just like that?"

Lucky said, "Not exactly, Bigman. We'll be on board the Agrav ship and we'll continue it there."

"No sir," the commander said flatly, "You will not be on board. Don't think that for an instant."

Lucky said, "Who will be on board, Commander? Yourself, I presume?"

"Myself. Also Panner, as chief engineer. Two of my officers, five other engineers, and five ordinary crewmen. All these were chosen some time ago. Myself and Panner, as responsible heads of the project; the five engineers to handle the ship itself; the remainder in return for their services to the project."

Lucky said thoughtfully, "What type of service?"

Panner interrupted to say, "The best example of what the commander is talking about is Harry Norrich, who—"

Bigman stiffened in surprise. "You mean the blind fellow?"

Panner said, "You know him then?"

"We met him last evening," said Lucky.

"Well," said Panner, "Norrich was here at the very beginning of the project. He lost his sight when he threw himself between two contacts to keep a force field from buckling. He was in the hospital five months and his eyes were the one part of him that couldn't be restored. By his act of bravery, he kept the satellite from having a chunk the size of a mountain blown out of it. He saved the lives of two hundred people *and* he saved the project, since a major accident at the beginning might have made it impossible to get further appropriations out of Congress. That sort of thing is what earns one the honor of a place on the maiden voyage of the Agrav ship."

"It's a shame he won't be able to see Jupiter up close," said Bigman. Then, his eyes narrowing, "How'll he get around on board ship?"

Panner said, "We'll be taking Mutt, I'm sure. He's a well-behaved dog."

"That's all I want to know then," said Bigman heatedly. "If you cobbers can take a dog, you can take Lucky and me."

Commander Donahue was looking at his wristwatch impatiently. Now he put the palms of his hands flat on the table and made as though to rise. "We have finished our business then, gentlemen."

"Not quite," Lucky said. "There's one little point to be cleared up. Bigman puts it crudely, but he's quite right. He and I will be on the Agrav ship when it leaves."

"No," said Commander Donahue. "Impossible."

"Is the added mass of two individuals too great for the ship to handle?"

Panner laughed. "We could move a mountain."

"Do you lack room then?"

The commander stared at Lucky in hard displeasure. "I will not give any reason. You are not being taken only because it is my decision that you not be taken. Is that clear?"

There was a glint of satisfaction in his eyes, and Lucky did not find it hard to guess that he was squaring accounts for the tongue-lashing Lucky had given him aboard the *Lucky Starr*.

Lucky said quietly, "You had better take us, Commander."

Donahue smiled sardonically. "Why? Am I to be relieved of duty at the orders of the Council of Science? You won't be able to communicate with Earth till I return, and after that they can relieve me of duty if they wish."

"I don't think you've thought it through, Commander," said Lucky. "They might relieve you of duty retroactive to this moment. In fact, I assure you they will do so. As far as the government records are concerned, then, it will appear that Agrav ship made its first flight not under your command but under the command, officially, of your successor, whoever he might be. The records of the trip might even be adjusted to show, officially, that you were not on board."

Commander Donahue went white. He rose and for a moment seemed on the point of throwing himself bodily at Lucky.

Lucky said, "Your decision, Commander?"

Donahue's voice was most unnatural when it finally came. "You may come."

Lucky spent the remainder of the day in the record rooms, studying the files on various men employed on the project, while Bigman, under Panner's guidance, was taken from laboratory to laboratory and through tremendous testing rooms.

It was only after the evening meal when they returned to quarters that they had a chance to be alone together.

Lucky's silence then was not extraordinary, since the young councilman was never talkative at the best of times, but there was a small crease between his eyes that Bigman recognized as a sure sign of concern.

Bigman said, "We aren't making any progress, are we, Lucky?"

Lucky shook his head, "Nothing startling, I'll admit."

He had brought a book-film with him from the project's library, and Bigman caught a flash of its title: *Advanced Robotics.* Methodically Lucky threaded the beginnings of the film through the viewer.

Bigman stirred restlessly. "Are you going to be all tied up with that film, Lucky?"

"I'm afraid so, Bigman."

"Do you mind then if I visit Norrich next door for company?"

"Go ahead." Lucky had the viewer over his eyes and he was leaning back, his arms crossed loosely across his chest.

Bigman closed the door and remained standing just outside for a moment, a little nervous. He should discuss this with Lucky first, he knew he should, and yet the temptation . . .

He told himself: I'm not going to do anything. I'll just check something. If I'm wrong, I'm wrong and why bother Lucky? But if it checks out, then I'll *really* have something to tell him.

The door opened at once when he rang, and there was Norrich, blind eyes fixed in the direction of the doorway, seated before a desk on which a checkerboard design carried odd figures.

He said, "Yes?"

"This is Bigman," said the little Martian.

"Bigman! Come in. Sit down. Is Councilman Starr with you?"

The door closed again, and Bigman looked about in the brightly lit room. His mouth tightened. "He's busy. But as for me, I'm filled up on Agrav today. Dr. Panner took me all over, only I don't understand a thing of it hardly."

Norrich smiled. "You're not exactly in a minority, but if you ignore the mathematics, some of it isn't too hard to understand."

"No? Mind explaining it then?" Bigman sat down in a large chair and bent to look under Norrich's workbench. Mutt lay there with his head between his forepaws and one eye brightly fixed on Bigman.

(Keep him talking, thought Bigman. Keep him talking till I find a hole, or make one.)

"Look here," Norrich said. He held up one of the round counters he had been holding. "Gravity is a form of energy. An object such as this piece I'm holding which is under the influence of a gravitational field but is not allowed to move is said to have potential energy. If I were to release the piece, that potential energy would be converted to motion—or kinetic energy, as it is called. Since it continues under the influence of the gravitational field as it falls, it falls faster and faster and faster." He dropped the counter at this point, and it fell.

"Until, splash," said Bigman. The counter hit the floor and rolled.

Norrich bent as though to retrieve it and then said, "Would you get it for me, Bigman? I'm not sure where it rolled."

Bigman suppressed his disappointment. He picked it up and returned it.

Norrich said, "Now until recently that was the only thing that could be done with potential energy: it could be converted into kinetic energy. Of course the kinetic energy could be used further. For instance, the falling water of Niagara Falls could be used to form electricity, but that's a different thing. In space, gravity results in motion and that ends it.

"Consider the Jovian system of moons. We're at Jupiter Nine, way out. Fifteen million miles out. With respect to Jupiter, we've got a tremendous quantity of potential energy. If we try to travel to Jupiter One, the satellite Io, which is only 285,000 miles from Jupiter, we are in a way, falling all those millions of miles. We pick up tremendous speeds which we must continually counteract by pushing in the opposite direction with a hyperatomic motor. It takes enormous energy. Then, if we miss our mark by a bit, we're in constant danger of continuing to fall, in which case there's only one place to go, and that's Jupiter —and Jupiter is instant death. *Then*, even if we land safely on Io, there's the problem of getting back to Jupiter Nine, which means lifting ourselves all those millions of miles against Jupiter's gravity. The amount of energy required to maneuver among Jupiter's moons is just prohibitive."

"And Agrav?" asked Bigman.

"Ah! Now that's a different thing. Once you use an Agrav converter, potential energy can be converted into forms of energy *other* than kinetic energy. In the Agrav corridor, for instance, the force of gravity in one direction is used to charge the gravitational field in the other direction as you fall. People falling in one direction provide the energy for people falling in the other. By bleeding off the energy that way, you yourself, while falling, need never speed up. You can fall at any velocity less than the natural falling velocity. You see?"

Bigman wasn't quite sure he did but he said, "Go on."

"In space it's different. There's no second gravitational field to shift the energy to. Instead, it is converted to hyperatomic field energy and stored so. By doing this, a space ship can drop from Jupiter Nine to Io at any speed less than the natural falling speed without having to use any energy to decelerate. Virtually no energy is expended except in the final adjustment to Io's orbital speed. And safety is complete, since the ship is always under perfect control. Jupiter's gravity could be completely blanketed, if necessary.

"Going back to Jupiter Nine still requires energy. There is no getting around that. But now you can use the energy you had previously stored in the hyperatomic field condenser to get you back. The energy of Jupiter's own gravitational field is used to kick you back."

Bigman said, "It sounds good." He squirmed in his seat. He wasn't getting anywhere. Suddenly he said, "What's that you're fooling with on your desk?"

"Chess," said Norrich. "Do you play?"

"A little," Bigman confessed. "Lucky taught me, but it's no fun playing with him. He always wins." Then he asked, offhand, "How can *you* play chess?"

"You mean because I'm blind?"

"Uh—"

"It's all right. I'm not sensitive about being blind. . . . It's easy enough to explain. This board is magnetized and the pieces are made of a light magnetic alloy so that they stick where they're put and don't go tumbling if I move my arm about carelessly. Here, try it, Bigman."

Bigman reached for one of the pieces. It came up as though stuck in syrup for a quarter of an inch or so, then was free.

"And you see," said Norrich, "they're not ordinary chess pieces."

"More like checkers," grunted Bigman.

"Again so I don't knock them over. They're not completely flat, though. They've got raised designs which I can identify easily enough by touch and which resemble the ordinary pieces closely enough so that other people can learn them in a moment and play with me. See for yourself."

Bigman had no trouble. The circle of raised points was obviously the queen, while the little cross in the center of another piece signified the king. The pieces with grooves slanting across were the bishops, the raised circle of squares the rooks, the pointed horse's ears the knights, and the simple round knobs the pawns.

Bigman felt stymied. He said, "What are you doing now? Playing a game by yourself?"

"No, solving a problem. The pieces are arranged just so, you see, and there's one way and only one in which white can win the game in exactly three moves and I'm trying to find that way."

Bigman said suddenly, "How can you tell white from black?"

Norrich laughed. "If you'll look closely, you'll see the white pieces are grooved along the rims and the black pieces aren't."

"Oh. Then you have to remember where all the pieces are, don't you?"

"That's not hard," Norrich said. "It sounds as though you would need a photographic memory, but actually all I have to do is pass my hand over the board and check the pieces any time. You'll notice the squares are marked off by little grooves, too."

Bigman found himself breathing hard. He had forgotten about the squares on the checkerboard, and they *were* grooved off. He felt as though he were playing a kind of a chess game of his own, one in which he was being badly beaten.

"Mind if I watch?" he said sharply. "Maybe I can figure out the right moves."

"By all means," said Norrich. "I wish you could. I've been at this for half an hour and I'm getting frustrated."

There was silence for a minute or more, and then Bigman rose, his body tense and catlike in its effort to make no noise. He drew a small flashlight from one pocket and stepped toward the wall in little motions. Norrich never moved from his bowed position over the chessboard. Bigman threw a quick glance toward Mutt, but the dog made no move, either.

Bigman reached the wall and, hardly breathing, put one hand lightly and noiselessly over the light patch. At once, the light in the room went out and a profound darkness rested everywhere.

Bigman remembered the direction in which Norrich's chair was. He raised the flashlight.

He heard a muted thump and then Norrich's voice calling out in surprise and a little displeasure, "Why did you put out the light, Bigman?"

"That does it," yelled Bigman in triumph. He let the flashlight's beam shine full on Norrich's broad face. "You're not blind at all, you spy."

9

The Agrav Ship

Norrich cried out, "I don't know what you're doing, but Space, man, don't do anything sudden or Mutt will jump you!"

"You know exactly what I'm doing," said Bigman, "because you can see well enough I'm drawing my needle-gun, and I think you've heard I'm a dead shot. If your dog moves in my direction, it's the end for him."

"Don't hurt Mutt. Please!"

Bigman was taken aback by the sudden anguish in the other's voice. He said, "Just keep him quiet then and come with me and no one will be hurt. We'll go see Lucky. And if we pass anyone in the corridor, don't you say anything but 'Good day.' I'll be right beside you, you know."

Norrich said, "I can't go without Mutt."

"Sure you can," said Bigman. "It's only five steps down the corridor. Even if you were really blind, you could manage that—a fellow who can do threedees and all."

• • •

Lucky lifted the viewer from his head at the sound of the door opening and said, "Good day, Norrich. Where's Mutt?"

Bigman spoke before the other had a chance to answer. "Mutt's in Norrich's room, and Norrich doesn't need him. Sands of Mars. Lucky, Norrich isn't any blinder than we are!"

"What?"

Norrich began, "Your friend is quite mistaken, Mr. Starr. I want to say—"

Bigman snapped, "Quiet, you! I'll talk, and then when you're invited, you can make some remarks."

Lucky folded his arms. "If you don't mind, Mr. Norrich, I'd like to hear what Bigman has on his mind. And meanwhile, Bigman, suppose you put away the needle-gun."

Bigman did so with a grimace. He said, "Look, Lucky, I suspected this cobber from the beginning. Those threedee puzzles of his set me to thinking. He was just a little too good. I got to wondering right away that he might be the spy."

"That's the second time you've called me a spy," Norrich cried. "I won't stand for that."

"Look, Lucky," said Bigman, ignoring Norrich's outcry, "it would be a clever move to have a spy a supposed blind man. He could see an awful lot no one would think he was seeing. People wouldn't cover up. They wouldn't hide things. He could be staring right at some vital document and they'd think, 'It's only poor Norrich. He can't see.' More likely they wouldn't give it a thought at all. Sands of Mars, it would be a perfect setup!"

Norrich was looking more astonished with every moment. "But I *am* blind. If it's the threedee puzzles or the chess, I've explained—"

"Oh, sure, you've explained," Bigman said scornfully.

"You've been practicing explanations for years. How come you sit in the privacy of your room with the lights on, though? When I walked in, Lucky, about half an hour ago, the light was on. He hadn't just put it on for me. The switch was too far away from where he was sitting. Why?"

"Why not?" said Norrich. "It makes no difference to me whether it's on or not, so it might as well be on as long as I'm awake for the convenience of those who come visiting, like you."

"All right," said Bigman. "That shows how he can think up an explanation for everything—how he can play chess, how he can identify the pieces, everything. Once he almost forgot himself. He dropped one of his chess pieces and bent to pick it up when he remembered just in time and asked me to do it for him."

"Usually," said Norrich, "I can tell where something drops by the sound. This piece rolled."

"Go on, explain," said Bigman. "It won't help you because there's one thing you *can't* explain. Lucky, I was going to test him. I was going to put out the light, then flash my pocketlight in his eyes at full intensity. If he weren't blind, he'd be bound to jump or blink his eyes anyway. I was sure I'd get him. But I didn't even have to go that far. As soon as I put out the light, the poor cobber forgets himself and says, 'Why did you put out the light?' . . . How did he know I put out the light, Lucky? *How did he know?*"

"But—" Norrich began.

Bigman drove on. "He can feel chess pieces and threedee puzzles and all that but he can't feel light going out. He had to *see* that."

Lucky said, "I think it's time to let Mr. Norrich say something."

Norrich said, "Thank you. I may be blind, Councilman, but my dog is not. When I put out the light at night, it makes no difference to me, as I said before, but to Mutt it signals bedtime and he goes to his own corner. Now I heard Bigman tiptoe to the wall in the direction of the light switch. He was trying to move without sound, but a man who has been blind for five years can hear the lightest tiptoe. A moment after he stopped walking I heard Mutt jump into his corner. It didn't take much brain power to figure out what had happened. Bigman was standing at the light switch and Mutt was turning in for the night. Obviously he had put out the light."

The engineer turned his sightless face in the direction first of Bigman, then of Lucky, as though straining his ears for an answer.

Lucky said, "Yes, I see. It seems we owe you an apology."

Bigman's gnomelike face screwed up unhappily. "But Lucky—"

Lucky shook his head. "Let go, Bigman! Never hang on to a theory after it's been exploded. I hope you understand, Mr. Norrich, that Bigman was only doing what he felt to be his duty."

"I wish he had asked a few questions before acting," said Norrich, coldly, "Now may I go? Do you mind?"

"You may go. As an official request, however, please make no mention of what has occurred to anyone. That's quite important."

Norrich said, "It comes under the heading of false arrest, I imagine, but we'll let it go. I won't mention this." He walked to the door, reached the signal patch with a minimum of fumbling, and walked out.

Bigman turned almost at once to Lucky. "It was a trick. You shouldn't have let him go."

Lucky rested his chin on the palm of his right hand, and his calm, brown eyes were thoughtful. "No, Bigman, he isn't the man we're after."

"But he's *got* to be, Lucky. Even if he's blind, *really* blind, it's an argument against him. Sure, Lucky," Bigman grew excited again, his small hands clumping into fists, "he could get close to the V-frog without seeing it. He could kill it."

Lucky shook his head. "No, Bigman. The V-frog's mental influence doesn't depend on its being seen. It's direct mental contact. That's the one fact we can't get around." He said slowly, "It had to be a robot who did that. It had to be, and Norrich is no robot."

"Well, how do you know he—?" But Bigman stopped.

"I see you've answered your own question. We sensed his emotion during our first meeting, when the V-frog was still with us. He has emotions, so he's not the robot and he's not the man we're looking for."

But even as he said so, there was a look of deep trouble on his face and he tossed the book-film on advanced robotics to one side as though despairing of help from it.

The first Agrav ship ever to be built was named *Jovian Moon* and it was not like any ship Lucky had ever seen. It was large enough to be a luxury liner of space, but the crew and passenger quarters were abnormally crowded forward, since nine tenths of the ship's volume consisted of the Agrav converter and the hyperatomic force-field condensers. From the midsection, curved vanes, ridged into a vague resemblance to bat's wings, extended on either side. Five to one side, five to the other, ten in all.

Lucky had been told that these vanes, in cutting the lines of force of the gravitational field, converted the gravity into hyperatomic energy. It was as prosaic as that, and yet they gave the ship an almost sinister appearance.

The ship rested now in a gigantic pit dug into Jupiter Nine. The lid, of reinforced concrete, had been retracted, and the whole area was under normal Jupiter Nine gravity and exposed to the normal airlessness of Jupiter Nine's surface.

Nevertheless the entire personnel of the project, nearly a thousand men, were gathered in this natural amphitheater. Lucky had never seen so many men in space suits at one time. There was a certain natural excitement because of the occasion; a certain almost hysterical restlessness that manifested itself in horseplay made possible by the low gravity.

Lucky thought grimly: And one of those men in space suits is no man at all.

But which one? And how could he tell?

Commander Donahue made his short speech of dedication to a group of men grown silent, impressed despite themselves; while Lucky, looking up at Jupiter, glanced at a small object near it that was not a star but a tiny sliver of light, curved like the paring of a small fingernail, almost too small for the curve to be seen. If there had been any air in the way, instead of Jupiter Nine's airless vacuum, that small curve would have been blurred into a formless spot of light.

Lucky knew the tiny crescent to be Ganymede, Jupiter Three, Jupiter's largest satellite and worthy moon of the giant planet. It was nearly three times the size of Earth's moon; it was larger than the planet Mercury. It was almost as large as Mars. With the Agrav fleet completed, Ganymede would quickly become a major world of the solar system.

Commander Donahue christened the ship at last in a voice husky with emotion, and then the assembled audience, in groups of five and six, entered the air-filled interior of the satellite through the various locks.

Only those who were to be aboard the *Jovian Moon* remained. One by one they climbed the ramp to the entrance lock, Commander Donahue first.

Lucky and Bigman were last to board. Commander Donahue turned away from the air lock as they entered, stiffly unfriendly.

Bigman leaned toward Lucky, to say tightly, "Did you notice, Lucky, that Red Summers is on board?"

"I know."

"He's the cobber who tried to kill you."

"I know, Bigman."

The ship was lifting now in what was at first a majestic creep. The surface gravity of Jupiter Nine was only one eightieth of Earth, and though the weight of the ship was still in the hundreds of tons, that was not the cause of the initial slowness. Even were gravity absent altogether, the ship would still retain its full content of matter and all the inertia that went with it. It would still be just as hard to put all that matter into motion, or, if it came to that, to stop it or change its direction of travel, once it had begun moving.

But first slowly, then more and more rapidly, the pit was left behind. Jupiter Nine shrank beneath them and became visible in the visiplates as a rugged gray rock. The constellations powdered the black sky and Jupiter was a bright marble.

James Panner approached them and placed an arm on the shoulder of each man. "Would you two gentlemen care to join me in my cabin for a meal? There'll be nothing to watch here in the viewing room for a while." His wide mouth pulled back in a grin that swelled the cords of his thick neck and made it seem no neck at all but a mere continuation of head.

"Thank you," Lucky said. "It's kind of you to invite us."

"Well," said Panner, "the commander isn't going to

and the men are a little leery of you, too. I don't want you to get too lonely. It will be a long trip."

"Aren't you leery of me, Dr. Panner?" Lucky asked dryly.

"Of course not. You tested me, remember, and I passed."

Panner's cabin was a small one in which the three barely fitted. It was obvious that the quarters in this, the first Agrav ship, were as cramped as engineering ingenuity could make them. Panner broke out three cans of ship-ration, the concentrated food that was universally eaten on space ships. It was almost home to Lucky and Bigman; the smell of heating rations, the feeling of crowding walls, outside of which was the infinite emptiness of space, and, sounding through those walls, the steady vibrating hum of hyperatomic motors converting field energies into a directional thrust or, at the very least, powering the energy-consuming innards of the ship.

If ever the ancient belief of the "music of the spheres" could be said to have come literally true, it was in that hum of hyperatomics that was the very essential of space flight.

Panner said, "We're past Jupiter Nine's escape velocity now, which means we can coast without danger of falling back to its surface."

Lucky said, "That means we're in free fall down to Jupiter."

"With fifteen million miles to fall, yes. Once we've piled up enough velocity to make it worthwhile, we'll shift to Agrav."

He took a watch out of his pocket as he spoke. It was a large disc of gleaming, featureless metal. He pressed a small catch, and luminous figures appeared upon its face. A glowing line of white encircled it, turning red in a sweeping arc until the redness closed in upon itself and the arc turned white again.

Lucky said, "Are we scheduled to enter Agrav so soon?"

"Not very long," said Panner. He placed the watch on the table, and they ate silently.

Panner lifted the watch again. "A little under a minute. It should be completely automatic." Although the chief engineer spoke calmly enough, the hand that held the watch trembled very slightly.

Panner said, "Now," and there was silence. Complete silence.

The hum of the hyperatomics had stopped. The very power to keep the ship's lights on and its pseudo-grav field in operation were now coming from Jupiter's gravitational field.

Panner said, "On the nose! Perfect!" He put away his watch, and though the smile on his broad, homely face was a restrained one, it virtually shouted relief. "We're actually on an Agrav ship now in full Agrav operation."

Lucky was smiling, too. "Congratulations. I'm pleased to be on board."

"I imagine you are. You worked hard enough for it. Poor Donahue."

Lucky said gravely, "I'm sorry I had to push the commander so hard, but I had no choice. One way or another, I had to be on board."

Panner's eyes narrowed at the sudden gravity in Lucky's voice. "*Had* to be?"

"Had to be! It seems almost certain to me that on board this ship at the present moment is the spy we're looking for."

10

In the Vitals of the Ship

Panner stared blankly. Then, "Why?"

"The Sirians would certainly want to know how the ship actually worked. If their method of spying is fool-proof, as it has been till now, why not continue it on board the ship?"

"What you're saying, then, is that one of the fourteen men on board the *Jovian Moon* is a robot?"

"That is exactly what I mean."

"But the men aboard ship have been chosen long since."

"The Sirians would know the reasons for choosing and the method of choice just as they know everything else about the project and they would maneuver their human-oid robot so as to have him chosen."

"That's giving them a lot of credit," muttered Panner.

"I admit it," said Lucky. "There is an alternative."

"Which is?"

"That the humanoid robot is aboard as a stowaway."

"Very unlikely," said Panner.

"But quite possible. It might easily have boarded the ship in the confusion before the commander made his christening speech. I tried to watch the ship then, but it was impossible. Furthermore, nine tenths of the ship seems to be made up of engine compartment, so there must be plenty of room to hide."

Panner thought about it. "Not as much room as you might think."

"Still we must search the ship. Will you do that, Dr. Panner?"

"I?"

"Certainly. As chief engineer, you would know the contents of the engine compartment better than anyone else. We'll go with you."

"Wait. It's a fool's errand."

"If there is no stowaway, Dr. Panner, we have still gained something. We'll know we can restrict our consideration to the men legally aboard ship."

"Just three of us?"

Lucky said quietly, "Whom can we trust to help us, when anyone we might ask might be the robot we're looking for? Let us not discuss this any further, Dr. Panner. Are you willing to help us search the ship? I am asking your help in my capacity as a member of the Council of Science."

Reluctantly Panner got to his feet. "I suppose I must then."

They clambered down the hand holds of the narrow shaft leading to the first engine level. The light was subdued and, naturally, indirect, so that the huge structures on either side cast no shadow.

There was no sound, no slightest hum to indicate activity or to show that vast forces were being trapped and dealt with. Bigman, looking about, was appalled to find that nothing seemed familiar; that of the ordinary workings of a space ship, such as that of their own *Shooting Starr*, nothing seemed left.

"Everything's closed in," he said.

Panner nodded and said in a low voice, "Everything is as automatic as possible. The need for human intervention has been cut to the minimum."

"What about repairs?"

"There shouldn't have to be any," the engineer said grimly. "We have alternate circuits and duplicated equipment at every step, all allowing for automatic cut-in after self-check."

Panner moved ahead, guiding them through the narrow openings but moving always slowly as though at any moment he expected someone, or some thing, to hurl itself murderously upon them.

Level by level, methodically moving out from the central shaft along the side channels, Panner probed each bit of room with the sureness of the expert.

Eventually they came to a halt at the very bottom, hard against the large tail jets through which the glowing hyperatomic forces (when the ship was in ordinary flight) pressed backward to push the ship forward.

From within the ship the test jets showed as four smooth pipes, each twice as thick as a man, burrowing into the ship and ending in the tremendous featureless structures that housed the hyperatomic motors.

Bigman said, "Hey, the jets! Inside!"

"No," said Panner.

"Why not? A robot could hide there fine. It's open space, but what's that to a robot?"

"Hyperatomic thrusts," said Lucky, "would be plenty to it and there've been a number of those till an hour ago. No, the jets are out."

"Well, then," said Panner, "there's no one anywhere in the engine compartments. No thing, either."

"You're sure?"

"Yes. There isn't a place we haven't looked, and the route I followed made it impossible for anything to get around and behind us."

Their voices made small echoes in the lengths of shafts behind them.

Bigman said, "Sands of Mars, that leaves us with the fourteen regulars."

Lucky said thoughtfully, "Less than that. Three of the men aboard ship showed emotion: Commander Donahue, Harry Norrich, Red Summers. That leaves eleven."

Panner said, "Don't forget me. I disobeyed an order. That leaves ten."

"That raises an interesting point," said Lucky. "Do you know anything about robotics?"

"I?" said Panner. "Never dealt with a robot in my life."

"Exactly," said Lucky. "Earthmen invented the positronic robot and developed most of the refinements, yet, except for a few specialists, the Earth technician knows nothing about robotics, simply because we don't use robots to any extent. It isn't taught in the schools and it doesn't come up in practice. I myself know the Three Laws and not too much more. Commander Donahue couldn't even quote the Three Laws. The Sirians, on the other hand, with a robot-saturated economy, must be past masters at all the subtleties of robotics.

"Now I spent a good deal of time yesterday and today with a book-film on advanced robotics that I found in the project library. It was the only book on the subject, by the way."

"So?" said Panner.

"It became obvious to me that the Three Laws aren't as simple as one might think. . . . Let us move on, by the way. We can give the engine levels a double check on the way back." He was moving across this lowest level as he spoke, looking with keen interest at his surroundings.

Lucky continued, "For instance, I might think it would only be necessary to give each man on the ship a ridiculous order and note whether it be obeyed. As a matter of fact, I did think so. But that isn't necessarily true. It is theoretically possible to adjust the positronic brain of a robot to obey only those orders that belong naturally to the line of its duties. Orders that are contrary to those duties or irrelevant to them may still be obeyed provided that they are preceded by certain words which act as a code or by the person who gives the orders identifying himself in a certain way. In this manner a robot can be handled in all ways by its proper overseers and yet be insensitive to strangers."

Panner, who had placed his hands on the holds that would guide the men up to the next higher level, released them. He turned to face Lucky.

He said, "You mean when you told me to take off my shirt and I didn't obey, that meant nothing?"

"I say it could have meant nothing, Dr. Panner, since taking off your shirt at that moment was no part of your regular duties, and my order might not have been stated in the proper form."

"Then you're accusing me of being a robot?"

"No. It isn't likely that you are. The Sirians, in choosing some member of the project to replace by a robot, would scarcely choose the chief engineer. For the robot to do that job properly, it would have to know so much about Agrav that the Sirians couldn't supply the knowledge. Or, if they could, they would have no need to spy."

"Thanks," said Panner, sourly, turning toward the hand holds again, but now Bigman's voice rang out.

"Hold it, Panner!" The small Martian had his ready needle-gun in his fist. He said, "Wait a minute, Lucky, how do we know he knows anything about Agrav? We're just assuming that. He never showed us any knowledge. When the *Jovian Moon* shifted to Agrav, where was he? Sitting on his squatter in his quarters with us, that's where he was."

Lucky said, "I thought of that, too, Bigman, and that's one reason I brought Panner down here. He's obviously acquainted with the engines. I've watched him inspect everything and he couldn't have done it with such assurance if he weren't an expert on the workings."

"Does that suit you, Martian?" Panner demanded with suppressed anger.

Bigman put his needle-gun away, and without a further word Panner scrambled up the ladder.

They stopped off at the next level, working through it a second time.

Panner said, "All right, that leaves ten men: two army officers, four engineers, four workmen. What do you propose to do? X-ray each of them separately? Something like that?"

Lucky shook his head. "That's too risky. Apparently the Sirians have been known to use a cute little trick to protect themselves. They've been known to use robots to carry messages or to perform tasks which the individual giving the orders wanted to be kept secret. Now obviously a robot can't keep a secret if a human being asks him, in the proper fashion, to reveal it. What the Sirians do, then, is to install an explosive device in the robot which is triggered by any attempt to force the robot to give away the secret."

"You mean if you put an X-ray on the robot, it will explode?"

"There's a very good chance that it would. Its greatest secret is its identity, and it may be triggered for every attempt to discover that identity that the Sirians could think of." Lucky added regretfully, "They hadn't counted on a V-frog; there was no trigger against that. They had to order the robot to kill the V-frog directly. Or that might have been preferable anyway, since it managed to keep the robot alive undetected."

"Wouldn't the robot be harming humans nearby if it exploded? Wouldn't it be breaking First Law?" asked Panner with a trace of sarcasm.

"*It* wouldn't. It would have no control over the explosion. The triggering would be the result of the sound of a certain question or the sight of a certain action, not the result of anything the robot itself would do."

They crawled up to still another level.

"Then what do you expect to do, Councilman?" demanded Panner.

"I don't know," Lucky said frankly. "The robot must be made to give itself away somehow. The Three Laws, however modified and fancified, *must* apply. It's only a question of being sufficiently acquainted with robotics to know how to take advantage of those Laws. If I knew how to force the robot into some action that would show it to be non-human without activating any explosive device with which it might be equipped; if I could manipulate the Three Laws so as to force one to conflict with another sufficiently strongly to paralyze the creature completely; if I—"

Panner broke in impatiently, "Well, if you expect help from me, Councilman, it's no use. I've told you already I know nothing of robotics." He whirled suddenly. "What's that?"

Bigman looked about, too. "I didn't hear anything."

Wordlessly Panner squeezed past them, dwarfed by the bending metal tube on either side.

He had gone almost as far as he could, the other two

following, when he muttered, "Someone might have squeezed in among the rectifiers. Let me pass again."

Lucky stared, frowning, into what was almost a forest of twisting cables that enclosed them in a complete dead end.

Lucky said, "It seems clear to me."

"We can test it for sure," Panner said tightly. He had opened a panel in the wall nearby and now he reached in cautiously, looking over his shoulder.

"Don't move," he said.

Bigman said testily, "Nothing's happened. There's nothing there."

Panner relaxed. "I know it. I asked you not to move because I didn't want to slice an arm off when I established the force field."

"What force field?"

"I've shorted a force field right across the corridor. You can't move out of there any more than you could if you were encased in solid steel three feet thick."

Bigman yelled, "Sands of Mars, Lucky, he *is* the robot!" His hand lunged.

Panner cried at once, "Don't try the needle-gun. Kill me and how do you ever get out?" He stared at them, dark eyes sparking, his broad shoulders hunched. "Remember, energy can get through a force field but matter can't, not even air molecules. You're airtight in there. Kill me and you'll suffocate long before anyone happens to come across you down here."

"I said he was the robot," said Bigman in raging despair.

Panner laughed shortly, "You're wrong. I'm not a robot. But if there *is* one, I know who it is."

11

Down the Line of Moons

"Who?" Bigman demanded at once.

But it was Lucky who answered, "Obviously he thinks it's one of us."

"Thanks!" said Panner. "How would *you* explain it? You mentioned stowaways; you talked about people forcing their way on board the *Jovian Moon*. Talk about nerve! Aren't there two people who did force their way on board? Didn't I witness the process? *You two!*"

"True enough," said Lucky.

"And you brought me down here so you could investigate every inch of the ship's workings. You tried to keep me busy with stories about robots hoping I wouldn't notice that you two were going over the whole ship with a microscope."

Bigman said, "We have a right to do it. This is Lucky Starr!"

"He *says* he's Lucky Starr. If he's a member of the Council of Science, he can prove it and he knows how. If I had any brains, I'd have demanded identification before taking you down."

"It's not too late now," Lucky said calmly. "Can you

see clearly from that distance?" He held up one arm, palm forward, and peeled the sleeve back.

"I'm not coming any closer," Panner said angrily.

Lucky said nothing to that. He let his wrist tell the story. The skin along the inner surface of his wrist seemed merely exposed skin, but years before it had been treated hormonally in a most complicated fashion. Responding to nothing more than a disciplined effort of Lucky's will, an oval spot on the wrist darkened and slowly turned black. Within it, little yellow specks formed in the familiar patterns of the Big Dipper and of Orion.

Panner gasped as though the breath had been forcibly knocked out of his lungs. Few human beings had the occasion to see this sign of the Council, but all above the age of childhood knew it for what it was—the final and unforgeable identification insigne of the councilman of science.

Panner was left with no choice. Silently, reluctantly, he released the force field and stepped back.

Bigman came out, raging, "I ought to bend in your skull, you lopsided—"

Lucky pulled him back. "Forget it, Bigman. The man had as much right to suspect us as we had to suspect him. Settle down."

Panner shrugged. "It seemed logical."

"I admit it did. I think we can trust each other now."

"You, maybe," the chief engineer said pointedly. "You're identified. What about this little loudmouth with you? Who identifies him?"

Bigman squawked incoherently and Lucky stepped in between the two. "I identify him and take full responsibility for him. . . . Now I propose that we get back to passenger quarters before a search is organized for us. Everything that went on down here is, of course, strictly confidential."

Then, as though nothing had happened, they resumed the climb upward.

The room assigned to them contained a two-decker bed and a washstand out of which a small trickle of water could be urged. Nothing more. Even the cramped and Spartan quarters on board the *Shooting Starr* were luxury to this.

Bigman sat cross-legged on the upper bed, while Lucky sponged his neck and shoulders. They talked in whispers, conscious of the listening ears that might be present on the other side of the walls.

Bigman said, "Look, Lucky, suppose I go up to each person on board ship; I mean, each of the ten we don't know about? Suppose I deliberately pick a fight with each one, call them a few names, things like that? Wouldn't it turn out that the guy who doesn't take a punch at me is the robot?"

"Not at all. He might not want to break shipboard discipline, or he might know what a handy fellow you are with a needle-gun, or he might not want to get into a wrangle with the Council of Science, or he might just not like to hit a man smaller than himself."

"Aw, come on, Lucky." Bigman was silent for a minute, then he said cautiously, "I've been thinking: how can you be *sure* the robot is aboard ship? I keep thinking maybe it stayed back on Jupiter Nine. It's possible."

"I know it's possible and yet I'm sure the robot is here on board ship. That's just it. I'm sure and I don't know why I'm sure," said Lucky, his eyes dark with thought. He leaned against the bed and tapped his teeth with the knuckle of one finger. "That first day we landed on Jupiter Nine, something happened."

"What?"

"If I only knew! I had it; I knew what it was, or

thought I did, just before I went to sleep that night, and it vanished. I haven't been able to get it back. If I were on Earth, I'd submit to a psycho-probe. Great Galaxy, I swear I would!

"I've tried every trick I could. Thinking hard, getting my mind off it altogether. When we were with Panner down in the engine levels, I tried talking my fool head off. I thought if I would just keep discussing every aspect of the matter, the thought was bound to pop into my head. It didn't.

"But it's there just the same. It's because of the thought that I must feel so sure the robot is one of the men aboard ship. I've made the subconscious deduction. If I could only put my finger on it, I'd have the whole answer. If I could only put my finger on it."

He sounded almost despairing.

Bigman had never seen Lucky with quite that look of frustrated loss in his face. He said, worried, "Hey, we'd better get some sleep."

"Yes, we'd better."

Minutes later, in the darkness, Bigman whispered, "Hey, Lucky, what makes you so sure I'm not the robot myself?"

Lucky whispered back, "Because the Sirians couldn't bear to build a robot with such an ugly face," and lifted his elbow to ward off a flying pillow.

The days passed. Halfway to Jupiter, they passed the inner and more sparsely populated belt of small moons, of which only Six, Seven, and Ten were numbered. Jupiter Seven was visible as a bright star, but the others were far enough away to melt into the background of the constellations.

Jupiter itself had grown to the size of the moon as seen from Earth. And because the ship was approaching the planet with the sun squarely to its rear, Jupiter remained in the "full" phase. Its entire visible surface was ablaze with sunlight. There was no shadow of night advancing across it.

Yet though the size of the moon, it was not so bright as the moon by any means. Its cloud-decked surface reflected eight times as much of the light that reached it, as did the bare powdered rock of the moon. The trouble was that Jupiter only received one twenty-seventh of the light per square mile that the moon did. The result was that it was only one third as bright at that moment as the moon appeared to be to human beings on Earth.

Yet it was more spectacular than the moon. Its belts had become quite distinct, brownish streaks with soft fuzzy edges against a creamy-white background. It was even easy to make out the flattened straw-colored oval that was the Great Red Spot as it appeared at one edge, crossed the face of the planet, then disappeared at the other.

Bigman said, "Hey, Lucky, Jupiter looks as though it isn't really round. Is that just an optical illusion?"

"Not at all," said Lucky. "Jupiter *really* isn't round. It's flattened at the poles. You've heard that Earth is flattened at the poles, haven't you?"

"Sure. But not enough to notice."

"Of course not. Consider! Earth is twenty-five thousand miles about its equator and rotates in twenty-four hours, so that a spot on its equator moves just over a thousand miles an hour. The resulting centrifugal force bulges the equator outward so that the diameter of the Earth across its middle is about twenty-seven miles more than the diameter from North Pole to South Pole. The difference in the two diameters is only about a third of one per cent so that from space Earth looks like a perfect sphere."

"Oh."

"Now take Jupiter. It is 276,000 miles about its equator, eleven times the circumference of Earth, yet it rotates about its axis in only ten hours; five minutes less than that, to be exact. A point on its equator is moving at a speed of almost twenty-eight thousand miles an hour; or twenty-eight times as fast as any point on Earth. There's a great deal more centrifugal force and a much larger equatorial bulge, especially since the material in Jupiter's outer layers is much lighter than that in the Earth's crust. Jupiter's diameter across its equator is nearly six thousand miles more than its diameter from North Pole to South Pole. The difference in the diameters is a full fifteen per cent, and that's an easy thing to see."

Bigman stared at the flattened circle of light that was Jupiter and muttered, "Sands of Mars!"

The sun remained behind them and unseen as they sank toward Jupiter. They crossed the orbit of Callisto, Jupiter Four, outermost of Jupiter's major satellites, but did not see it to advantage. It was a world one and a half million miles from Jupiter and as large as Mercury, but it was on the other side of its orbit, a small pea close to Jupiter and heading into eclipse in its shadow.

Ganymede, which was Jupiter Three, was close enough to show a disc one third as wide as the moon seen from Earth. It lay off to one side so that part of its night surface could be seen. It was three quarters full even so, pale white, and featureless.

Lucky and Bigman found themselves ignored by the rest of the crew. The commander never spoke to them or even looked at them, but moved past with eyes fixed on nothingness. Norrich, when he was led past by Mutt, nodded cheerfully as he always did when he detected the presence of humans. When Bigman answered the greeting, however, the pleasant look vanished from his face. A gentle pressure on Mutt's harness started the dog moving and he was gone.

The two found it more comfortable to eat in their own quarters.

Bigman grumbled. "Who in space do they think they are? Even that guy Panner gets busy all at once when I'm around."

Lucky said, "In the first place, Bigman, when the commander makes it so obvious that we're in his bad books, subordinates don't fall over themselves being friendly. Secondly, our dealings with a few of the men have been unpleasant."

Bigman said thoughtfully, "I met Red Summers today, the cobber. There he was coming out of the engine room and there I was, facing him."

"What happened? You didn't . . ."

"I didn't do anything. I just stood there waiting for him to start something, *hoping* he would start something, but he just smiled and moved around me."

Everyone aboard the *Jovian Moon* was watching the day Ganymede eclipsed Jupiter. It wasn't a true eclipse. Ganymede covered only a tiny part of Jupiter. Ganymede was 600,000 miles away, not quite half the size of the moon as seen from Earth. Jupiter was twice the distance, but it was a swollen globe now, fourteen times as wide as Ganymede, menacing and frightening.

Ganymede met Jupiter a little below the latter's equator, and slowly the two globes seemed to melt together. Where Ganymede cut in, it made a circle of dimmer light, for Ganymede had far less of an atmosphere than Jupiter had and reflected a considerably smaller portion of the light it received. Even if that had not been so, it would have been visible as it cut across Jupiter's belts.

The remarkable part was the crescent of blackness that hugged Ganymede's rear as the satellite moved completely onto Jupiter's disk. As the men explained to one another in breathless whispers, it was Ganymede's shadow falling on Jupiter.

The shadow, only its edge seen, moved with Ganymede, but slowly gained on it. The sliver of black cut finer and finer until in the mid-eclipse region, when Jupiter, Ganymede, and the *Jovian Moon* all made a straight line with the sun, the shadow was completely gone, covered by the world that cast it.

Thereafter, as Ganymede continued to move on, the shadow began to advance, appearing before it, first a sliver, then a thicker crescent, until both left Jupiter's globe.

The entire eclipse lasted three hours.

The *Jovian Moon* reached and passed the orbit of Ganymede when that satellite was at the other end of its seven-day orbit about Jupiter.

There was a special celebration when that happened. Men with ordinary ships (not often, to be sure) had reached Ganymede and landed on it, but no one, not one human being, had ever penetrated closer than that to Jupiter. And now the *Jovian Moon* did.

The ship passed within one hundred thousand miles of Europa, Jupiter Two. It was the smallest of Jupiter's major satellites, only nineteen hundred miles in diameter. It was slightly smaller than the moon, but its closeness made it appear twice the size of the moon as seen from Earth. Dark markings could be made out that might have been mountain ranges. Ship's telescopes proved they were exactly that. The mountains resembled those on Mercury, and there was no sign of moon-like craters. There were brilliant patches, too, resembling ice fields.

And still they sank downward, and left Europa's orbit behind.

Io was the innermost of Jupiter's major satellites, in size almost exactly equal to Earth's moon. Its distance from Jupiter, moreover, was only 285,000 miles, or little more than that of the moon from Earth.

But there the kinship ended. Whereas Earth's gentle gravitational field moved the moon about itself in the space of four weeks, Io, caught in Jupiter's gravity, whipped about in its slightly larger orbit in the space of forty-two hours. Where the moon moved about Earth at a speed of a trifle over a thousand miles an hour, Io moved about Jupiter at a speed of twenty-two thousand miles an hour, and a landing upon it was that much more difficult.

The ship, however, maneuvered perfectly. It cut in ahead of Io and wiped out Agrav at just the proper moment.

With a bound, the hum of the hyperatomics was back, filling the ship with what seemed a cascade of sound after the silence of the past weeks.

The *Jovian Moon* curved out of its path, finally, subject once again to the accelerating effect of a gravitational field, that of Io. It was established in an orbit about the satellite at a distance of less than ten thousand miles, so that Io's globe filled the sky.

They circled about it from dayside to nightside, coming lower and lower. The ship's batlike Agrav fins were retracted in order that they might not be torn off by Io's thin atmosphere.

Then, eventually, there was the keen whistling that came with the friction of ship against the outermost wisps of that atmosphere.

Velocity dropped and dropped; so did altitude. The ship's sidejets curved it to face stern-downward toward Io, and the hyperatomic jets sprang into life, cushioning the fall. Finally, with one last bit of drop and the softest jar, the *Jovian Moon* came to rest on the surface of Io.

There was wild hysteria on board the *Jovian Moon*. Even Lucky and Bigman had their backs pounded by men who had been avoiding them constantly all voyage long.

One hour later, in the darkness of Io's night, with Commander Donahue in the lead, the men of the *Jovian Moon*, each in his space suit, emerged one by one onto the surface of Jupiter One.

Sixteen men. The first human beings ever to land on Io!

Correction, thought Lucky. Fifteen men.

And one robot!

12

The Skies and Snows of Io

It was Jupiter they stopped to look at. It was Jupiter that held them frozen. There was no talk about it, no babble over the helmet radios. It was beyond talk.

Jupiter was a giant globe which, from rim to rim, extended one eighth of the way across the visible sky. Had it been full, it would have been two thousand times as bright as the Earth's full moon, but the night shadow cut a third of it away.

The bright zones and dark belts that crossed it were not merely brown now. They were close enough to show full clear color: pink, green, blue, and purple, amazingly bright. The edges of the bands were ragged and slowly changed shape as they watched, as though the atmosphere were being whipped into gigantic and turbulent storms, as most probably it was. Io's clear, thin atmosphere didn't obscure the smallest detail of that colored shifting surface.

The Great Red Spot was heaving ponderously into sight. It gave the impression of a funnel of gas, swirling lazily.

They watched for a long time, and Jupiter did not

change position. The stars moved past it, but Jupiter remained fixed where it was, low in the western sky. It could not move, since Io presented only one side to Jupiter as it revolved. On nearly half of Io's surface Jupiter never rose, and on nearly half it never set. In an in-between region of the satellite, a region making up nearly a fifth of the total surface, Jupiter remained forever on the horizon, part showing, part hidden.

"What a place for a telescope!" murmured Bigman on the wave length allotted to Lucky during the pre-landing briefing.

Lucky said, "They'll have one soon and a lot of other equipment."

Bigman touched Lucky's face-plate to attract his attention and pointed quickly. "Look at Norrich. Poor guy, he can't see any of this!"

Lucky said, "I noticed him before. He's got Mutt with him."

"Yes. Sands of Mars, they go to trouble for that Norrich! That dog suit is a special job. I was watching them put it on the dog when you were keeping tabs on the landing. They had to test to make sure he could hear the orders and obey them and if he'd let Norrich use him once Norrich got into a space suit. Apparently it all worked out."

Lucky nodded. On impulse he moved rapidly in Norrich's direction. Io's gravity was just a trifle over that of the moon, and both he and Bigman could handle that neatly.

A few long, flat strides did the job. "Norrich," said Lucky, shifting to the engineer's wave length.

One cannot tell direction of a sound when it comes out of earphones, of course, and Norrich's blind eyes looked about helplessly. "Who is it?"

"Lucky Starr." He was facing the blind man, and

through the face-plate could make out clearly the look of intense joy on Norrich's face. "You're happy to be here?"

"Happy? You might call it that. Is Jupiter very beautiful?"

"Very. Would you want me to describe it to you?"

"No. You don't have to. I've seen it by telescope when —when I had eyes, and I can see it in my mind now. It's just that . . . I don't know if I can make you understand. We're some of the few people to stand on a new world for the first time. Do you realize what a special group that makes us?"

His hand reached down to stroke Mutt's head and contacted only the metal of the dog's helmet, of course. Through the curved face-plate, Lucky could see the dog's lolling tongue, and his uneasy eyes turning restlessly this way and that, as though disturbed by the strange surroundings or by the presence of his master's voice without the familiar body that went with it.

Norrich said quietly, "Poor Mutt! The low gravity has him all confused. I won't keep him out much longer."

Then, with an increase of passion again, "Think of all the trillions of people in the galaxy. Think how few of them have had the luck to be the first on a world. You can almost name them all off. Janofski and Sterling were the first men on the moon, Ching the first man on Mars, Lubell and Smith on Venus. Add them all up. Even count in all the asteroids and all the planets outside the solar system. Add up all the firsts and see how few there are. And we're among those few. I'm among those few."

He flung his arms out as though he were ready to embrace the whole satellite. "And I owe that to Summers, too. When he worked out a new technique for manufacturing the lead contact point—it was just a matter of a bent rotor, but it saved two million dollars and a year's time, and he not even a trained mechanic—they offered to let him be in the party as reward. You know what he said. He said I deserved it in his place. They said sure, but I was blind, and he reminded them why I was blind and said he wouldn't go without me. So they took us both. I know you two don't think much of Summers, but that's what I think of when *I* think of him."

The commander's voice sounded ringingly in all helmets: "Let's get to work, men. Jupiter will stay where it is. Look at it later."

For hours the ship was unloaded, equipment was set up, tents unfurled. Temporary air tights were prepared for possible use as oxygen-supplied headquarters outside the ship.

The men were not to be kept from watching the unusual sky, though. As it happened, all three of Jupiter's other large satellites were in the sky.

Europa was closest, appearing somewhat smaller than Earth's moon. It was a crescent, near the eastern horizon. Ganymede, appearing smaller still, was nearer zenith and half full. Callisto, only a quarter the width of Earth's moon, was nudging close to Jupiter and, like Jupiter, was some two thirds full. All three together gave not one quarter the light of Earth's full moon and were completely inconspicuous in the presence of Jupiter.

Bigman said exactly that.

Lucky looked down at his small Martian friend after having studied the eastern horizon thoughtfully. "You think nothing could beat Jupiter, do you?"

"Not out here," Bigman said stoutly.

"Then keep watching," said Lucky.

In Io's thin atmosphere there was no twilight to speak of and no warning. There was a diamondlike sparkle along the frost-covered top-line of the ridge of low hills, and seven seconds later the sun had topped the horizon.

It was a tiny seed-pearl of a sun, a little circle of brilliant white, and for all the light that giant Jupiter cast, the pigmy sun cast much, much more.

They got the telescope up in time to catch Callisto vanishing behind Jupiter. One by one, all three satellites would do the same. Io, although it kept only one face to Jupiter, revolved about it in forty-two hours. That meant that the sun and all the stars seemed to march around Io's skies in those forty-two hours.

As for the satellites, Io moved faster than any of them, so it kept overtaking them in the race about Jupiter. It overtook the farthest and slowest, Callisto, most rapidly; so Callisto circled Io's heavens in two days. Ganymede took four days and Europa seven. Each traveled from east to west and each in due turn was to pass behind Jupiter.

The excitement in the case of the Callisto eclipse, which was the first to be witnessed, was extreme. Even Mutt seemed to be affected by it. He had grown increasingly used to low gravity, and Norrich gave him periods of freedom during which he floundered grotesquely about and tried vainly to inspect by nose the numerous strange things he encountered. And in the end, when Callisto reached Jupiter's glowing curve and passed behind, and all the men grew silent, Mutt, too, sat on his swathed haunches and, tongue lolling, stared upward at the sky.

But it was the sun they were really waiting for. Its apparent motion was faster than that of any of the satellites. It gained on Europa (whose crescent thinned to nothingness) and passed behind it, remaining in eclipse for something less than thirty seconds. It emerged, and then Europa was a crescent again, with its horns facing in the other direction now.

Ganymede had plunged behind Jupiter before the sun

could reach it, and Callisto, having emerged from behind Jupiter, was below the horizon.

It was the sun and Jupiter now, those two.

The men watched greedily as the seed-pearl sun climbed higher in the sky. As it did, Jupiter's phase grew narrower, its lighted portion always, of course, facing the sun. Jupiter became a "half-moon," then a fat crescent, then a thin one.

In Io's thin atmosphere the sunlit sky was a deep purple, and only the dimmer stars had been blotted out. Against that background there burnt the gigantic crescent in the sky, bulging out toward the relentlessly approaching sun.

It was like David's pebble hurled from some cosmic slingshot toward Goliath's forehead.

The light of Jupiter shrank still further and became a yellowish curved thread. The sun was almost touching.

It did touch and the men cheered. They had masked their face-plates in order to watch, but now that was no longer necessary, for the light had dimmed to bearable dimensions.

Yet it had not vanished entirely. The sun had moved behind the edge of Jupiter but it still shone murkily through that giant planet's thick, deep atmosphere of hydrogen and helium.

Jupiter itself was now completely blanked out, but its atmosphere had sprung to life, refracting and bending the sunlight through itself and around the curve of the planet, a smoothly bending film of milky light.

The film of light spread as the sun moved farther behind Jupiter. It curved back on itself until faintly, very faintly, the two horns of light met on Jupiter's other side. Jupiter's vanished body was outlined in light and one side bulged with it. It was a diamond ring in the sky, big enough to hold two thousand globes the size of the moon as seen from Earth.

And still the sun moved farther behind Jupiter so that the light began to fade and grow dim, and dimmer, until finally it was gone and, except for the pale crescent of Europa, the sky was black and belonged to the stars.

"It will stay like this five hours," said Lucky to Bigman. "Then everything will repeat itself in reverse as the sun comes out."

"And this happens every forty-two hours?" said Bigman, awed.

"That's right," said Lucky.

Panner approached them the next day and called out to them, "How are you? We're almost done here." He spread his arm about in a broad circle to indicate the Ioan valley, now littered with equipment. "We'll be leaving soon, you know, and we'll leave most of this stuff here."

"We will?" said Bigman, surprised.

"Why not? There's nothing living on the satellite to disturb the stuff and there's no weather to speak of. Everything's coated for protection against the ammonia in the atmosphere and it will keep nicely till a second expedition comes round." His voice was suddenly lower. "Is there anyone else on your private wave length, Councilman?"

"My receivers don't detect anyone."

"Do you want to take a walk with me?" He headed out, out of the shallow valley and up the gentle slope of the surrounding hills. The other two followed.

Panner said, "I must ask your pardon if I seemed unfriendly on board ship. I thought it better so."

"There are no hard feelings," Lucky assured him.

"I thought I'd try an investigation of my own, you see, and I thought it safer not to seem hand in glove with you.

I was sure that if I only watched carefully, I would catch someone giving himself away, doing something non-human, if you know what I mean. I failed, I'm afraid."

They had reached the top of the first rise and Panner looked back. He said with amusement, "Look at that dog, will you? He's getting the real feel of low gravity."

Mutt had learned a lot in the past few days. His body arched and straightened as he lunged in low, twenty-foot leaps, and he seemed to indulge in them for the sheerest pleasure.

Panner switched his radio to the wave length that had been reserved for Norrich's use in calling Mutt and shouted, "Hey, Mutt, hey, boy, come, Mutt," and whistled.

The dog heard, of course, and bounded high in the air. Lucky switched to the dog's wave length and heard his delighted barking.

Panner waved his arm and the dog headed toward them, then stopped and looked back as though wondering if he did right to leave his master. He approached more slowly.

The men walked onward again. Lucky said, "A Sirian robot built to fool a man would be a thorough job. Casual examination wouldn't detect the fraud."

"Mine wasn't casual examination," protested Panner.

Lucky's voice held more than a tinge of bitterness. "I'm beginning to think that the examination by anyone but an experienced robotics man can be nothing *but* casual."

They were passing over a drift of snowlike material, glittering in Jupiter light, and Bigman looked down upon it in amazement.

"This thing melts if you look at it," he said. He picked some up in his gauntleted hand, and it melted down and ran off like butter on a stove. He looked back, and where the three had stepped were deep indentations.

Lucky said, "It's not snow, it's frozen ammonia, Bigman. Ammonia melts at a temperature eighty degrees lower than ice does, and the heat radiating from our suits melts it that much faster."

Bigman lunged forward to where the drifts lay deeper, gouging holes wherever he stepped, and shouted, "This is fun."

Lucky called, "Make sure your heater is on if you're going to play in the snow."

"It's on," yelled Bigman, and running down a ridge with long low leaps, he flung himself headlong into a bank. He moved like a diver in slow motion, hit the drifted ammonia, and, for a moment, disappeared. He floundered to his feet.

"It's like diving into a cloud, Lucky. You hear me? Come on, try it. More fun than sand skiing on the moon."

"Later, Bigman," Lucky said. Then he turned to Panner. "For instance, did you try in any way to test any of the men?"

Out of the corner of his eye Lucky could see Bigman plunging into a bank for a second time, and, after a few moments had elapsed, his eyes turned full in that direction. Another moment and he called out anxiously, "Bigman!" Then, more loudly and much more anxiously, *"Bigman!"*

He started running.

Bigman's voice came, weak and gasping. "Breath . . . knocked out . . . hit rock . . . river down here . . ."

"Hold on, I'll be with you." Lucky and Panner, too, were devouring space with their strides.

Lucky knew what had happened, of course. The surface temperature of Io was not far removed from the melting point of ammonia. Underneath the ammonia drifts, melting ammonia could be feeding hidden rivers of that foul-smelling, choking substance that existed so copiously on the outer planets and their satellites.

There was the rattle of Bigman's coughing in his ear. "Break in air hose . . . ammonia getting in . . . choking."

Lucky reached the hole left by Bigman's diving body and looked down. The ammonia river was plainly visible, bubbling slowly downhill over sharp crags. It must have been against one of those that Bigman's air hose had been damaged.

"Where are you, Bigman?"

And though Bigman answered feebly, "Here," he was nowhere to be seen.

13

Fall!

Lucky jumped recklessly into the exposed river, drifting gently downward under the pull of Io's weak gravity. He was angry at the slowness of his fall, at Bigman for the childish enthusiasms that seized him so suddenly, and—unpredictably—at himself for not having stopped Bigman when he might.

Lucky hit the stream, and ammonia sprayed high in the air, then fell back with surprising quickness. Io's thin atmosphere could not support the small droplets even at low gravity.

There was no sense of buoyancy to the ammonia river. Lucky had not expected any to speak of. Liquid ammonia was less dense than water and had less lifting power. Nor was the force of the current great under Io's weak pull. Had Bigman not damaged his air hose, it would have been only a matter of walking out of the river and through any of the drifts that might have packed it round.

As it was . . .

Lucky splashed downstream furiously. Somewhere ahead the small Martian must be struggling feebly against the poisonous ammonia. If the break in the hose was large enough, or had grown large enough, to allow liquid ammonia to enter, Lucky would be too late.

He might be too late, already, and his chest constricted and tightened at the thought.

A form streaked past Lucky, burying itself in the powdered ammonia. It disappeared, leaving a tunnel into which ammonia slowly collapsed.

"Panner," Lucky said tentatively.

"Here I am." The engineer's arm fell upon Lucky's shoulder from behind. "That was Mutt. He came running when you yelled. We were both on his wave length."

Together they forged through the ammonia on the track of the dog. They met him, returning.

Lucky cried eagerly, "He's got Bigman."

Bigman's arms feebly enfolded the dog's suit-encased haunches, and though that hampered Mutt's movements, low gravity enabled the dog to make respectable headway through use of shoulder muscles alone.

Even as Lucky bent for Bigman, the little Martian's straining hold relaxed and he fell.

Lucky scooped him up. He wasted no time on investigation or talk. There was only one thing to do. He turned up Bigman's oxygen flow to full capacity, slung him over his shoulders, and ran for the ship. Even allowing for Io's gravity he had never run so recklessly in his life. With such haste did he kick the ground away when coming down from each hurtling, horizontal stride that the effect was almost one of low-level flying.

Panner pumped along in the rear, and Mutt stayed excitedly at Lucky's heels.

Lucky used the communal wave length to alert the others even as he was running and one of the air tights was made ready.

Lucky hurtled inside the air tight, scarcely breaking his stride. The flap closed behind him and the interior flooded with additional air under pressure to make up the loss during the flap's opening.

With flying fingers he unbuckled Bigman's helmet, then more slowly drew off the rest of the suit.

He felt for the heartbeat and, to his relief, found it. The air tight was equipped, of course, with a first-aid kit. He made the necessary injections for general stimulation and waited for warmth and plentiful oxygen to do the rest.

And eventually Bigman's eyes fluttered and focused with difficulty on Lucky. His lips moved and made the word "Lucky," though no sound was involved.

Lucky laughed with relief and finally took the time to remove his own space suit.

On board the *Jovian Moon* Harry Norrich stopped at the open door of the compartment within which Bigman was completing his recuperation. His unseeing, china-blue eyes were warm with pleasure.

"How's the invalid?"

Bigman struggled up in his bunk and shouted, "Fine! Sands of Mars, I feel great! If it weren't that Lucky wants to keep me down, I'd be up and around."

Lucky grunted his disbelief.

Bigman ignored that. He said, "Hey, let Mutt come in. Good old Mutt! Here, boy, here!"

Mutt, the hold on his harness released, trotted over to Bigman, his tail wagging furiously and his intelligent eyes doing everything but talk a greeting.

Bigman's small arm embraced the dog's neck in a bear hug. "Boy, *there's* a friend. You heard what he did, Norrich, didn't you?"

"Everyone did," and it was plain to see that Norrich took a great personal pride in his dog's accomplishment.

"I just barely remember it," Bigman said, "before I blacked out altogether. I got that lungful of ammonia and couldn't seem to straighten out. I rolled downhill, just going through the ammonia snow as though it were nothing. Then there was this thing coming at me and I was sure it was Lucky when I heard the sound of something moving. But he knocked enough of the snow off us to let some of the Jupiter light come in and I could just make out it was Mutt. The last thing I remember was grabbing him."

"And a good thing, too," Lucky said. "The extra time that would have been required for me to find you would have been your finish."

Bigman shrugged. "Aw, Lucky, you make such a big deal out of it. Nothing would have happened if I hadn't just caught the hose on a rock and torn it. At that if I had had enough brains to turn up my oxygen pressure, I could have kept the ammonia out. It was just the first lungful that seemed to put me out of kilter. I couldn't think."

Panner passed by, just then, and looked. "How are you, Bigman?"

"Sands of Mars! Looks like everyone thinks I'm an invalid or something. There's nothing wrong with me. Even the commander stopped by and managed to find his tongue long enough to grunt at me."

"Well," said Panner, "maybe he's getting over his mad."

"Never," said Bigman. "He just wants to make sure his first flight won't be spoiled by a casualty. He wants his record pure white, that's all."

Panner laughed. "All set for the take-off?"

Lucky said, "Are we leaving Io?"

"Any hour. The men are reloading the equipment we're taking with us and securing what we leave behind. If you two can make the pilot room once we're underway, do so. We'll get a better look at Jupiter than ever."

He tickled Mutt behind one ear and left.

They radioed Jupiter Nine that they were leaving Io,

as days earlier they had radioed that they had surfaced on the satellite.

Bigman said, "Why don't we call Earth? Chief Councilman Conway ought to know we've made it."

"Officially," said Lucky, "we haven't made it all the way until we've returned to Jupiter Nine."

He did not add aloud that he was not at all anxious to return to Jupiter Nine, still less anxious to talk to Conway. He had, after all, accomplished nothing on this trip.

His brown eyes surveyed the control room. The engineers and crewmen were at their stations for the takeoff. The commander, his two officers and Panner, however, were in the control room.

Lucky wondered again about the officers as time and again he had wondered about each of the ten men whom the V-frog had not had a chance to eliminate. He had spoken to each of them on occasion, as had Panner even more frequently. He had searched their quarters. He and Panner together had gone over their records. Nothing had resulted.

He would be going back to Jupiter Nine with the robot unlocated, and thereafter location would be harder than ever and he might have to report back to Council headquarters with news of failure.

Once more, desperately, the thought of X rays entered his mind, or some other means of forceful inspection. As always, he thought at once of the possibility of triggering off an explosion, probably a nuclear explosion.

It would destroy the robot. It would also kill thirteen men and blow up a priceless ship. Worst of all, it would show no safe way of detecting the humanoid robots which, Lucky felt certain, were preying in other parts of the Solar Confederation.

He was startled by Panner's sudden cry, "Here we go!"

There was the familiar distant *whoosh* of the initial thrust, the gathering backward press of acceleration, and Io's surface dropped away, faster and faster.

The visiplate could not center Jupiter in its entirety: it was too large. It centered the Great Red Spot instead and followed it in its rotation about the globe.

Panner said, "We've gone into Agrav again, yes, but it's only temporary, just to let Io pull away from us."

"But we're still falling toward Jupiter," Bigman said.

"That's right, but only till the proper moment is reached. Then we go into hyperatomic drive and plunge toward Jupiter on a hyperbolic orbit. Once that is established, we cut the drive and let Jupiter do the work. Our closest approach will be about 150,000 miles. Jupiter's gravity will zoom us around as though we were a pebble in a slingshot and shoot us out again. At the proper point our hyperatomic drive cuts in again. By taking advantage of the slingshot effect, we actually save a bit on energy over the alternative of leaving directly from Io, *and* we get some super close-ups of Jupiter."

He looked at his watch. "Five minutes," he said.

He was referring, as Lucky knew, to the moment when the ship would switch from Agrav to hyperatomic drive and begin to curve off into the planned orbit about Jupiter.

Still staring at his watch, Panner said, "The time is selected so that we come out heading toward Jupiter Nine as squarely as possible. The fewer side adjustments we have to make, the more energy we save. We've got to come back to Jupiter Nine with as much of our original energy store as possible. The more we come back with, the better Agrav looks. I've set my goals at eighty-five per cent. If we can come back with ninety, that would be superlative."

Bigman said, "Suppose you come back with more energy than you had when you left? How would that be?"

"Super-superlative, Bigman, but impossible. There's something called the second law of thermodynamics that stands in the way of making a profit on the deal or, for that matter, of breaking even. We've got to take some loss." He smiled broadly and said, "One minute."

And at the appropriate second the sound of the hyperatomics filled the ship with its muted murmurings, and Panner placed his watch in his pocket with a satisfied expression.

"From here on in," he said, "until actual landing maneuvers at the Jupiter Nine approach, everything is quite automatic."

He had no sooner said that when the humming ceased again, the lights in the room flickered and went out. Almost at once they went on again, but now there was a little red sign on the control panel that said, EMERGENCY.

Panner sprang to his feet. "What in Space . . . ?"

He left the pilot room at a run, leaving the others staring after him and at one another in various degrees of horror. The commander had gone dead-white, his lined face a tired mask.

Lucky, with sudden decision, followed Panner, and Bigman, of course, followed Lucky.

They came upon one of the engineers clambering out of the engine compartment. He was panting. "Sir!"

"What is it, man?" snapped Panner.

"The Agrav is off, sir. It can't be activated."

"What about the hyperatomics?"

"The main reserve is shorted. We cut it just in time to keep it from blowing. If we touch it, the whole ship will go up. Every bit of the stored energy will blow."

"Then we're working on the emergency reservoir?"

"That's right."

Panner's swarthy face was congested with blood. "What good is that? We can't set up an orbit about Jupiter with the emergency reservoir. Out of the way. Let me down there."

The engineer stepped aside, and Panner swung into the shaft. Lucky and Bigman were at his heels.

Lucky and Bigman had not been in the engine compartment since that first day aboard the *Jovian Moon*. The scene was different now. There was no august silence, no sensation of mighty forces quietly at work.

Instead, the puny sound of men rose high about them.

Panner sprang off into the third level. "Now what's wrong?" he called. "Exactly what's wrong?"

Men parted to let him through and they all huddled over the gutted insides of a complex mechanism, pointing things out in tones of mingled despair and anger.

There were sounds of other footsteps coming down the rungs of the shaft, and then the Commander himself made his appearance.

He spoke to Lucky, who was standing gravely to one side. "What is it, Councilman?" It was the first time he had addressed Lucky since they had left Jupiter Nine.

Lucky said, "Serious damage of some sort, Commander."

"How did it happen? *Panner!*"

Panner looked up from the close examination of something that had been held out to him. He shouted in annoyance, "What in space do you want?"

Commander Donahue's nostrils flared. "Why has something been allowed to go wrong?"

"Nothing has been *allowed* to go wrong."

"Then what do you call this?"

"Sabotage, Commander. Deliberate, murdering sabotage!"

"*What!*"

"Five gravitic relays have been completely smashed and the necessary replacements have been removed and can't be located. The hyperatomic thrust-control has been fused and shorted beyond repair. None of it happened by accident."

The commander stared at his chief engineer. He said, hollowly, "Can anything be done?"

"Maybe the five relay replacements can be located or cannibalized out of the rest of the ship. I'm not sure. Maybe a makeshift thrust-control can be set up. It would take days anyway and I couldn't guarantee results."

"Days!" cried the commander. "It can't take days. *We're falling toward Jupiter!*"

There was a complete silence for a few moments, and then Panner put into words what all of them knew. "That's right, Commander. We're falling toward Jupiter and we can't stop ourselves in time. It means we're through, Commander. We're all dead men!"

14

Jupiter Close Up

It was Lucky who broke the deadly silence that followed, in sharp, incisive tones. "No man is dead while he has a mind capable of thought. Who can handle this ship's computer most rapidly?"

Commander Donahue said, "Major Brant. He's the regular trajectory man."

"Is he up in the control room?"

"Yes."

"Let's get to him. I want the detailed *Planetary Ephemerae* . . . Panner, you stay here with the men and get to work cannibalizing and improvising."

"What good will it—?" Panner began.

Lucky cut in at once. "Perhaps no good at all. If so, we'll hit Jupiter and you'll die after having wasted a few hours of labor. Now I've given you an order. Get to work!"

"But . . ." Commander Donahue seemed stuck after that one word.

Lucky said, "As councilman of science, I'm assuming command of this vessel. If you wish to dispute that, I'll have Bigman lock you in your cabin and you can argue it out at the court-martial proceedings, assuming we survive."

Lucky turned away and moved quickly up the central shaft. Bigman motioned Commander Donahue up with a quick jerk of his thumb and followed last.

Panner looked after them scowling, turned savagely to the engineers, and said, "All right, you bunch of corpses. No use waiting for it with our fingers in our mouths. Hop to it."

Lucky strode into the control room.

The officer at the controls said, "What's wrong down there?" His lips were white.

"You're Major Brant," said Lucky, "We haven't been formally introduced, but never mind that. I'm Councilman David Starr, and you're taking orders from me. Get at that computer and do what you're told with all the speed you have."

Lucky had the *Planetary Ephemerae* before him. Like all great reference works, it was in book form rather than film. The turning of pages, after all, made for the more rapid location of a specific piece of information, than did the long-drawn-out unwinding of film from end to end.

He turned the pages now with practiced hand, searching among the rows and columns of numbers that located the position of every chunk of matter in the solar system over ten miles in diameter (and some under) at certain standard times, together with their planes of revolution and velocity of motion.

Lucky said, "Take the following co-ordinates as I call them out, together with the line of motion, and calculate the characteristics of the orbit and the position of the point at this moment and for succeeding moments for the space of forty-eight hours."

The major's fingers flew as figures were converted by

the special punch machine into a coded tape which was fed into the computer.

Even while that was taking place, Lucky said, "Calculate from our present position and velocity our orbit with respect to Jupiter and the point of intersection with the object whose orbit you have just calculated."

Again the major worked.

The computer spat out its results in coded tape that wound on to a spool and dictated the tapping of a typewriter that spelled out the results in figures.

Lucky said, "At the point of intersection, what is time discrepancy between our ship and the object?"

Again the major worked. He said, "We miss it by four hours, twenty-one minutes, and forty-four seconds."

"Calculate how the velocity of the ship must be altered in order to hit the point squarely. Use one hour from now as the starting time."

Commander Donahue broke in. "We can't do anything this close to Jupiter, Councilman. The emergency power won't break us away. Don't you understand that?"

"I'm not asking the major to break us away, Commander. I'm asking him to accelerate the ship toward Jupiter, for whatever our reserve power is worth."

The commander rocked back on his heels. "*Toward* Jupiter?"

The computer was making the calculation and the results were coming in. Lucky said, "Can you accelerate by that much on the power available?"

Major Brant said shakily, "I think so."

"Then do it."

Commander Donahue said again, "*Toward* Jupiter?"

"Yes. Exactly. Io isn't the innermost of Jupiter's satellites. Amalthea is closer, Jupiter Five. If we can intersect its orbit properly, we can land on it. If we miss it, well, then, we will have hurried death by two hours."

Bigman felt a surge of sudden hope. He could never entirely despair while Lucky was in action, but until that moment he had not seen what it was that Lucky intended doing. He remembered now his earlier conversation with Lucky on the subject. The satellites were numbered in order of discovery. Amalthea was a small satellite, just a hundred miles in diameter, and it was discovered only after the four major satellites were known. So, though the closest to Jupiter, it was Jupiter Five. Somehow one tended to forget that. Because Io was called Jupiter One, there was always the tendency to think there was nothing between it and the planet itself.

And one hour later the *Jovian Moon* began a carefully plotted acceleration toward Jupiter, hastening toward the death trap.

They no longer centered the visiplate on any part of Jupiter. Though the latter swelled hourly, the center of sight remained on a portion of the star field a considerable distance from Jupiter's rim. The star field was under maximum magnification. At that point should be Jupiter Five, streaking for its rendezvous with a ship which was hurtling and straining down, down toward Jupiter. Either the ship would be caught by the speck of rock and saved, or it would miss and be lost forever.

"There it is," said Bigman in excitement. "That star shows a visible disk."

"Calculate observed position and motion," ordered Lucky, "and check with the computed orbit."

This was done.

"Any correction?" Lucky asked.

"We'll have to slow down by—"

"Never mind the figures. Do it!"

Jupiter Five circled Jupiter in twelve hours, moving in its orbit at a speed of nearly three thousand miles an hour.

This was one and a half times as rapid as Io's motion and its gravitational field was only one twentieth that of Io. For both reasons, it made the harder target.

Major Brant's fists trembled on the controls as the all-important side thrusts bent the *Jovian Moon's* orbit ever so slightly to meet the onrushing Jupiter Five, slip behind it and round, matching speeds for just those vital moments that would enable the satellite's gravity to establish the ship in an orbit about itself.

Jupiter Five was a large, brilliant object now. If it stayed so, good. If it began to grow smaller, they had missed.

Major Brant whispered, "We've made it," and his head fell forward into his shaking palms as he released the controls.

Even Lucky closed his eyes momentarily in a kind of weary relief.

In one way the situation on Jupiter Five was far different from what it had been on Io. There, all the crew had been sight-seers; the consideration of the heavens had taken precedence over the leisurely preparations in the valley.

Here on Jupiter Five, however, no one emerged from the *Jovian Moon*. What there was to see, no one saw.

The men stayed aboard the ship and worked on the repair of the engines. Nothing else mattered. If they failed, the landing on Jupiter Five could only postpone doom and stretch it out into greater agony.

No normal ship could land on Jupiter Five to rescue them, and no other Agrav ship existed or would exist for a year at least. If they failed, there would be time enough to watch Jupiter and the vision of the skies while they waited for death.

Yet under less urgent conditions the vision would have

been worth watching. It was Io all over again with everything doubled and tripled.

From the point at which the *Jovian Moon* landed, Jupiter's lower rim seemed to sweep the flat, powdery horizon. The giant looked so close in the airlessness that a watcher would have imagined he could reach out his hand and bury it in that circle of light.

From the horizon Jupiter stretched upward, halfway to zenith. At the moment the *Jovian Moon* landed, Jupiter was almost full, and within the unbearable circle of brilliant stripes and colors nearly ten thousand full moons Earth variety, could have been placed. Almost one sixteenth of the entire vault of the sky was covered by Jupiter.

And because Jupiter Five circled Jupiter in twelve hours, the visible moons—there were four here rather than three as on Io, since Io itself was now a moon—moved three times as fast as they did on Io. So did all the stars and everything else in the sky, except for frozen Jupiter, which one side of the satellite eternally faced and which therefore never moved.

In five hours the sun would rise and it would be exactly the same in appearance as on Io; it would be the one thing that hadn't changed. But it would race toward a four-times-as-large Jupiter at three times the speed and make an eclipse a hundred times as terrifyingly beautiful.

But no one saw it. It took place twice while the *Jovian Moon* stayed and no one saw it. No one had the time. No one had the heart.

Panner finally sat down and stared out of bleary eyes. The flesh around them was red and puffy. His voice was a hoarse whisper.

"All right. Everyone to your normal stations. We'll have a dry run." He hadn't slept in forty hours. The others had worked in shifts, but Panner had stopped neither to eat nor to sleep.

Bigman, who had confined himself to unskilled labor, to fetching and carrying, to reading dials under direction and holding levers according to instruction, had no place in a dry run, no station, no duties. So he wandered somberly about the ship in search of Lucky and found him in the control room with Commander Donahue.

Lucky had his shirt off and was wiping his shoulders, forearms, and face on a large plastofluff towel.

As soon as he saw Bigman, he said briskly, "The ship will be moving, Bigman. We'll be taking off soon."

Bigman's eyes raised. "We're only doing a dry run, Lucky."

"It will work. That Jim Panner worked miracles."

Commander Donahue said stiffly, "Councilman Starr, you have saved my ship."

"No, no. Panner deserves the credit. I think half the engine is being held together with copper wire and mucilage, but it will work."

"You know what I mean, Councilman. You drove us on to Jupiter Five when the rest of us were ready to give up and panic. You saved my ship, and I will report that fact fully when I stand court-martial on Earth for having failed to co-operate with you on Jupiter Nine."

Lucky flushed in embarrassment. "I can't allow that, Commander. It is important that councilmen avoid publicity. As far as the official record is concerned, you will have remained in command at all times. There will be no mention of any actions of mine."

"Impossible. I couldn't allow myself to be praised for what you have done."

"You will have to. It's an order. And let's have no talk of court-martials."

Commander Donahue drew himself up with a kind of

pride. "I deserve court-martial. You warned me of the presence of Sirian agents. I did not listen and as a result my ship was sabotaged."

"The blame is mine, too," Lucky said calmly. "I was on board ship and did not prevent it. Nevertheless, if we can bring back the saboteur, there will be no question of court-martial."

The commander said, "The saboteur, of course, is the robot you warned me of. How I could be so blind!"

"I'm afraid you still don't see entirely. It wasn't the robot."

"*Not* the robot?"

"A robot could not have sabotaged the ship. It would have been bringing harm to humans and that would have meant breaking the First Law."

The commander frowned as he considered that. "It might not have been aware that it was doing harm."

"Everyone aboard ship, including the humanoid, understands Agrav. The robot would have known it was doing harm. In any case I think we have the identity of the saboteur, or will have in a moment."

"Oh? Who is he, Councilman Starr?"

"Well, consider this for a moment. If a man so sabotages a ship as to insure that it will either blow up or fall into Jupiter, he would be either a madman or a superhumanly dedicated person to stay on board that ship."

"Yes, I suppose so."

"Since the time we left Io, the air locks have never opened. If they had there would have been slight drops in air pressure, and the ship's barometer indicates no such drops. You see, then, the saboteur must never have gotten on the ship at Io. He's still there, unless he's been taken off."

"How could he be taken off? No ship could get to Io, except this one."

Lucky smiled grimly. "No *Earth* ship."

The commander's eyes widened. "Surely no Sirian ship, either."

"Are you sure?"

"Yes, I'm sure." The commander frowned. "And for that matter, wait a moment. Everyone reported on board before we left Io. We wouldn't have left without everyone reported present."

"In that case everyone is still on board."

"I would presume so."

"Well," said Lucky, "Panner has ordered all men to stations under emergency conditions. The whereabouts of every man should be fixed during this dry run. Call Panner and ask if anyone is missing."

Commander Donahue turned to the intercom, and signaled Panner.

There was some delay, and then Panner's voice, infinitely tired, answered. "I was about to call, Commander. The run was successful. We can take off. If we're lucky, things will hold till we're back on Jupiter Nine."

The commander said, "Very good. Your work will be properly acknowledged, Panner. Meanwhile, are all men at stations?"

Panner's face on the visiplate above the intercom seemed to harden all at once. "*No!* By Space, I meant to tell you! We can't locate Summers."

"Red Summers," Bigman cried in sudden excitement. "That murdering cobber. Lucky . . ."

"One moment, Bigman," Lucky said. "Dr. Panner, you mean Summers isn't in his quarters?"

"He isn't anywhere. Except that it's impossible, I'd say he wasn't on board."

"Thank you." Lucky reached over to break contact. "Well, Commander."

Bigman said, "Listen, Lucky. You remember once I

told you I met him coming out of the engine room? What was he doing down there?"

"We know now," said Lucky.

"And we know enough to get him," said the commander, white-faced. "We're landing on Io and . . ."

"Wait," said Lucky, "first things first. There is something more important even than a traitor."

"What?"

"The matter of the robot."

"That can wait."

"Perhaps not. Commander, you said that all men reported on board the *Jovian Moon* before we left Io. If so, the report was obviously a false one."

"Well?"

"I think we ought to try to find the source of the false report. A robot can't sabotage a ship, but if a man has sabotaged the ship without the robot's knowledge, it would be very simple for the robot to help that man remain off the ship if its help is requested."

"You mean whoever is responsible for the false report that Summers was on board ship is the robot?"

Lucky paused. He tried not to allow himself to grow too hopeful or feel too triumphant, and yet the argument seemed perfect.

He said, "It seems so."

15

Traitor!

Commander Donahue said, "Major Levinson, then." His eyes darkened. "And yet I find that impossible to believe."

"Find what impossible to believe?" Lucky asked.

"That he is a robot. He's the man who took the report. He keeps our records. I know him well and I swear that he *can't* be a robot."

"We'll question him, Commander. And one thing—" Lucky's expression was somber. "Don't accuse him of being a robot; don't ask him if he's one or even imply that he might be one. Do nothing to make him feel he's under suspicion."

The commander looked astonished. "Why not?"

"The Sirians have a way of protecting their robots. Open suspicion may trigger some explosive device within the major if he is indeed a robot."

The commander exhaled explosively. "Space!"

Major Levinson showed the signs of strain that were universal among the men aboard the *Jovian Moon*, but he stood at brisk military attention. "Yes, sir."

The commander said cautiously, "Councilman Starr has a few questions to ask."

Major Levinson shifted to face Lucky. He was quite tall, topping even Lucky's inches, with fair hair, blue eyes, and a narrow face.

Lucky said, "All men were reported on board the *Jovian Moon* at the time of take-off from Io, and you prepared that report. Is that right, major?"

"Yes, sir."

"Did you see each man individually?"

"No, sir. I used the intercom. Each man answered at take-off station or in his cabin."

"Each man? Did you hear each man's voice? Each individual voice?"

Major Levinson looked astonished. "I suppose so. That's not the sort of thing one remembers, really."

"Nevertheless it's quite important and I'm asking you to remember."

The major frowned and bent his head. "Well, now wait. Come to think of it, Norrich answered for Summers because Summers was in the bathroom." Then, with a sudden spark of excitement, he added, "Hold on, they're looking for Summers right now."

Lucky held up a palm. "Never mind that, Major. Would you get Norrich and send him up?"

Norrich came in on Major Levinson's arm. He looked bewildered. He said, "Commander, no one seems to be able to find Red Summers. What's happened to him?"

Lucky forestalled the commander's answer. He said, "We're trying to find out. Did you report Summers present when Major Levinson checked those aboard before we left Io?"

The blind engineer reddened. He said tightly, "Yes."

"The major says you said Summers was in the bathroom. Was he?"

"Well . . . No, he wasn't, Councilman. He had gotten off ship for a moment to pick up some item of equipment he had left behind. He didn't want the commander chewing him out—pardon me, sir—for carelessness, and he asked me to cover for him. He said he would be back well before take-off."

"Was he?"

"I . . . I thought . . . I had the impression he was. Mutt barked, I think, and I was sure Summers was coming back, but there isn't anything for me to do at take-off, so I was turning in for a nap and I guess I just didn't give the matter too much thought at the moment. Then there was the mess in the engine room almost right away, and after that there was no time to think of anything."

Panner's voice came over the central intercom with sudden loudness. "Warning to all men. We are taking off. Everyone to stations."

The *Jovian Moon* was in space again, lifting itself against Jupiter's gravity with powerful surges. It was expending energy at a rate that would have bankrupted five ordinary vessels and only the faint tremor in the sound of the hyperatomics remained to show that the ship's mechanism depended, in part, on makeshift devices.

Panner gloomily pondered on the poor showing the ship would now make energy-wise. He said, "As is, I'll get back with only seventy per cent of original energy, when it could have been eighty-five or ninety. If we land on Io and make another take-off, we'll get back with only fifty. And I don't know if we can stand another take-off."

But Lucky said, "We must get Summers, and you know why."

· · ·

With Io growing large-sized once again in the visiplate, Lucky said thoughtfully, "It's not entirely certain we can find him, Bigman."

Bigman said incredulously, "You don't think the Sirians actually picked him up, do you?"

"No, but Io's a big place. If he wanders off to some rendezvous, we might never locate him. I'm counting on his staying put. He'd have to carry air, food, and water with him if he moved, so it would be most logical for him to stay put. Particularly when he'd have no reason to expect us to come back."

Bigman said, "We should have known it was that cobber all along, Lucky. He tried to kill you first thing. Why should he want to do that, if he weren't playing along with the Sirians?"

"True enough, Bigman, but remember this: we were looking for a spy. Summers couldn't be the spy. He had no access to the leaked information. Once it was clear to me that the spy was a robot, that cleared Summers on another account. The V-frog had detected emotion in him, so he couldn't be a robot and therefore couldn't be the spy. Of course that didn't prevent him from being a traitor and saboteur, and I should not have allowed the search for a spy to blind me to that possibility."

He shook his head and added, "This seems to be a case riddled with disappointment. If it had been anyone else *but* Norrich who had covered for Summers, we would have had our robot. The trouble is that Norrich is the only man who could have had convincingly innocent reason to co-operate with Summers. He was friendly with Summers; we know that. Then, too, Norrich could innocently be ignorant that Summers never returned before take-off. After all, he's blind."

Bigman said, "Besides which, he showed emotion, too, so he can't be the robot."

Lucky nodded. "True enough." Yet he frowned and grew silent.

Down, down they came to Io's surface, landing almost in the marks of their previous take-off. The dots and smeared shadows in the valley resolved themselves into the equipment they had set up as they approached.

Lucky was surveying the surface intently through the visiplate. "Were any air tights left behind on Io?"

"No," said the commander.

"Then we may have our man. One air tight, as you may notice, is fully expanded behind that rock formation. Do you have the list of material unaccounted for on board?"

The commander delivered a sheet of paper without comment, and Lucky studied it. He said, "Bigman and I will go out after him. I doubt that we'll need help."

The tiny sun was high in the sky, and Bigman and Lucky walked on their own shadows. Jupiter was a thinnish crescent.

Lucky spoke on Bigman's wave length. "He must have seen the ship unless he's sleeping."

"Or unless he's gone," said Bigman.

"I doubt that he's gone."

And almost at once Bigman cried, "Sands of Mars, Lucky, look up there!"

A figure appeared at the top of the line of rock. It stood out blackly against the thinning yellow line of Jupiter.

"Don't move," came a low, tired voice on Lucky's own wave length. "I'm holding a blaster."

"Summers," said Lucky, "come down and surrender."

A note of bitter mockery entered the other's strained voice. "I guessed the right wave length, didn't I, Councilman? Though it was an easy guess from the size of your friend . . . Get back to your ship or I'll kill you both."

Lucky said, "Don't bluff pointlessly. At this distance you couldn't hit us in a dozen tries."

Bigman added with tenor fury, "And I'm armed, too, and I can hit you even at *this* distance. Just remember that and don't even move a finger near the activating button."

Lucky said, "Throw down your blaster and surrender."

"Never!" said Summers.

"Why not? To whom are you being loyal?" Lucky demanded. "The Sirians? Did they promise to pick you up? If so, they lied to you and betrayed you. They're not worth loyalty. Tell me where the Sirians' base in the Jupiter system is located."

"You know so much! Figure it out for yourself."

"What subwave combination do you use to contact them?"

"Figure that out, too . . . Don't move any closer."

Lucky said, "Help us out now, Summers, and I'll do my best to get you mild treatment on Earth."

Summers laughed weakly. "The word of a councilman?"

"Yes."

"I wouldn't take it. Get back to your ship."

"Why have you turned against your own world, Summers? What have the Sirians offered you? Money?"

"Money!" The other's voice was suddenly furious. "Do you want to know what they offered me? I'll tell you. A chance at a decent life." They could hear the tiny gritting sound Summers made as his teeth ground together. "What did I have on Earth? Misery all my life. A crowded planet with no decent chance at making a name and a position for myself. Everywhere I went I was surrounded by millions of people clawing at each other for existence, and when I tried to claw also, I was put in jail. I made up my mind that if ever I could do anything to get back at Earth, I would."

"What do you expect to get from Sirius in the way of a decent life?"

"They invited me to emigrate to the Sirian planets, if you must know." He paused, and his breathing made small whistling noises. "New worlds out there. Clean worlds. There's room for men there; they need men and talent. I'd have a chance there."

"You'll never get there. When are they coming for you?"

Summers was silent.

Lucky said, "Face it, man. They're not coming for you. They have no decent life for you; no life at all for you. Only death for you. You expected them before this, didn't you?"

"I didn't."

"Don't lie. It won't improve the situation for you. We've checked the supplies missing from the *Jovian Moon*. We know exactly how much oxygen you smuggled off the ship. Oxygen cylinders are clumsy things to carry even under Io's gravity when you have to sneak them off without being caught and in a hurry. Your air supply is almost gone now, isn't it?"

"I have plenty of air," said Summers.

Lucky said, "I say it's almost gone. Don't you see the Sirians aren't coming for you? They can't come for you without Agrav and they haven't got Agrav. Great Galaxy, man, have you let yourself get so hungry for the Sirian worlds that you'll let them kill you in as open and crude a double-cross as I've ever seen? Now, tell me, what have you done for them?"

Summers said, "I did what they asked me to do and

that wasn't much. And if I have any regrets," he shouted in sudden, breathless bravado, "it's only that I didn't get the *Jovian Moon*. How did you get away, anyway? I fixed it. I *fixed* the rotten, slimy . . ." he ended, choking.

Lucky motioned to Bigman and broke into the soaring lope characteristic of running on low-gravity worlds. Bigman followed, veering off so as not to offer a single target.

Summers' blaster came up and made a thin popping sound, all that was possible in Io's thin wisps of atmosphere. Sand kicked up and around, and a crater formed yards from Lucky's fleeting figure.

"You won't catch me," Summers yelled with a kind of weak violence. "I'm not coming back to Earth. They'll come for me. The Sirians will come for me."

"Up, Bigman," said Lucky. He had reached the rock formation. Jumping upward, he caught a projection and hurled himself further upward. At sixth-normal gravity, a man, even in a space suit, could outdo a mountain goat in climbing.

Summers screamed thinly. His hands moved up to his helmet and he leaped backward and disappeared.

Lucky and Bigman reached the top. The rock formation was nearly sheer on the other side, with sharp outcroppings breaking the clifflike face. Summers was a spread-eagled figure, dropping slowly downward, striking against the face of the rock, and rebounding.

Bigman said, "Let's get him, Lucky," and jumped far outward, wide of the cliff. Lucky followed.

It would have been a killing leap on Earth, even on Mars. On Io it was little more than a tooth-jarring drop.

They hit with bent knees and let themselves roll to take up some of the force of impact. Lucky was on his feet first and made for Summers, who lay prone and unmoving.

Bigman came up panting. "Hey, that wasn't the easiest jump I— What's the matter with the cobber?"

Lucky said grimly. "He's dead. I knew his oxygen was low from the way he sounded. He was almost unconscious. It's why I rushed him."

"You could go a long time being unconscious," said Bigman.

Lucky shook his head. "He made sure. He really didn't want to be taken. Just before he jumped, he opened his helmet to Io's poison air and he hit the cliff."

He stepped aside and Bigman caught a glimpse of the smashed face.

Lucky said, "Poor fool!"

"Poor *traitor!*" Bigman raged. "He might have had the answer and he wouldn't tell us. Now he can't tell us."

Lucky said, "He doesn't have to, Bigman. I think I know the answer now."

16

Robot!

"You do?" The little Martian's voice rose to a squeak. "What is it, Lucky?"

But Lucky said, "Not now." He gazed down at Summers, whose dead eyes stared sightlessly toward the alien heavens. He said, "Summers has one distinction. He is the first man ever to die on Io."

He looked up. The sun was edging behind Jupiter. The planet was becoming only a faint silvery circle of twilit atmosphere.

Lucky said, "It will be dark. Let's go back to the ship."

Bigman paced the floor of their cabin. It took only three steps one way, three steps the other, but he paced. He said, "But if you *know,* Lucky, why don't you . . ."

Lucky said, "I can't take ordinary action and risk explosion. Let me do it in my own time and my own way, Bigman."

There was a firmness in his tone that quite subdued Bigman. He changed the subject and said, "Well, then, why waste any more time on Io because of that cobber out there? He's dead. There's nothing more to do about him."

"One thing," said Lucky. The door signal flashed and he added, "Open it, Bigman. It should be Norrich."

It was. The blind engineer stepped in, his dog, Mutt, going before.

Norrich's blue, unseeing eyes blinked rapidly. He said, "I've heard about Summers, Councilman. It's a terrible thing to think he tried to . . . to . . . Terrible that he was a traitor. Yet somehow I'm sorry for him."

Lucky nodded. "I knew you would be. It's why I asked you to come here. It's dark out on Io now. The sun's in eclipse. When the eclipse is over, will you come out with me to bury Summers?"

"Gladly. We should do that much for any man, shouldn't we?" Norrich's hand dropped as if for consolation on Mutt's muzzle, and the dog came close and moved softly against his master as though feeling some dim need to offer sympathy.

Lucky said, "I thought you would want to come along. After all, you were his friend. You might want to pay your last respects."

"Thank you. I would like to." Norrich's blind eyes were moist.

Lucky said to Commander Donahue just before he placed the helmet over his head, "It will be our last trip out. When we return, we will take off for Jupiter Nine."

"Good," the commander said, and there seemed some unspoken understanding as their eyes met.

Lucky put on his helmet and in another corner of the pilot room, Norrich's sensitive fingers moved delicately over Mutt's flexible space suit, making sure all fastenings were secure. Inside the glass-fronted, odd-shaped helmet that fitted over Mutt's head, Mutt's jaws moved in a faintly heard bark. It was obvious the dog knew he was headed for a trip into low gravity and that he enjoyed the prospect.

· · ·

The first grave on Io was done. It had been dug out of hard, rocky soil by the use of force diggers. It was filled in with a mound of gravel and topped by an oval boulder as a marker.

The three men stood round it while Mutt wandered off in the distance, trying vainly, as always, to examine his surroundings, though metal and glass blocked the use of his sense of smell.

Bigman, who knew what Lucky expected him to do but didn't know why, waited tensely.

Norrich stood with his head bowed and said softly, "This was a man who wanted something very much, did wrong for that reason, and has paid for it."

"He did what the Sirians asked him to do," Lucky added. "That was his crime. He committed sabotage and . . ."

Norrich stiffened as the pause in Lucky's remarks lengthened. He said, "And *what?*"

"And he got *you* on board ship. He refused to join the crew without you. You yourself told me that it was only through him that you were assigned to the *Jovian Moon.*"

Lucky's voice grew stern. "You are a robot spy placed here by the Sirians. Your blindness makes you seem innocent to the others on the project, but you don't need a sense of sight. You killed the V-frog and covered for Summers to get him off the ship. Your own death meant nothing to you in the face of orders, as Third Law states. And, finally, you fooled me by the display of emotion I caught through the V-frog, a synthetic emotion built into you by the Sirians."

This was the cue for which Bigman had been waiting. Lifting the butt of his blaster high, he hurled himself at Norrich, whose incoherent protestations did not coalesce into words.

"I knew it was you," Bigman shrieked, "and I'm smashing you."

"It's not true," Norrich wailed, finding his voice. He threw up his hands and stumbled backward.

And suddenly Mutt was a streak in the pale, white light. He hurled himself furiously across the quarter mile that separated him from the men, aiming with desperate passion at Bigman.

Bigman paid no attention. One hand caught at Norrich's shoulder. The other swung the blaster upward.

Then Mutt collapsed!

While he was still ten feet from the struggling pair, his legs stiffened uselessly and he tumbled and rolled past them, coming to a frozen halt at last. Through the glass of his helmet his jaws could be seen hanging open, as though in mid-bark.

Bigman held his threatening position over Norrich as though he, too, were frozen.

Lucky approached the animal with quick steps. He used his force shovel as a kind of unwieldy knife and slit Mutt's space suit lengthwise from neck to tail.

Then, tensely, he slit through the skin at the back of the neck and probed deftly with his mail-shod fingers. They closed on a small sphere that was not bone. He lifted the sphere and met resistance. Holding his breath, he snapped the wires that held it in place and stood up, almost weak with relief. The base of the brain had been the logical place for a mechanism to be activated by the brain, and he had found it. Mutt could endanger no one now.

Norrich cried out, as though through instinctive knowledge of his loss.

"My dog! What are you doing to my dog?"

Lucky said softly, "It's no dog, Norrich. Never was. It

was a robot. Come, Bigman, lead him back to the ship. I'll carry Mutt."

Lucky and Bigman were in Panner's room. The *Jovian Moon* was in flight again, and Io was falling rapidly away, already only a bright coin in the sky.

"What gave it away?" said Panner.

Lucky said somberly, "A number of things which I never saw. Every clue pointed firmly to Mutt, but I was so intent on finding a humanoid robot, so inwardly convinced that a robot had to look human, that I looked past the truth though it stared me in the face."

"Then when *did* you see?"

"When Summers killed himself by jumping off the rock. I stared at him, lying there, and thought of Bigman falling through the ammonia snow and nearly dying. I thought: There's no Mutt that can save this one. . . . And that did it."

"How? I don't understand."

"How *did* Mutt save Bigman? When the dog came running up past us, Bigman was somewhere under the ice, nowhere to be seen. Yet Mutt plunged in, made for Bigman without hesitation, and dragged him out. We accepted that without thought because we somehow expect dogs to find what can't be seen through their sense of smell. But Mutt's head was enclosed. He could neither see nor smell Bigman, yet had no trouble locating him. We ought to have seen that unusual sense perception was involved. We'll find out exactly which when our roboticists work over the carcass."

"Now that you explain," said Panner, "it looks plain enough. The dog had to give itself away because First Law compelled it not to allow a human being to come to harm."

"That's right," said Lucky. "Once suspicions of Mutt finally penetrated, a few other things started falling into place. Summers had maneuvered Norrich on board, yes, but in doing so, he also got Mutt on board. Moreover, Summers was the one who got Mutt for Norrich in the first place. The chances are that there is a spy ring on Earth whose only task is to distribute these robot dogs to people working in or near critical research centers.

"Dogs are perfect spies. If you find a dog nosing through your papers or walking through a super-secret section of a laboratory, are you concerned? Chances are you pet the dog and feed him a dog biscuit. I checked through Mutt as best I could and I think he has a built-in subetheric transmitter which keeps him in contact with his Sirian masters. They can see what he sees, hear what he hears. For instance, they saw the V-frog through Mutt's eyes, recognized its danger, and directed him to kill it. He could be made to handle an energy projector with which to fuse the lock of a door. Even if he was caught in the act, there was a good chance we would put it all down to the accidental happenings of a dog playing with a weapon he had found.

"But once all this had occurred to me, I was only at the beginning of the practical problem. I had to try to take the dog intact. I was sure that any obvious suspicion of Mutt would trigger an explosion inside him. So first I brought Norrich and Mutt to a safe distance from the ship by suggesting we dig Summers' grave. In that way if Mutt did explode, the ship, at least, and its men would escape. Naturally I left a note with Commander Donahue, to be opened in case I did not return, so that Earth would at least investigate dogs in research centers.

"I then accused Norrich . . ."

Bigman broke in, "Sands of Mars, Lucky, for a while I thought you really meant it when you said Norrich had killed the V-frog and fooled us with built-in emotion."

Lucky shook his head. "No, Bigman. If he could fool

us with built-in emotion, why bother to kill the V-frog? No, I was making sure that if Sirians were listening through Mutt's senses, they would be convinced I was on the wrong track. In addition, I was setting up a situation for Mutt's benefit.

"You see, Bigman, under instructions, attacked Norrich. As a Seeing Eye dog, Mutt was built with strong orders to defend his master against attack, and obedience to orders are Second Law. Usually there's no problem here. Few people attack a blind man and those who do will usually stop if the dog simply growls and bares its fangs.

"But Bigman persisted in his attack, and Mutt, for the first time since being built, had to carry through all the way. But how could he? He couldn't hurt Bigman. First Law. Yet he couldn't allow Norrich to be hurt either. It was a complete dilemma and Mutt went out of commission. Once that happened, I gambled that any bomb he contained could no longer be triggered. So I removed it and after that we were safe."

Panner took a deep breath. "Very neat."

Lucky snorted. "Neat? I could have done this the first day I landed on Jupiter Nine, if I had my wits about me. I almost had it, at that. The thought was at the edge of my mind constantly and I never caught it."

Bigman said, "What was it, Lucky? I still don't know."

"It was simple enough. The V-frog detected animal emotion as well as human emotion. We had an example of that when we first landed on Jupiter Nine. We detected hunger in the mind of a cat. Then, later, we met Norrich and he urged you to aim a blow at him in order to show off Mutt's protectiveness. You did so. I detected Norrich's emotions and yours, Bigman, through the V-frog, but although Mutt showed every outward sign of anger, I detected no trace of such an emotion. There was the absolute proof as early as that, that Mutt had no emotions and was therefore no dog but a robot. Yet I was so convinced that I was looking for some human that my mind refused to see that point. . . . Well, let's go to dinner and visit Norrich on the way. I want to promise him that we'll get him another dog, a real one."

They arose, and Bigman said, "Anyway, Lucky, maybe it took some time, but we've stopped the Sirians."

Lucky said quietly, "I don't know that we've stopped them, but certainly we've slowed them down."

Lucky Starr
and the
Rings of Saturn

CONTENTS

Preface

Back in the 1950s, I wrote a series of six derring-do novels about David "Lucky" Starr and his battles against malefactors within the Solar System. Each of the six took place in a different region of the system, and in each case I made use of the astronomical facts—as they were then known.

LUCKY STARR AND THE RINGS OF SATURN was written in 1957, but in 1967, a French astronomer, Audouin Dollfus, discovered a tenth satellite of Saturn, one that was closer to the planet than any of the others, 22,000 miles closer to Saturn than Mimas is. This new satellite has been named Janus.

If I were writing the book today, I would certainly mention that satellite and I might have used it instead of Mimas.

Moreover, it was not until 1977 that astronomers discovered that Saturn was not the only ringed planet. Uranus, it turns out, also has rings. They are very thin rings and very faint ones—but they're there. I would surely have mentioned that in this book if I were writing it today.

I hope my Gentle Readers enjoy the book anyway, as an adventure story, but please don't forget that the advance of science can outdate even the most conscientious science-fiction writer and that my astronomical descriptions are no longer accurate in all respects.

ISAAC ASIMOV

TO THE MEMORY OF
HENRY KUTTNER
AND
CYRIL KORNBLUTH

1

The Invaders

The Sun was a brilliant diamond in the sky, just large enough to the naked eye to be made out as something more than a star; as a tiny white-hot pea-sized globe.

Out here in the vastness of space, near the second largest planet of the Solar System, the Sun gave out only one per cent of the light it cast on man's home planet. It was still, however, the brightest object in the sky, as bright as four thousand full Moons would be.

Lucky Starr gazed thoughtfully at the visiplate which centered the image of the distant Sun. John Bigman Jones watched with him, an odd contrast to Lucky's tall and rangy figure. When John Bigman Jones stretched himself to his full height, he stood five foot two exactly. But the little man did not measure himself in inches and he allowed people to call him by his middle name only: Bigman.

Bigman said, "You know, Lucky, it's nearly nine hundred million miles away. The Sun, I mean. I've never been out this far."

The third man in the cabin, Councilman Ben Wessilewsky, grinned over his shoulder from his place at the controls. He was another large man, though not as tall as Lucky, and his shock of yellow hair topped a face that had grown space-brown in the service of the Council of Science.

He said, "What's the matter, Bigman? Scared way out here?"

Bigman squawked, "Sands of Mars, Wess, you get your hands off those controls and say that again."

He had dodged around Lucky and was making for the Councilman, when Lucky's hands came down on Bigman's shoulders and lifted him bodily. Bigman's legs still pumped, as though carrying him toward Wess at a charge, but Lucky put his Mars-born friend back in his original position.

"Stay put, Bigman."

"But, Lucky, you heard him. This long cobber thinks there's more *to* a man just because there's more *of* him. If that Wess is six feet tall, that just means there's an extra foot of flab——"

"All right, Bigman," said Lucky. "And, Wess, let's save the humor for the Sirians."

He spoke quietly to both, but there was no questioning his authority.

Bigman cleared his throat and said, "Where's Mars?"

"On the other side of the Sun from us."

"Wouldn't you know," said the little fellow disgustedly. Then, brightening, "But hold on, Lucky, we're a hundred million miles below the plane of the Ecliptic. We ought to be able to see Mars below the Sun; peeking out from behind, sort of."

"Uh-huh, we should. Actually, it's a degree or so away from the Sun, but that's close enough for it to be drowned out in the glare. You can make out Earth, though, I think."

Bigman allowed a look of haughty disgust to cross his face. "Who in space wants to see Earth? There isn't anything there but people; mostly ground hogs who've never even been a hundred miles off the surface. I wouldn't look at it if that were all there was in the sky to look at. You let Wess look at it. That's his speed."

He walked moodily away from the visiplate.

Wess said, "Hey, Lucky, how about getting Saturn on and taking a good look at it from this angle? Come on, I've been promising myself a treat."

"I don't know," said Lucky, "that the sight of Saturn these days is exactly what you might call a treat."

He said it lightly, but for a moment silence fell uneasily within the confined pilot room of *The Shooting Starr*.

All three felt the change in atmosphere. Saturn meant danger. Saturn had taken on a new face of doom to the peoples of the Terrestrial Federation. To six billion people on Earth, to additional millions on Mars, the Moon, and Venus, to scientific stations on Mercury, Ceres, and the outer moons of Jupiter, Saturn had become something newly and unexpectedly deadly.

Lucky was the first to shrug off that moment of depression, and, obedient to the touch of his fingers, the sensitive electronic scanners set into the hull of *The Shooting Starr* rotated smoothly on their universal gimbals. As that happened, the field of vision in the visiplate shifted.

The stars marched across the visiplate in steady procession, and Bigman said with a curl of hatred in his upper lip, "Any of those things Sirius, Lucky?"

"No," said Lucky, "we're working through the Southern Celestial Hemisphere and Sirius is in the Northern. Would you like to see Canopus?"

"No," said Bigman. "Why should I?"

"I just thought you might be interested. It's the second brightest star and you could pretend it was Sirius." Lucky smiled slightly. It always amused him that the patriotic Bigman should be so annoyed because Sirius, home star of the great enemies of the Solar System (though themselves descendants of Earthmen), was the brightest star in Earth's heavens.

Bigman said, "Very funny. Come on, Lucky, let's see Saturn, and then when we get back to Earth you can get on some comedy show and panic everybody."

The stars kept their smooth motion, then slowed and stopped. Lucky said, "There it is—unmagnified, too."

Wess locked the controls and twirled in the pilot's seat so that he might see also.

It was a half-moon in appearance, somewhat bulging into more than half, just large enough to be seen as such, bright with a soft yellow light that was dimmer in the center than along the edges.

"How far away are we?" Bigman asked in astonishment.

Lucky said, "About a hundred million miles, I think."

"Something's wrong," Bigman said. "Where are the rings? I've been counting on a good look."

The Shooting Starr was high above the south pole of Saturn. From that position it should see the rings broad on.

Lucky said, "The rings are blurred into the globe of the planet, Bigman, because of the distance. Suppose we magnify the image and take a closer look."

The spot of light that was Saturn expanded and stretched in every direction, growing. And the half-moon that it had seemed to be broke up into three segments.

There was still a central globe, half-mooned. Around it, however, touching the globe at no point, was a circularly curved ribbon of light, divided into two unequal halves by a dark line. As the ribbon curved about Saturn and entered its shadow, it was cut off in darkness.

"Yes, sir, Bigman," said Wess, lecturing, "Saturn itself

is only seventy-eight thousand miles in diameter. At a hundred million miles, it would just be a dot of light, but count in the rings and there are nearly two hundred thousand miles of reflecting surface from one end to the other."

"I know all that," said Bigman indignantly.

"And what's more," continued Wess, unheeding, "at a hundred million miles, the seven-thousand-mile break between Saturn's surface and the innermost portion of the rings just couldn't be seen; let alone the twenty-five-hundred-mile break that divides the rings in two. That black line is called Cassini's division, you know, Bigman."

"I said I know," roared Bigman. "Listen, Lucky, that cobber is trying to make out I didn't go to school. Maybe I didn't get much schooling, but there isn't anything he has to tell me about space. Say the word, Lucky; say you'll let him stop hiding behind you and I'll squash him like a bug."

Lucky said, "You can make out Titan."

At once Bigman and Wess said in chorus, "Where?"

"Right there." Titan showed as a tiny half-moon about the size, under current magnification, that Saturn and its ring system had appeared to be without magnification. It was near the edge of the visiplate.

Titan was the only sizable moon in the Saturnian system. But it wasn't its size that made Wess stare at it with curiosity and Bigman with hate.

It was, instead, that the three were almost certain that Titan was the only world in the Solar System populated by men who did not acknowledge the overlordship of Earth. Suddenly and unexpectedly it had been revealed as a world of the enemy.

It brought the danger suddenly closer. "When do we get inside the Saturnian system, Lucky?"

Lucky said, "There's no real definition as to what is

the Saturnian system, Bigman. Most people consider a world's system to include all the space out to the distance where the farthermost body is moving under the gravitational influence of that world. If that's so, we're still outside the Saturnian system."

"The Sirians say, though——" began Wess.

"To Sun-center with the Sirian cobbers!" roared Bigman, slapping his high boots in anger. "Who cares what they say?" He slapped his boots again as though every Sirian in the system were under the force of his blows. His boots were the most truly Martian thing about him. Their raucous coloring, orange and black in a curving checkerboard design, was the loud proclamation that their owner had been born and bred among the Martian farms and domed cities.

Lucky blanked out the visiplate. The detectors on the ship's hulls retracted, leaving the ship's outer skin smooth, gleaming, and unbroken except for the bulge that ringed the stern and held *The Shooting Starr*'s Agrav* attachment.

Lucky said, "We can't allow ourselves the luxury of the who-cares-what-they-say attitude, Bigman. At the moment the Sirians have the upper hand. Maybe we'll get them out of the Solar System eventually, but right now the only thing we can do is to play it their way for the while."

Bigman muttered rebelliously, "We're in our own system."

"Sure, but Sirius is occupying this part of it and, pending an interstellar conference, there isn't anything Earth can do about it, unless it's willing to start a war."

There was nothing to be said to that. Wess returned to his controls, and *The Shooting Starr*, with minimum ex-

* See *LUCKY STARR AND THE MOONS OF JUPITER.*

penditure of thrust, making use of Saturn's gravity to the maximum, continued to sink rapidly toward the polar regions of the planet.

Down, down, deeper into the grip of what was now a Sirian world, its space swarming with Sirian ships some fifty trillion miles from their home planet and only seven hundred million miles from Earth. In one giant step Sirius had covered 99.999 per cent of the distance between itself and Earth and established a military base on Earth's very doorstep.

If Sirius were allowed to remain there, then in one sudden moment Earth would sink to the status of second-class power at Sirius's mercy. And the interstellar political situation was such that for the moment all of Earth's giant military establishment, all of her mighty ships and weapons were helpless to deal with the situation.

Only three men in one small ship, on their own initiative and unauthorized by Earth, were left to try, by skill and craft, to reverse the situation, knowing that if they were caught they could be executed out of hand as spies —in their own Solar System by invaders of that Solar System—and that Earth could not do a solitary thing to save them.

2

Pursuit

As little as a month ago there had been no thought of the danger, no barest notion, until it exploded in the face of Earth's government. Steadily and methodically the Council of Science had been cleaning up the nest of robot spies that had riddled Earth and its possessions and whose power had been broken by Lucky Starr on the snows of Io.*

It had been a grim job and, in a way, a frightening one, for the espionage had been thorough and efficient and, moreover, had come within an ace of succeeding and damaging Earth desperately.

Then, at the moment when the situation seemed completely in the clear at last, a crack appeared in the healing structure, and Hector Conway, Chief Councilman, awakened Lucky in the small hours one night. He showed signs of hurried dressing, and his fine white hair was in rumpled disarray.

Lucky, blinking sleep out of his eyes, offered coffee and said in amazement, "Great Galaxy, Uncle Hector"

* See *LUCKY STARR AND THE MOONS OF JUPITER.*

(Lucky had called him that since his early orphaned days, when Conway and Augustus Henree had been his guardians), "are the visiphone circuits out?"

"I dared not trust the visiphone, my boy. We're in a dreadful mess."

"In what way?" Lucky asked the question quietly, but he removed the upper half of his pajamas and began washing.

Bigman came in, stretching and yawning. "Hey, what's all this Mars-forsaken noise about?" Recognizing the Chief Councilman, he snapped into wakefulness. "Trouble, sir?"

"We've let Agent X slip through our fingers."

"Agent X? The mysterious Sirian?" Lucky's eyes narrowed a bit. "The last I heard of him, the Council had decided he didn't exist."

"That was before the robot spy business turned up. He's been clever, Lucky, darned clever. It takes a clever spy to convince the Council he doesn't exist. I should have put you on his track, but there always seemed something else you had to do. Anyway——"

"Yes?"

"You know how all this robot spy business showed there must be a central clearing agency for the information being gathered and that it pointed to a position on Earth itself as the location of the agency. That got us on the trail of Agent X all over again, and one of the strong possibilities for that role was a man named Jack Dorrance at Acme Air Products right here in International City."

"I hadn't known this."

"There were many other candidates for the job. But then Dorrance took a private ship off Earth and blasted right through an emergency block. It was a stroke of luck we had a Councilman at Port Center who took the right action at once and followed. Once the report of the ship's block-blasting reached us, it took only minutes to find that of all the suspects only Dorrance was out of surveillance check. He'd gotten past us. A few other matters fit in then and—anyway, he's Agent X. We're sure of it now."

"Very well, then, Uncle Hector. Where's the harm? He's gone."

"We know one more thing now. He's taken a personal capsule with him, and we have no doubt that that capsule contains information he has managed to collect from the spy network over the Federation, and, presumably, has not yet had time to deliver to his Sirian bosses. Space knows exactly what he has, but there must be enough there to blow our security to pieces if it gets into Sirian hands."

"You say he was followed. Has he been brought back?"

"No." The harassed Chief Councilman turned pettish. "Would I be here if he had been?"

Lucky asked suddenly, "Is the ship he took equipped to make the Jump?"

"No," cried the ruddy-faced Chief Councilman, and he smoothed his silvered thatch of hair as though it had risen in horror at the very thought of the Jump.

Lucky drew a deep breath of relief too. The Jump was, of course, the leap through hyperspace, a movement that carried a ship outside ordinary space and brought it back again into a point in space many light-years away, all in an instant.

In such a ship Agent X would, very likely, get away.

Conway said, "He worked solo; his getaway was solo. That was part of the reason he slipped through our fingers. And the ship he took was an interplanetary cruiser designed for one-man operation."

"And ships equipped with hyperspatials don't come designed for one-man operation. Not yet, anyway. But,

Uncle Hector, if he's taken an interplanetary cruiser, then I suppose that's all he needs."

Lucky had finished washing and was dressing himself rapidly. He turned to Bigman suddenly. "And how about you? Snap into your clothes, Bigman."

Bigman, who was sitting on the edge of the couch, virtually turned a somersault getting off it.

Lucky said, "Probably, waiting for him somewhere in space, is a Sirian-manned ship that is equipped with hyperspatials."

"Right. And he's got a fast ship, and with his start and speed, we may not catch him or even get within weapons range. And that leaves——"

"*The Shooting Starr.* I'm ahead of you, Uncle Hector. I'll be on the *Shooter* in an hour, and Bigman with me, assuming he can drag his clothes on. Just get me the present location and course of the pursuing ships and the identifying data on Agent X's ship and we'll be on our way."

"Good." Conway's harried face smoothed out a bit. "And, David"—he used Lucky's real name, as he always did in moments of emotion—"you *will* be careful?"

"Did you ask that of the personnel on the other ten ships too, Uncle Hector?" Lucky asked, but his voice was soft and affectionate.

Bigman had one hip boot pulled up now and the other in his hand. He patted the small holster on the velvety inner surface of the free boot. "Are we on our way, Lucky?" The light of action glowed in his eyes, and his puckish little face was wrinkled in a fierce grin.

"We're on our way," said Lucky, reaching out to tousle Bigman's sandy hair. "We've been rusting on Earth for how long? Six weeks? Well, that's long enough."

"And how," agreed Bigman joyfully, and pulled on the other boot.

• • •

They were out past the orbit of Mars before they made satisfactory sub-etheric contact with the pursuing ships, using the tightest scrambling.

It was Councilman Ben Wessilewsky on board the T.S.S. *Harpoon* who answered.

He shouted, "Lucky! Are you joining us? Swell!" His face grinned out of the visiplate and he winked. "Got room to squash Bigman's ugly puss into a corner of your screen? Or isn't he with you?"

"I'm with him," howled Bigman as he plunged between Lucky and the transmitter. "Think Councilman Conway would let this big lunk go anywhere without me to keep an eye on him so's he doesn't trip over his big feet?"

Lucky picked Bigman up and tucked him, squawking, under one arm. He said, "Seems to be a noisy connection, Wess. What's the position of the ship we're after?"

Wess, sobering, gave it. He said, "The ship's *The Net of Space*. It's privately owned, with a legitimate record of manufacture and sale. Agent X must have bought it under a dummy name and prepared for emergency a long time ago. It's a sweet ship and it's been accelerating ever since it took off. We're falling behind."

"What's its power capacity?"

"We've thought of that. We've checked the manufacturer's record of the craft, and at the rate he's expending power, he can't go much farther without either cutting motors or sacrificing maneuverability once he reaches destination. We're counting on driving him into that exact hole."

"Presumably, though, he may have had the sense to rev up the ship's power capacity."

"Probably," said Wess, "but even so he can't keep this up forever. The thing I worry about is the possibility that he might evade our mass detectors by asteroid-skipping. If he can get the breaks in the asteroid belt, we may lose him."

Lucky knew that trick. Place an asteroid between yourself and a pursuer, and the pursuer's mass detectors locate the asteroid rather than the ship. When a second asteroid comes within reach, the ship shifts from one to the other, leaving the pursuer with his instrument still fastened on the first rock.

Lucky said, "He's moving too fast to make the maneuver. He'd have to decelerate for half a day."

"It would take a miracle," agreed Wess frankly, "but it took a miracle to put us on his trail, and so I almost expect another miracle to cancel the first."

"What was the first miracle? The Chief said something about an emergency block."

"That's right." Wess told the story crisply, and it didn't take long. Dorrance, or Agent X (Wess called him by either name), had slipped surveillance by using an instrument that distorted the spy-beam into uselessness. (The instrument had been located, but its workings were fused and it could not even be determined if it was of Sirian manufacture.) He reached his getaway ship, *The Net of Space*, without trouble. He was ready to take off with his proton micro-reactor activated, his motor and controls checked, clear space above—and then a limping freight ship, meteor-struck and unable to radio ahead, had appeared in the stratosphere, signaling desperately for a clear field.

The emergency block was flashed. All ships in port were held fast. Any ship in the process of take-off, unless it was already in actual motion, had to abandon take-off procedure.

The Net of Space ought to have abandoned take-off, but it did not. Lucky Starr could well understand what the feelings of Agent X aboard must have been. The hottest item in the Solar System was in his possession, and every second counted. Now that he had made his actual move he could not rely on too long a time before the Council would be on his heels. If he abandoned take-off it would mean an untold delay while a riddled ship limped down and ambulances slowly emptied it. Then, when the field was cleared again, it would mean reactivation of the micro-reactor and another controls check. He could not afford the delay.

So his jets blasted and up he went.

And still Agent X might have escaped. The alarm sounded, the port police put out wild messages to *The Net of Space,* but it was Councilman Wessilewsky, serving a routine hitch at Port Center, who took proper action. He had played his part in the search for Agent X, and a ship that blasted off against an emergency block somehow smelled wildly of just enough desperation to mean Agent X. It was the wildest possible guess, but he acted.

With the authority of the Council of Science behind him (which superseded all other authority except that contained in a direct order from the President of the Terrestrial Federation), he ordered Space Guard ships into space, contacted Council Headquarters, and then boarded the T.S.S. *Harpoon* to guide the pursuit. He had already been in space for hours before the Council as a whole caught up with events. But then the message came through that he was indeed pursuing Agent X and that other ships would be joining him.

Lucky listened gravely and said, "It was a chance that paid off, Wess. And the right thing to do. Good work."

Wess grinned. Councilmen traditionally avoided publicity and the trappings of fame, but the approval of one's fellows in the Council was something greatly to be desired.

Lucky said, "I'm moving on. Have one of your ships maintain mass contact with me."

He broke visual contact, and his strong, finely formed hands closed almost caressingly on his ship's controls—his *Shooting Starr*, which in so many ways was the sweetest vessel in space.

The Shooting Starr had the most powerful proton microreactors that could be inserted into a ship of its size; reactors almost powerful enough to accelerate a battle cruiser at fleet-regulation pace; reactors almost powerful enough to manage the Jump through hyperspace. The ship had an ion drive that cut out most of the apparent effects of acceleration by acting simultaneously on all atoms aboard ship, including those that made up the living bodies of Lucky and Bigman. It even had an Agrav, recently developed and still experimental, which enabled it to maneuver freely in the intense gravitational fields of the major planets.

And now *The Shooting Starr's* mighty motors hummed smoothly into a higher pitch, just heard, and Lucky felt the slight pressure of such backward drag as was not completely compensated for by the ion drive. The ship bounded outward into the far reaches of the Solar System, faster, faster, still faster. . . .

And still Agent X maintained his lead, and *The Shooting Starr* gained too slowly. With the main body of the asteroid belt far behind, Lucky said, "It looks bad, Bigman."

Bigman looked surprised. "We'll get him, Lucky."

"It's where he's heading. I was sure it would be a Sirian mother-ship waiting to pick him up and make the Jump homeward. But such a ship would be either way out of the plane of the Ecliptic or it would be hidden in the asteroid belt. Either way, it could count on not being detected. But Agent X stays in the Ecliptic and heads beyond the asteroids."

"Maybe he's just trying to shake us before he heads for the ship."

"Maybe," said Lucky, "and maybe the Sirians have a base on the outer planets."

"Come on, Lucky." The small Martian cackled his derision. "Right under our noses?"

"It's hard to see under our noses sometimes. His course is aimed right at Saturn."

Bigman checked the ship's computers, which were keeping constant tab on the other's course. He said, "Look, Lucky, the cobber is still on a ballistic course. He hasn't touched his motors in twenty million miles. Maybe he's out of power."

"And maybe he's saving his power for maneuvers in the Saturnian system. There'll be a heavy gravitational drag there. At least I *hope* he's saving power. Great Galaxy, I hope he is." Lucky's lean, handsome face was grave now and his lips were pressed together tightly.

Bigman looked at him with astonishment. "Sands of Mars, Lucky, why?"

"Because if there is a Sirian base in Saturn's system, we'll need Agent X to lead us to that base. Saturn has one tremendous satellite, eight sizable ones, and dozens of splinter worlds. It would help to know exactly where it was."

Bigman frowned. "The cobber wouldn't be dumb enough to lead us there."

"Or maybe to let us catch him. . . . Bigman, calculate his course forward to the point of intersection with Saturn's orbit."

Bigman did so. It was a routine moment of work for the computer.

Lucky said, "And how about Saturn's position at the

moment of intersection? How far will Saturn be from Agent X's ship?"

There was the short pause necessary for getting the elements of Saturn's orbit from the Ephemeris, and then Bigman punched it in. A few seconds of calculation and Bigman suddenly rose to his feet in alarm. "Lucky! Sands of Mars!"

Lucky did not need to ask the details. He said, "I'm thinking that Agent X may have decided on the one way to keep from leading us to the Sirian base. If he continues on ballistic course exactly as he is now, he will strike Saturn itself—and sure death."

3

Death in the Rings

There came to be no possible doubt about it as the hours passed. Even the pursuing guard ships, far behind *The Shooting Starr*, too far off to get completely accurate fixes on their mass detectors, were perturbed.

Councilman Wessilewsky contacted Lucky Starr. "Space, Lucky," he said, "where's he going?"

"Saturn itself, it seems," said Lucky.

"Do you suppose a ship might be waiting for him on Saturn? I know it has thousands of miles of atmosphere with million-ton pressures, and without Agrav motors they couldn't—— Lucky! Do you suppose they *have* Agrav motors and forcefield bubbles?"

"I think he may be simply crashing to keep us from catching him."

Wess said dryly, "If he's all that anxious to die, why doesn't he turn and fight, force us to destroy him and maybe take one or two of us with him?"

"I know," said Lucky, "or why not short-circuit his motors, leaving Saturn a hundred million miles off course? In fact, it bothers me that he should be attracting attention to Saturn this way." He fell into a thoughtful silence.

Wess broke in! "Well, then, can you cut him off, Lucky? Space knows *we're* too far away."

Bigman shouted from his place at the control panel, "Sands of Mars, Wess, if we rev up enough ion beam to catch him, we'll be moving too fast to maneuver him away from Saturn."

"Do *something*."

"Space, there's an intelligent order," said Bigman. "Real helpful. 'Do something.' "

Lucky said, "Just keep on the move, Wess. I'll do something."

He broke contact and turned to Bigman. "Has he answered our signals at all, Bigman?"

"Not one word."

"Forget that for now and concentrate on tapping his communication beam."

"I don't think he's using one, Lucky."

"He may at the last minute. He'll have to take a chance then if he has anything to say at all. Meanwhile we're going for him."

"How?"

"Missile. Just a small pea-shot."

It was his turn to bend over the computer. While *The Net of Space* moved in an unpowered orbit, it required no great computation to direct a pellet at the proper moment and velocity to strike the fleeing ship.

Lucky readied the pellet. It was not designed to explode. It didn't have to. It was only a quarter of an inch in diameter, but the energy of the proton micro-pile would hurl it outward at five hundred miles a second. Nothing in space would diminish that velocity, and the pellet would pass through the hull of *The Net of Space* as though it were butter.

Lucky did not expect it would, however. The pellet would be large enough to be picked up on its quarry's mass detectors. *The Net of Space* would automatically correct course to avoid the pellet, and that would throw it off the direct course to Saturn. The time lost by Agent X in computing the new course and correcting it back to the old one might yet allow *The Shooting Starr* to come close enough to make use of a magnetic grapple.

It all added up to a slim chance, perhaps vanishingly slim, but there seemed no other possible course of action.

Lucky touched a contact. The pellet sped out in a soundless flash, and the ship's mass-detector needles jumped, then quieted rapidly, as the pellet receded.

Lucky sat back. It would take two hours for the pellet to make (or almost make) contact. It occurred to him that Agent X might be completely out of power; that the automatic procedures might direct a course change which could not be followed through; that the pellet would penetrate, blow up the ship, perhaps, and in any case leave its course unchanged and still marked for Saturn.

He dismissed the idea almost at once. It would be incredible to suppose that Agent X would run out of the last bit of power at the moment his ship took on the precise collision course. It was infinitely more likely that some power was left him.

The hours of waiting were deadly. Even Hector Conway, far back on Earth, grew impatient with the periodic bulletins and made direct contact on the sub-ether.

"But where in the Saturnian system do you suppose the base might be?" he asked worriedly.

"If there is one," said Lucky cautiously, "if what Agent X is doing is not a tremendous effort to mislead us, I would say the most obvious choice is Titan. It's Saturn's one really large satellite, with three times the mass of our own Moon and over twice the surface area. If the Sirians have holed up underground, trying to dredge all of Titan for them would take a long time."

"It's hard to believe that they would have dared do this. It's virtually an act of war."

"Maybe so, Uncle Hector, but it wasn't so long ago that they tried to establish a base on Ganymede."*

Bigman called out sharply, "Lucky, he's moving."

Lucky looked up in surprise. "Who's moving?"

"*The Net of Space.* The Sirian cobber."

Lucky said hastily, "I'll get in touch with you later, Uncle Hector," and broke contact. He said, "But he can't be moving, Bigman. He can't possibly have detected the pellet yet."

"Look and see for yourself, Lucky. I tell you he's moving."

Lucky, in one stride, was at the mass detectors of *The Shooting Starr*. For a long time now it had had a fix on the fleeing quarry. It had been adjusted for the ship's unpowered motion through space, and the blob that represented the detectable mass had been a small bright star mark on the screen.

But now the mark was drifting. It was a short line.

Lucky's voice was softly intense. "Great Galaxy, *of course!* Now it makes sense. How could I think his first duty would be merely to avoid capture? Bigman——"

"Sure, Lucky. What?" The little Martian was ready for anything.

"We're being outmaneuvered. We've got to destroy him now even if it means crashing into Saturn ourselves." For the first time since the ion-beam jets had been placed aboard *The Shooting Starr* the year before, Lucky added the emergency thrusts to the main drive. The ship reeled

* See *LUCKY STARR AND THE PIRATES OF THE ASTEROIDS.*

as every last atom of power it carried was turned into a giant thrust backward that all but burned it out.

Bigman struggled for breath. "But what's it all about, Lucky?"

"It's not Saturn he's headed for, Bigman. He was just making use of the full power of its gravitational field to help him keep ahead of us. Now he's cutting around the planet to get into orbit. It's the rings he's headed for. Saturn's rings." The young Councilman's face was drawn with tension. "Keep after that communication beam, Bigman. He'll have to talk now. Now or never."

Bigman bent over his wave analyzer with a quickening heartbeat, though for the life of him he could not understand why the thought of Saturn's rings should so disturb Lucky.

The Shooting Starr's pellet came nowhere near its mark, not within fifty thousand miles. But now it was *The Shooting Starr* itself that was a pellet, striving for junction; and it, too, would miss.

Lucky groaned. "We'll never make it. There's not enough room left to make it."

Saturn was a giant in the sky now, with its rings a thin gash across its face. Saturn's yellow globe was almost at the full as *The Shooting Starr* burned toward it from the direction of the Sun.

And Bigman suddenly exploded, "Why, the dirty cobber! He's melting into the rings, Lucky. Now I see what got you about the rings."

He worked furiously at the mass detector, but it was hopeless. As a portion of the rings came into focus, each of the countless solid masses that composed them formed its own star mark on the screen. The screen turned pure white and *The Net of Space* was gone.

Lucky shook his head. "That's not an insoluble problem. We're close enough to get a visual fix now. It's something else that I'm sure is coming."

Lucky, pale and engrossed, had the visiplate under maximum telescopic enlargement. *The Net of Space* was a tiny metal cylinder obscured but not hidden by the material of the rings. The individual particles in the rings were no larger than coarse gravel and were only sparkles as they caught and threw back the light of the distant Sun.

Bigman said, "Lucky! I've got his communications beam. . . . No, no, wait now. . . . Yes, I have it."

There was a wavering voice crackling in the control room now, obscured and distorted. Bigman's deft fingers worked at the unscrambler, trying to fit it better and ever better with the unknown characteristics of the Sirian scrambling system.

The words would die out, then come back. There was silence except for the faint hum of the recorder taking down permanently whatever came through.

". . . not . . . wor . . . hither . . ." (Quite a pause while Bigman fought frantically with his detectors). ". . . on trail and . . . couldn't shake . . . done for and I must transmit . . . rn's rings in normal orb . . . dy launch . . . stics of or . . . follow . . . co-ordinate read thus . . ."

It broke off altogether at that precise point; the voice, the static, everything.

Bigman yelled, "Sands of Mars, something's blown!"

"Nothing here," said Lucky. "It's *The Net of Space*."

He had seen it happen two seconds after transmission ceased. Transmission through the sub-ether was at virtually infinite velocity. The light that he saw through the visiplate traveled at only 186,000 miles a second.

It took two seconds for the sight of it to reach Lucky. He saw the rear end of *The Net of Space* glow a cherry-red, then open and spatter into a flower of melting metal.

Bigman caught the tail end of it, and he and Lucky watched wordlessly until radiation cooled the spectacle.

Lucky shook his head. "That close to the rings, even though you're outside the main body of them, space has more than its share of speeding material. Maybe he had no further power to turn the ship out of the way of one of those bits. Or maybe two pieces converged at him from slightly different directions. In any case, he was a brave man and clever enemy."

"I don't get it, Lucky. What was he doing?"

"Don't you see even now? While it was important for him not to fall into our hands, it wasn't enough for him to die. I should have seen that earlier myself. His most important task was to get the stolen information in his possession to Sirius. He didn't dare risk the sub-ether for reeling off what may have been thousands of words of information—with ships in pursuit and possibly tapping his beam. He had to restrict his message to the briefest essentials and see to it that the capsule was placed bodily in the grip of the Sirians."

"How could he do that?"

"What we caught of his message contains the syllable "orb"—probably for "orbit"—and "dy launch," meaning "already launched."

Bigman caught at Lucky's arms, his small fingers pinching tightly on the other's sinewy wrists. "He launched the capsule into the rings; is that it, Lucky? It'll be a piece of gravel along with a zillion other pieces, like —like a pebble on the Moon——or a water drop in an ocean."

"Or," said Lucky, "like a piece of gravel in Saturn's rings, which is worst of all. Of course he was destroyed before he could give the co-ordinates of the orbit he had chosen for the capsule, so the Sirians and we start even, and we had better make the most of that without delay."

"Start looking? Now?"

"Now! If he was ready to give the co-ordinates, knowing I was hot after him, he must also have known the Sirians were close by. . . . Contact the ships, Bigman, and give them the news."

Bigman turned to the transmitter but never touched it. The reception button was glowing with intercepted radio waves. Radio! Ordinary etheric communication! Obviously someone was close by (certainly within the Saturnian system), and someone, moreover, felt not the least desire for secrecy, since a radio beam, unlike sub-etheric communication, was childishly simple to tap.

Lucky's eyes narrowed. "Let's receive, Bigman."

The voice came through with that trace of accent, that broadening of vowels and sharpening of consonants. It was a Sirian voice.

It said, "—fy yourselves before we are forced to place a grapple on you and take you into custody. You have fourteen minutes to acknowledge reception." There was a minute's pause. "By authority of the Central Body, you are ordered to identify yourself before we are forced to place a grapple on you and take you into custody. You have thirteen minutes to acknowledge reception."

Lucky said coldly, "Reception acknowledged. This is *The Shooting Starr* of the Terrestrial Federation, orbiting peacefully in the spatial volume of the Terrestrial Federation. No authority other than that of the Federation exists in these spaces."

There was a second or two of silence (radio waves travel with only the speed of light) and the voice retorted, "The authority of the Terrestrial Federation is not recognized on a world colonized by the Sirian peoples."

"Which world is that?" asked Lucky.

"The uninhabited Saturnian system has been taken possession of in the name of our government under the interstellar law that awards any uninhabited world to those who colonize it."

"Not any uninhabited world. Any uninhabited stellar system."

There was no answer. The voice said stolidly, "You are now within the Saturnian system and you are requested to leave forthwith. Any delay in acceleration outward will result in our taking you into custody. Any further ships of the Terrestrial Federation entering our territory will be taken into custody without additional warning. Your acceleration out of the Saturnian system must begin within eight minutes or we will take action."

Bigman, his face twisted with unholy glee, whispered, "Let's go in and get them, Lucky. Let's show them the old *Shooter* can fight."

But Lucky paid no attention. He said into the transmitter, "Your remark is noted. We do not accept Sirian authority, but we choose, of our own will, to leave and will now do so." He snapped off contact.

Bigman was appalled. "Sands of Mars, Lucky! Are we going to run from a bunch of *Sirians?* Are we going to leave that capsule in Saturn's rings for the Sirians to pick up?"

Lucky said, "Right now, Bigman, we have to." His head was bent and his face was pale and strained, but there was something in his eyes that was not quite that of a man backing down. Anything but that.

4

Between Jupiter and Saturn

The ranking officer in the pursuing squadron (not counting Councilman Wessilewsky, of course) was Captain
Myron Bernold. He was a four-striper, still under fifty,
and with the physique of a man ten years younger. His
hair was graying, but his eyebrows were still their original
black and his beard showed blue about his shaven chin.

He stared at the much younger Lucky Starr with un-
disguised scorn. "*And you backed away?*"

The Shooting Starr, having headed inward toward the
Sun again, had met the ships of the squadron approxi-
mately halfway between the orbits of Jupiter and Saturn.
Lucky had boarded the flagship.

He said now quietly, "I did what was necessary to be
done."

"When the enemy has invaded our home system, retreat can never be necessary. You might have been blown
out of space, but you would have had time to warn us and
we would have been there to take over."

"With how much power left in your micro-pile units,
Captain?"

The captain flushed. "Nor would it matter if we got

blasted out of space. That couldn't have been done before we had, in our turn, alerted home base."

"And started a war?"

"*They*'ve started the war. The Sirians. . . . It is now my intention to move on to Saturn and attack."

Lucky's own rangy figure stiffened. He was taller than the captain, and his cool glance did not waver. "As full Councilman of the Council of Science, Captain, I outrank you and you know it. I will give no orders to attack. The orders I give you are to return to Earth."

"I would sooner——" The captain was visibly struggling with his temper. His fists clenched. He said in a strangled voice, "May I ask the reason for the order, sir?" He emphasized the syllable of respect with heavy irony. "If, sir, you would be so good as to explain the excellent reason you no doubt have, sir. My own reasoning is based on a small tradition that the fleet happens to have. A tradition, sir, that the fleet does not retreat, sir."

Lucky said, "If you want my reasons, Captain, sit down and I'll give them to you. And don't tell me the fleet does not retreat. Retreat is a part of the maneuver of war, and a commanding officer who would rather have his ships destroyed than retreat has no business in command. I think it's only your anger that's speaking. Now, Captain, are we ready to start a war?"

"I tell you they have already started. They have invaded the Terrestrial Federation."

"Not exactly. They've occupied an unoccupied world. The trouble is, Captain, that the Jump through hyperspace has made travel to the stars so simple that Earthmen have colonized the planets of other stars long before ever colonizing the remoter portions of our own Solar System."

"Terrestrials have landed on Titan. In the year——"

"I know about the flight of James Francis Hogg. He

landed on Oberon in the Uranian system also. But that was just exploration, not colonization. The Saturnian system was left empty, and an unoccupied world belongs to the first group that colonizes it."

"*If,*" said the captain heavily, "that unoccupied planet or planetary system is part of an unoccupied stellar system. Saturn isn't that, you'll admit. It's part of our Solar System, which, by the howling devils of space, is occupied."

"True, but I don't think there is any official agreement to that effect. Perhaps it may be decided that Sirius is within its rights in occupying Saturn."

The captain brought his fist down upon his knee. "I don't care what the space lawyers say. Saturn is ours, and any Earthman with blood in him will agree. We'll kick the Sirians off and let our weapons decide the law."

"But that's exactly what Sirius would want us to do!"

"Then let's give her what she wants."

"And we will be accused of aggression. . . . Captain, there are fifty worlds out there among the stars who never forget that they were our colonies once. We gave them their freedom without a war, but they forget that. They only remember we are still the most populous and most advanced of all the worlds. If Sirius shouts we have committed unprovoked aggression, she'll unite them against us. It is just for that reason that she is trying to provoke us to attack now, and it is just for that reason that I refused the invitation and came away."

The captain bit at his lower lip and would have answered, but Lucky drove on.

"On the other hand, if we do nothing, we can accuse the Sirians of aggression and we'll split public opinion in the outer worlds wide open. We can exploit that and bring them to our own side."

"The outer worlds to *our* side?"

"Why not? There isn't a stellar system in existence that doesn't have hundreds of unoccupied worlds of all sizes. They won't want to set up a precedent that would set every system to raiding every other system for bases. The only danger is that we will stampede them into opposition to us by making it look as if we are powerful Earth throwing our weight about against our former colonies."

The captain rose from his seat and strode the length of his quarters and then back. He said, "Repeat your orders."

Lucky said, "Do you understand my reason for retreat?"

"Yes. May I have my orders?"

"Very well. I order you to deliver this Capsule I now give you to Chief Councilman Hector Conway. You are not to discuss anything that has happened during this pursuit with anyone else, either on the sub-ether or in any other fashion. You are to take no hostile action—repeat, no hostile action—against any Sirian forces, unless directly attacked. And if you go out of your way to meet such forces, or if you deliberately provoke attack, I shall see you court-martialed and convicted. Is all clear?"

The captain stood frozen-faced. His lips moved as though they were carved out of wood and badly hinged. "With all due respect, sir, would it be possible for the Councilman to take over command of my ships and deliver the message himself?"

Lucky Starr shrugged slightly and said, "You are very obstinate, Captain, and I even admire you for it. There are times in battle when this kind of bulldoggedness can be useful. . . . It is impossible for me to deliver this message, since it is my intention to return to *The Shooting Starr* and blast off for Saturn again."

The captain's military rigidity came unstuck. "What? Howling space, *what?*"

"I thought my statement was plain, Captain. I have left something undone there. My first task was to see to it that Earth was warned of the terrible political danger we are facing. If you will take care of that warning for me, I can carry on where I now belong—back in the Saturnian system."

The captain was grinning broadly. "Well, now, that's different. I would like to come along with you."

"I know that, Captain. Sheering away from a fight is the harder task for you, and I'm asking you to do it because I expect you are used to hard tasks. Now I want each of your ships to transfer some of their power into the micro-pile units of *The Shooting Starr*. There'll be other supplies I'll need from your stores."

"You need only ask."

"Very good. I will return to my ship and I will ask Councilman Wessilewsky to join me in my mission."

He shook hands briefly with the now thoroughly friendly captain, and then Councilman Wessilewsky joined him as Lucky stepped into the inter-ship tube that snaked between the flagship and *The Shooting Starr*.

The inter-ship tube was at nearly its full extension, and it took several minutes to negotiate its length. The tube was airless, but the two Councilmen could maintain spacesuit contact easily and sound waves would travel along the metal to emerge squawkily but distinctly enough. And, after all, no form of communication is quite as private as sound waves over short range, so it was in the air tube that Lucky was able to speak briefly to the other.

Finally Wess, changing the subject slightly, said, "Listen, Lucky, if the Sirians are trying to start trouble, why did they let you go? Why not have harassed you till you were forced to turn and fight?"

"As for that, Wess, you listen to the recording of what

the Sirian ship had to say. There was a stiffness about the words; a failure to threaten actual harm, only magnetic grappling. I'm convinced it was a robot-piloted ship."

"Robots!" Wess's eyes widened.

"Yes. Judge from your own reaction what Earth's would be if that speculation got about. Earthmen are unreasonably frightened of robots. The fact is that those robot-piloted ships could have done no harm to a human-piloted ship. The First Law of Robotics—that no robot can harm a human—would have prevented it. And that just made the danger greater. If I had attacked, as they probably expected me to, the Sirians would have insisted that I had made a murderous and unprovoked assault on defenseless vessels. And the outer worlds appreciate the facts of robotics as Earth does not. No, Wess, the only way I could cross them was to leave, and I did."

With that, they were at the airlock of *The Shooting Starr*.

Bigman was waiting for them. There was the usual grin of relief on his face at meeting Lucky again after even the smallest separation.

"Hey," he said. "What do you know? You didn't fall out of the inter-ship tube after all and—— What's Wess doing here?"

"He's coming with us, Bigman."

The little Martian looked annoyed. "What for? This is a two-man ship we've got here."

"We'll manage a guest temporarily. And now we'd better get set to drain power from the other ships and receive equipment along the tube. After that we make ready for instant blast-off."

Lucky's voice was firm, his change of subject definite. Bigman knew better than to argue.

He muttered, "Sure thing," and stepped across into

the engine room after one malignant scowl in the direction of Councilman Wessilewsky.

Wess said, "Now what's eating him? I haven't said a word about his size."

Lucky said, "Well, you have to understand the little fellow. He's not a Councilman officially, although he is one for all practical purposes. He's the only one who doesn't realize that. Anyway, he thinks that because you're another Councilman we'll get chummy and cut him out; have our little secrets from him."

Wess nodded. "I see. Are you suggesting then that we tell him——"

"*No.*" The stress on the word was soft, but emphatic. "I'll tell him what has to be told. You say nothing."

At that moment Bigman stepped into the pilot room again and said, "She's sopping up the power," then looked from one to the other and growled, "Well, sorry I'm interrupting. Shall I leave the ship, gentlemen?"

Lucky said, "You'll have to knock me down first, Bigman."

Bigman made rapid sparring motions and said, "Oh boy, what a difficult task. You think an extra foot of clumped fat makes it any job?"

With blinding speed he was inside Lucky's arm as it was thrown out laughingly toward him, and his fists landed one-two, thwackingly, in Lucky's mid-section.

Lucky said, "Feel better?"

Bigman danced back. "I pulled my punch because I didn't want Councilman Conway bawling me out for hurting you."

Lucky laughed. "Thank you. Now, listen, I've got an orbit for you to calculate and send on to Captain Bernold."

"Sure thing." Bigman seemed quite at ease now, any rancor gone.

Wess said, "Listen, Lucky, I hate to act the wet blanket, but we're not very far from Saturn. It seems to me that the Sirians will have a fix on us right now and know exactly where we are, when we leave, and where we go."

"I think so too, Wess."

"Well, then, how in space do we leave the squadron and head back for Saturn without their knowing exactly where we are and heading us off too far from the system for our purposes?"

"Good question. I was wondering if you'd guess how. If you didn't, I was reasonably certain the Sirians wouldn't guess either, and they don't know the details of our system nearly as well as we do."

Wess leaned back in his pilot's chair. "Let's not make a mystery of it, Lucky."

"It's perfectly plain. All the ships, including ourselves, blast-off in tight formation, so that, considering the distance between the Sirians and ourselves, we'll register as a single spot on their mass detectors. We maintain that formation, flying on almost the minimum orbit to Earth, but just enough off course to make a reasonable approach to the asteroid Hidalgo, which is now moving out toward aphelion."

"Hidalgo?"

"Come on, Wess, you know it. It's a perfectly legitimate asteroid and known since the primeval days before space travel. The interesting thing about it is that it doesn't stay in the asteroid belt. At its closest to the Sun it moves in as close as the orbit of Mars, but at its farthest it moves out almost as far as Saturn's orbit. Now when we pass near it, Hidalgo will register on the Sirian mass-detection screens also, and from the strength with which it will register they'll know it to be an asteroid. Then they'll spot the mass of our ships moving on past Hidalgo toward Earth and they won't spot the less than ten per

cent total decrease in ship's mass that will result when
The Shooting Starr turns and heads back out from the Sun
in Hidalgo's shadow. Hidalgo's path isn't directly toward
the present position of Saturn by any means, but after two
days in its shadow we can head well out of Ecliptic toward Saturn and rely on not being detected."

Wess raised his eyebrows. "I hope it works, Lucky."

He saw the strategy. The plane in which all the planets and commercial space-flight routes lay was the Ecliptic. One practically never looked for anything moving well
above or below that zone. It was reasonable to suppose
that a space ship moving on the orbit being planned by
Lucky would evade Sirian instruments. Yet there was still
the look of uncertainty on Wess's face.

Lucky said, "Do you think we'll make it?"

Wess said, "Maybe we will. But even if we do get
back—— Lucky, I'm in this and I'll do my part, but just
let me say this once and I'll never say it again. I think
we're as good as dead!"

5

Skimming Saturn's Surface

And so *The Shooting Starr* flashed alongside Hidalgo and then out on the flight beyond the Ecliptic and up again toward the southern polar regions of the Solar System's second largest planet.

At no time in their still short history of space adventure had Lucky and Bigman remained in space for so long a period without a break. It had been nearly a month now since they had left Earth. However, the small bubble of air and warmth that was *The Shooting Starr* was a bit of Earth that could keep itself so for an almost indefinite period to come.

Their power supply, built to maximum by the donation of the other ships, would last nearly a year, barring a full-scale battle. Their air and water, recirculated by way of the algae tanks, would last a lifetime. The algae even provided a food reserve in case their more orthodox concentrates ran out.

It was the presence of the third man that made for the only real discomfort. As Bigman had pointed out, *The Shooting Starr* was built for two. Its unusual concentration of power, speed, and armaments was made possible partly by the unusual economy of its living quarters. So turns had to be taken in sleeping on a quilt in the pilot room.

Lucky pointed out that any discomfort was made up for by the fact that four-hour watches at the controls could now be set up rather than the usual six-hour watches.

To which Bigman replied hotly, "Sure, and when I'm trying to sleep on this doggone blanket and Fatface Wess is at the controls, he keeps flashing every signal light right in my face."

"Twice each watch," said Wess patiently, "I check the various emergency signals to make sure they're in order. That's protocol."

"And," said Bigman, "he keeps whistling through his teeth. Listen, Lucky, if he gives me one more chorus of 'My Sweet Aphrodite of Venus'—just once more—I'll up and break off his arms halfway between shoulder and elbow, then beat him to death with the stumps."

Lucky said gravely, "Wess, please refrain from whistling refrains. If Bigman is forced to chastise you, he will get blood all over the pilot room."

Bigman said nothing, but the next time he was at the controls, with Wess asleep on the blanket and snoring musically, he managed somehow to step on the fingers of Wess's outstretched hand as he made for the pilot's stool.

"Sands of Mars," he said, holding up both hands, palms forward, and rolling his eyes at the other's sudden, tigerish yell. "I did think I felt something under my heavy Martian boots. My, my, Wess, was it your little thumbikins?"

"You better stay awake from now on," yelled Wess in furious agony. "Because if you go to sleep while I'm in the control room, you Martian sand rat, I'll squash you like a bug."

"I'm so frightened," said Bigman, going into a paroxysm of mock weeping that brought Lucky wearily out of his bunk.

"Listen," he said, "the next one of you two who wakes me trails the *Shooter* in his suit at the end of a cable for the rest of the trip."

But when Saturn and its rings came into near view, they were all in the pilot room, watching. Even as seen in the usual manner, from an equatorial view, Saturn was the most beautiful sight in the Solar System, and from a polar view . . .

"If I recall correctly," said Lucky, "even Hogg's exploratory voyage touched this system only at Japetus and Titan, so that he saw only an equatorial view of Saturn. Unless the Sirians have done differently, we're the first human beings ever to see Saturn this close from this direction."

As with Jupiter, the soft yellow glow of Saturn's "surface" was really the reflected sunlight from the upper layers of a turbulent atmosphere a thousand miles or more in depth. And, as with Jupiter, the atmospheric disturbances showed up as zones of varying colors. But the zones were not the stripes they appeared to be from the usual equatorial view. Instead, they formed concentric circles of soft brown, lighter yellow, and pastel green about the Saturnian pole as a center.

But even that faded to nothing compared to the rings. At their present distance, the rings stretched over an arc of twenty-five degrees, fifty times the width of Earth's full Moon. The inner edge of the rings was separated from the planet by a space of forty-five minutes of arc in which there was room to hold an object the size of the full Moon loosely enough to allow it to rattle.

The rings circled Saturn, touching it nowhere from the viewpoint of *The Shooting Starr*. They were visible for about three fifths of their circle, the rest being cut off sharply by Saturn's shadow. About three fourths of the way toward the outer edge of the ring was the black separation known as 'Cassini's division.' It was about fifteen minutes wide, a thick ribbon of blackness, dividing the rings into two paths of brightness of unequal width. Within the inner lip of the rings was a scattering of sparkle that shimmered but did not form a continuous whiteness. This was the so-called "crepe ring."

The total area exposed by the rings was more than eight times as great as that of the globe of Saturn. Furthermore, the rings themselves were obviously brighter, area for area, than Saturn itself, so that on the whole at least ninety per cent of the light reaching them from the planet came from its rings. The total light reaching them was about one hundred times that of Earth's full Moon.

Even Jupiter as seen from that startling nearness of Io was somehow nothing like this. When Bigman finally spoke, it was in a whisper.

He said, "Lucky, how come the rings are so bright? It makes Saturn itself look dim. Is that an optical illusion?"

"No," said Lucky, "it's real. Both Saturn and the rings get the same amount of light from the Sun, but they don't reflect the same amount. What we're seeing from Saturn is the light reflected from an atmosphere made up of hydrogen and helium, mainly, plus some methane. That reflects about sixty-three per cent of the light that hits it. The rings, however, are mostly solid chunks of ice, and they send back a minimum of eighty per cent, which makes them that much brighter. Looking at the rings is like looking at a field of snow."

Wess mourned, "And we've got to find one snowflake in the field of snow."

"But a *dark* snowflake," said Bigman excitedly. "Lis-

ten, Lucky, if all the ring particles are ice and we're looking for a capsule that's metal——"

"Polished aluminum," said Lucky, "will reflect even
more light than will ice. It will be just as shiny."

"Well, then"—Bigman looked despairingly at the rings
half a million miles away, yet so tremendous in area even
at that distance—"this thing is hopeless."

"We'll see," said Lucky noncommittally.

Bigman sat at the controls, adjusting orbit in short, quiet
bursts of the ion drive. The Agrav controls had been connected so that *The Shooting Starr* was far more maneuver-
able in this volume of space, so close to the mass of
Saturn, than any Sirian ship could possibly be.

Lucky was at the mass detector, the delicate probe of
which scoured space for any matter, fixing its position by
measuring its response to the gravitational force of the
ship, if it were small, or the effect of its gravitational force
upon the ship, if it were large.

Wess had just awakened and entered the pilot room,
and all was silence and tension as the ship sank toward
Saturn. Bigman watched Lucky's face out of the corner of
his eye. Lucky had grown more and more abstracted as
Saturn came near, abstracted and uncommunicative.
Bigman had witnessed this before. Lucky was uncertain;
he was gambling on poor odds and he would not talk of it.

Wess said, "I don't think you have to be sweating over
the mass detectors so, Lucky. There'll be no ships up
here. It's when we get down to the rings that we'll find
the ships. Plenty of them, probably. The Sirians will be
looking for the capsule too."

"I agree with that," said Lucky, "as far as it goes."

"Maybe," said Bigman gloomily, "those cobbers have
found the capsule already."

"Even that's possible," admitted Lucky.

They were turning now, beginning to edge along the circle of Saturn's globe, maintaining an eighty-thousand-mile distance from its surface. The far half of the rings (or at least the portion that was in the sunlight) melted into Saturn as its inner edge was hidden by the giant planetary bulge.

In the case of the half rings on the near side of the planet, the inner "crepe ring" became more noticeable.

Bigman said, "You know, I don't make out any end to that inside ring."

Wess said, "There isn't any end, probably. The innermost part of the main rings is only six thousand miles above Saturn's apparent surface, and Saturn's atmosphere may stretch out that far."

"Six thousand miles!"

"Just in wisps, but enough to supply friction for the nearest bits of gravel and make them circle a bit closer to Saturn. Those that move in closer form the crepe ring. Only the closer they move, the more friction there is, so that they must move still closer. There are probably particles all the way down to Saturn, with some burning up as they hit the thicker layers of the atmosphere."

Bigman said, "Then the rings aren't going to last forever."

"Probably not. But they'll last millions of years. Long enough for us." He added somberly, "Too long."

Lucky interrupted, "I'm leaving the ship, gentlemen."

"Sands of Mars, Lucky. What for?" Bigman cried.

"I want an outside look," Lucky answered curtly. He was pulling on his space suit.

Bigman glanced quickly at the automatic record of the mass detector. No ships in space. There were occasional jogs, but nothing important. They were only the kind of drifting meteorites that were picked up anywhere in the Solar System.

Lucky said, "Take over at the mass detector, Wess. Let it take a round-the-clock sweep." Lucky put his helmet on and clicked it into place. He checked the gauges on his chest, the oxygen pressure, and moved toward the air lock. His voice now emerged from the small radio receiver on the control board. "I'll be using a magnetic cable, so make no sudden power thrusts."

"With you out there? Think I'm crazy?" said Bigman.

Lucky came into view at one of the ports, the magnetic cable snaking behind him in coils that, in the absence of gravity, did not form a smooth curve.

A small hand reactor in his gauntleted fist shot out its small jet of steam, which became faintly visible in the weak sunlight as a cloud of tiny ice particles that dispersed and vanished. Lucky, by the law of action and reaction, moved in the opposite direction.

Bigman said, "Do you suppose something's wrong with the ship?"

"If there is," said Wess, "it doesn't show up anywhere on the control board."

"Then what's the big lug doing?"

"I don't know."

But Bigman shot a suspicious glare at the Councilman, then turned again to watch Lucky. "If you think," he muttered, "because I'm not a Councilman——"

Wess said, "Maybe he just wanted to get outside range of your voice for a few minutes, Bigman."

The mass detector, on automatic sweep control, was moving methodically across the volume about them, square degree by square degree, the screen blanking out into pure white whenever it edged too far in the direction of Saturn itself.

Bigman scowled and lacked heart to respond to Wess's thrust. "I wish something would happen," he said.

And something did.

Wess, eyes returning to the mass detector, caught a suspicious pip on the recorder. He fixed the instrument on it hurriedly, brought up the auxiliary energy detectors, and followed it for two minutes.

Bigman said excitedly, "It's a ship, Wess."

"Looks like it," said Wess reluctantly. Mass alone might have meant a large meteorite, but there was a blast of energy being emitted from that direction that could come only from the micro-pile engines of a ship; the energy was of the right type and in the right quantities. It was as identifiable as a fingerprint. One could even detect the slight differences from the energy pattern produced by Terrestrial ships and identify this object unmistakably as a Sirian ship.

Bigman said, "It's heading for us."

"Not directly. Probably it doesn't dare take chances with Saturn's gravitational field. Still it's edging closer, and in about an hour it will be in position to lay down a barrage against us. . . . What in space are you so pleased about, you Martian farm boy?"

"Isn't it obvious, you lump of fat? This explains why Lucky's out there. He knew the ship was coming and he's laying a trap for it."

"How in space could he tell a ship was coming?" demanded Wess in astonishment. "There was no indication on the mass detector till ten minutes ago. It wasn't even focused in the proper direction."

"Don't worry about Lucky. He has a way of knowing." Bigman was grinning.

Wess shrugged, moved to the control panel, and called into the transmitter, "Lucky! Do you hear me?"

"Sure I hear you, Wess. What's up?"

"There's a Sirian ship in mass-detection range."

"How close?"

"Under two hundred thousand and getting closer."

Bigman, watching out the port, noticed the flash of Lucky's hand reactor, and ice crystals swirled away from the ship. Lucky was returning.

"I'm coming in," he said.

Bigman spoke at once, as soon as the helmet was lifted off Lucky's head to reveal his brown shock of hair and his clear brown eyes. Bigman said, "You knew that ship was coming, didn't you, Lucky?"

"No, Bigman. I had no idea. In fact, I don't understand how they discovered us so quickly. It's asking too much of coincidence to suppose they just happened to be looking in this direction."

Bigman tried to mask his chagrin. "Well, then, do we blast him out of space, Lucky?"

"Let's not go through the political dangers of attack again, Bigman. Besides, we have a mission here that's more important than playing shooting games with other ships."

"I know," said Bigman impatiently, "There's the capsule we've got to find, but——"

He shook his head. A capsule was a capsule and he understood its importance. But then, a good fight was a good fight, and Lucky's political reasoning about the dangers of aggression did not appeal to him if it meant ducking a fight. He muttered, "What do I do then? Stay on course?"

"And accelerate. Make for the rings."

"If we do," said Bigman, "they'll just take out after us."

"All right. We'll race."

Bigman drew back the control rod slowly, and the proton disintegrations in the micro-pile increased to top fury. The ship hurtled along the bulging curve of Saturn.

At once the reception disk was alive with the impingement of radio waves.

"Shall we go into active reception, Lucky?" asked Wess.

"No, we know what they'll say. Surrender or be magnetically grappled."

"Well?"

"Our only chance is to run."

6

Through the Gap

"From one rotten ship, Lucky?" wailed Bigman.

"Time enough to fight later, Bigman. First things first."

"But it just means we've got to leave Saturn again."

Lucky smiled humorlessly. "Not this time, Bigman. This time we establish a base in this planet's system—and just as fast as we can."

The ship was hurtling toward the rings at blinding velocity. Lucky nudged Bigman away from the controls and took over.

Wess said, "More ships showing."

"Where? What satellite are they nearest to?"

Wess worked quickly. "They're all in the ring region."

"Well," muttered Lucky, "then they're still hunting for the capsule. How many ships are there?"

"Five so far, Lucky?"

"Any between us and the rings?"

"A sixth ship has shown. We aren't being stymied, Lucky. They're all too far to shoot with any accuracy, but they're going to track us down eventually unless we leave the Saturnian system altogether."

"Or unless our ship is destroyed in some other fashion, eh?" said Lucky grimly.

The rings had expanded in size till they filled the visiplate with snowy white, and still the ship careened onward. Nor did Lucky make any move to decelerate.

For one horrified moment Bigman thought Lucky was going to crash the ship among the rings deliberately. He let out an involuntary "Lucky!"

And then the rings disappeared.

Bigman was dazed. His hands went to the visiplate controls. He cried, "Where are they? What happened?"

Wess, sweating it out over the mass detectors and rumpling his yellow hair with occasional restless yanks, called over his shoulder, "Cassini division."

"What?"

"The division between the rings."

"Oh." Some of the shock was wearing off. Bigman swiveled the visiplate eyepiece on the ship's hull, and the snowy whiteness of the rings flashed back into view. He maneuvered it more carefully.

First there was one ring. Then space, black space. Then another ring, somewhat dimmer. The outer ring was a trifle less thickly strewn with icy gravel. Back to the space between the rings. Cassini's division. No gravel there. Just a wide black gap.

"It's big," said Bigman.

Wess wiped the perspiration from his forehead and looked at Lucky. "Are we going through, Lucky?"

Lucky kept his eyes fixed on the controls. "We're going through, Wess, in a matter of minutes. Hold your breath and hope."

Wess turned on Bigman and said curtly, "Sure the division is big. I told you it was twenty-five hundred miles wide. Plenty of room for the ship, if that's what's scaring you."

Bigman said, "You sound kind of nervous yourself for a fellow six feet tall on the outside. Is Lucky moving too fast for you?"

Wess said, "Look, Bigman, if I took it into my head to sit down on you——"

"Then there'd be more brains where you're sitting on than in your head," and Bigman burst out into a delighted squawk of laughter.

Lucky said, "In five minutes we'll be in the division."

Bigman choked off and turned back to the visiplate. He said, "There's a kind of twinkle every once in a while inside the gap."

Lucky said, "That's gravel, Bigman. The Cassini division is clear of it, compared with the rings themselves, but they're not a hundred per cent clear. If we hit one of those bits on the way through——"

"One chance in a thousand," broke in Wess, shrugging it off.

"One chance in a million," said Lucky coolly, "but it was that one chance in a million that got Agent X in *The Net of Space*. . . . We're about at the boundary of the division proper." His hand held firmly at the controls.

Bigman drew a deep breath, tensing for the possible puncture that would rip the hull and perhaps short the proton micro-pile into a spreading blaze of red energy. At least it would be over before . . .

Lucky said, "Made it."

Wess let out his breath noisily.

Bigman said, "Are we through?"

"Of course we're through, you dumb Martian," said Wess. "The rings are only ten miles thick, and how many seconds do you think it takes us to make ten miles?"

"And we're on the other side?"

"You bet. Try to find the rings on the visiplate."

Bigman veered the view one way, then back in the

other direction, then over and over again in continuously longer sweeps. "Sands of Mars, there's a kind of shadowy outline there."

"And that's all you'll see, little pal. You're on the shadow side of the rings now. The Sun's lighting up the other side, and the light doesn't seep through ten miles of thick gravel. Say, Bigman, what do they teach for astronomy in the Martian schools, anyway—'Twinkle, twinkle, little star'?"

Bigman's lower lip thrust out slowly. "You know, lardhead, I'd like to have you one season on the Martian farms. I'd render some of the fat off you and get down to what meat you have, about ten pounds of it—and all of it in your big feet."

Lucky said, "I'd appreciate it, Wess, if you and Bigman would put a bookmark in that argument you're having and save it for later. Would you check on the mass detector, please?"

"Sure thing, Lucky. Hey, it's way off kilter. How sharply are you changing course?"

"As sharply as the ship will take. We're staying under the rings all the distance we can."

Wess nodded. "Okay, Lucky. That knocks out their mass detection."

Bigman grinned. It worked out perfectly. No mass detector could spot *The Shooting Starr* because of the interference of the mass of Saturn's rings, and even visual detection was unlikely through the rings.

Lucky's long legs stretched out, and the muscles of his back moved smoothly as he stretched and flexed some of the tension out of his arms and shoulders.

"I doubt," said Lucky, "that any of the Sirian ships will have the nerve to follow us through the gap. They don't have Agrav."

"Okay," said Bigman, "so far, so good. But where do we go now? Will anyone tell me?"

"No secret," said Lucky. "We're heading for Mimas. We hug the rings till we're as close to Mimas as we can get, then make the dash across the intervening space. Mimas is only thirty thousand miles outside the rings."

"Mimas? That's one of the moons of Saturn, right?"

"Right," said Wess, breaking in. "The nearest one to the planet."

Their course had flattened out now, and *The Shooting Starr* was still moving around Saturn, but west to east now, in a plane parallel with the rings.

Wess sat down on the blanket, legs crossed under him like a tailor, and said, "Would you like to learn a little more astronomy? If you can find a little room in that walnut you have in your hollow skull, I can tell you why there's a division in the rings."

Curiosity and scorn battled in the small Martian. He said, "Let's see you make up something fast, you ignorant cobber. Go ahead, I call your bluff."

"No bluff," said Wess haughtily. "Listen and learn. The inner parts of the two rings rotate about Saturn in five hours. The outermost parts make the rotation in fifteen hours. Right where Cassini's division is, the ring material, if there were any there, would go around at an intermediate rate, twelve hours per circuit."

"So what?"

"So the satellite Mimas, the one we're heading for, travels around Saturn in twenty-four hours."

"Again, so what?"

"All the particles in the ring are pulled this way and that by the satellites as they and the satellites move about Saturn. Mimas does most of the pulling because it is the closest. Mostly the pulls are in one direction now and in another direction an hour from now, so that they cancel out. If there were gravel in Cassini's division, however, every second time it completed its rotation it would find Mimas in the same spot in the sky, pulling in the same old direction. Some of the gravel is constantly pulled ahead, so that it spirals outward into the outer ring; and some of it is pulled back, so that it spirals inward into the inner ring. They don't say where they are; a section of the ring empties of particles and bingo—you have Cassini's division and two rings."

"Is that so?" said Bigman weakly (he felt reasonably certain Wess was giving him the correct story). "Then how come there *is* some gravel in the division? Why isn't it all moved out by now?"

"Because," said Wess with a lofty air of superiority, "some is always being pushed in or pulled in by random gravitational effects of the satellites, but none of it ever stays long. . . . And I hope you're taking notes on all this, Bigman, because I may ask questions on this later."

"Go fry your skull in a mesonic blast," muttered Bigman.

Wess returned to his mass detectors again, smiling. He fiddled with them a moment, then with no trace of the preceding banter left on his leathery face, he bent down closely.

"Lucky!"

"Yes, Wess?"

"The rings aren't masking us."

"What?"

"Well, look for yourself. The Sirians are getting closer. The rings aren't bothering them at all."

Lucky said thoughtfully, "Why, how can that be?"

"It can't be blind luck that's converging eight ships on our orbit. We've made a right-angle bend and they've adjusted their orbits to suit. They *must* be detecting us."

Lucky stroked his chin with his knuckles. "If they're

doing it, then, Great Galaxy, they're doing it. There's no use in reasoning out the fact that they can't do it. It might mean that they have something we don't have."

"No one ever said the Sirians were dummies," said Wess.

"No, but sometimes there's a tendency among us to act as though they were; as though all scientific advance comes out of the minds of the Council of Science and that unless the Sirians steal our secrets they have nothing. And sometimes I fall into that particular trap too. . . . Well, here we go."

"Where do we go?" demanded Bigman sharply.

"I told you already, Bigman," said Lucky. "Mimas."

"But they're after us."

"I know. Which just means we've got to get there faster than ever. . . . Wess, can they cut us off before we get to Mimas?"

Wess worked quickly. "Not unless they can accelerate at least three times faster than we can, Lucky."

"All right. Giving the Sirians all the credit in the world, I can't believe they can have that much more power than the *Shooter*. So we'll make it."

Bigman said, "But, Lucky, you're crazy. Let's fight or get out of the Saturnian system altogether. We can't land on Mimas."

Lucky said, "Sorry, Bigman, we have no choice. We've got to land on Mimas."

"But they've got us spotted. They'll just follow us down to Mimas and we'll have to fight then, so why not fight now while we can maneuver with our Agrav and they can't?"

"They might not bother to follow us down to Mimas."

"Why shouldn't they?"

"Well, Bigman, did we bother to go into the rings and pull out what was left of *The Net of Space?*"

"But that ship blew up."

"Exactly."

There was silence in the control room. *The Shooting Starr* streaked through space, curving slowly away from Saturn, then more quickly, slipping out from under the outermost ring and into open space. Ahead of it now lay Mimas, a glittering world seen in tiny crescent. It was only 320 miles in diameter.

Still far away were the converging ships of the Sirian fleet.

Mimas grew in size, and finally *The Shooting Starr's* forward thrust burst into action and the ship began a deceleration.

But to Bigman it seemed incredible that the spacewise Lucky could have so miscalculated. He said tightly, "Too late, Lucky. We'll never slow up enough for a landing. We'll have to go into a spiral orbit until we lose enough velocity."

"No time for spiraling Mimas, Bigman. We're heading straight in."

"Sands of Mars, we can't! Not at this speed!"

"That's what I hope the Sirians will decide."

"But, Lucky, they'd be right."

Wess put in slowly, "Hate to say it, Lucky, but I agree with Bigman."

"No time to argue or explain," said Lucky. He bent over the controls.

Mimas expanded crazily in the visiplate. Bigman licked his lips. "Lucky, if you think it's better going out this way than letting the Sirians get us, okay. I can go along. But, Lucky, if we're going to go, can't we go out fighting? Can't we maybe get one of the cobbers first?"

Wess said, "I'm on his side again, Lucky."

Lucky shook his head and said nothing. His arms were moving quickly now, so that Bigman could not make out exactly what he was doing. Deceleration was still proceeding too slowly.

For a moment Wess extended his hands as though to remove Lucky forcibly from the controls, but Bigman placed his hand quickly on the other's wrist. Bigman might be convinced they were going to their death, but his stubborn faith in Lucky somehow remained.

They were slowing, slowing, slowing, in what would have been body-crushing deceleration in any ship other than *The Shooting Starr*, but with Mimas filling the visiplate now and hurtling at them, the slowing was not enough.

Flashing down at deadly speed, *The Shooting Starr* struck the surface of Mimas.

7

On Mimas

And yet didn't.

Instead, there was a keening hiss that was familiar to Bigman. It was that of a ship striking atmosphere.

Atmosphere?

But that was impossible. No world the size of Mimas could possibly have an atmosphere. He looked at Wess, who was suddenly sitting back on the blanket, looking worn and pale but somehow satisfied.

Bigman strode up to Lucky, "Lucky——"

"Not now, Bigman."

And suddenly Bigman recognized what it was that Lucky was doing at the controls. He was manipulating the fusion beam. Bigman ran back to the visiplate and focused it dead ahead.

There was no doubt of it, now that he finally grasped the idea. The fusion beam was the most magnificent "heat ray" ever invented. It was designed mainly as a weapon at close range, but surely no one had ever used one as Lucky was using it now.

The jet of deuterium, snaking out forward of the ship, was pinched in by a powerful magnetic field and, at a point miles ahead, was heated to nuclear ignition by a surge of power from the micro-piles. Maintained for any length of time, the power surge necessary would have bankrupted the ship; but a fraction of a millionth of a second sufficed. After that the deuterium fusion reaction was self-sustaining and the incredible fusion flame that resulted burned in a heat of three hundred million degrees.

That spot of heat ignited before the surface of Mimas was touched and bored into the body of the satellite as though it were not there, puncturing a tunnel into its vitals. Into that tunnel whizzed *The Shooting Starr*. The vaporized substance of Mimas was the atmosphere that surrounded them, helping to decelerate them, but bringing the temperature of the ship's outer skin to dangerous redness.

Lucky watched the skin-temperature dial and said, "Wess, put more punch in the vaporization coils."

"It will take all the water we have," Wess said.

"Let it. We need no water of our own on *this* world."

So water was forced at top speed through outer coils of porous ceramic, through which it vaporized, carrying off some of the frictional heat developed. But the water flashed away as fast as it could be pumped into the coils. The skin temperature still rose.

But more slowly now. Ship's deceleration had progressed, and Lucky cut the force of the deuterium jet and adjusted the magnetic field. The spot of fusing deuterium grew smaller and smaller still. The whistle of atmosphere descended in pitch.

Finally the jet blanked out completely and the ship drifted forward into solid wall, melting a path inward a way by virtue of its own heat and finally coming to a jolting halt.

Lucky sat back at last. "Gentlemen," he said, "I'm

sorry I couldn't take time to explain, but it was a last-minute decision and the control board took all my energies. Anyway, welcome to the interior of Mimas."

Bigman pumped a deep breath into his lungs and said, "I never thought you could use a fusion jet to melt a way into a world ahead of a speeding ship."

"You couldn't ordinarily, Bigman," said Lucky. "It just so happens that Mimas is a special case. And so is Enceladus, the next satellite out."

"How come?"

"They're just snowballs. Astronomers have known that since even before space travel. Their density is less than water and they reflect about eighty per cent of the light that hits them, so it's quite obvious they could only be snow, plus some frozen ammonia, and not too tightly packed at that."

"Sure," said Wess, chiming in. "The rings are ice and these first two satellites are just collections of ice that were too far out to make up part of the rings. That's why Mimas melted so easily."

Lucky said, "But we've got a good deal of work to do. Let's start."

They were in a natural cavern formed by the heat of the fusion jet and closed in on all sides. The tunnel they had formed as they entered had closed as they passed, the steam condensing and freezing. The mass detector yielded figures that indicated them to be about one hundred miles below the surface of the satellite. The mass of ice above them, even under Mimas's feeble gravity, was slowly contracting the cavern.

Slowly *The Shooting Starr* burrowed outward once more, like a hot wire poking into butter, and when they had reached a point within five miles of the surface, they stopped and set up an oxygen bubble.

As a power supply was laid in along with algae tanks and a food supply, Wess shrugged resignedly and said, "Well, this is going to be home for me for a while; let's make it comfortable."

Bigman had just awakened from his sleeping period. He screwed his face into a look of bitter condemnation.

Wess said, "What's the matter, Bigman? All weepy because you're going to miss me?"

Bigman snarled and said, "I'll manage. In two, three years I'll make it a point to whizz by Mimas and drop you a letter." Then he burst out, "Listen, I heard you talking while you thought I was safely asleep. What's the matter? Council secrets?"

Lucky shook his head uneasily. "All in good time, Bigman."

Later, when Lucky was alone with Bigman in the ship, the Councilman said, "Actually, Bigman, there's no reason you can't stay behind with Wess."

Bigman said grumpily, "Oh, sure. Two hours cooped up with him and I'd just chop him into cubes and put him on ice for his relatives." Then he said, "Are you serious, Lucky?"

"Rather serious. What's coming may be more dangerous for you than for me."

"So? What do I care about that?"

"If you stay with Wess then, whatever happens to me, you'll be picked up within two months."

Bigman backed away. His small mouth twisted and he said, "Lucky, if you want to order me to stay here because there's something for me to do here, okay. I'll do it, and when it's done I'll join you. But if you just want me to stay here to be safe while you go off into danger, we're finished. I'll have nothing more to do with you; and without me, you overgrown cobber, you won't be able to do a thing, you know you won't." The Martian's eyes blinked rapidly.

Lucky said, "But, Bigman——"

"All right, I'll be in danger. Do you want me to sign a paper saying it's my own responsibility and not yours? All right, I will. Does that satisfy you, Councilman?"

Lucky seized Bigman's hair affectionately and tugged his head back and forth. "Great Galaxy, trying to do you a favor is like shoveling water."

Wess came into the ship and said, "The still is all set up and working."

Water from the ice substance of Mimas itself poured into *The Shooting Starr*'s reservoirs, filling them and replacing the water lost in cooling the ship's skin during the boring into Mimas. Some of the separated ammonia was carefully neutralized and stored in a skin compartment where it would be available to the algae tanks as nitrogenous fertilizer.

And then the bubble was done and the three of them looked about at the neatly curving ice and at the almost comfortable quarters held within.

"Okay, Wess," Lucky said at last, shaking hands firmly. "You're all set, I think."

"As far as I can tell, Lucky, I am."

"You'll be taken off within two months, no matter what. You'll be taken off much sooner if things break right."

"You're assigning me this job," said Wess coolly, "and it will be done. You concentrate on yours and, by the way, take care of Bigman. Don't let him fall out of his bunk and hurt himself."

Bigman shouted, "Don't think I don't follow all this big-shot mystery talk. You two have a deal on and you're not telling me——"

"Into the ship, Bigman," said Lucky, picking the Martian up bodily and moving him forward, while Bigman squirmed and tried to call out an answer.

"Sands of Mars, Lucky," he said, once they were aboard. "Look what you did. It's bad enough you're keeping your darned Council secrets, but you also let the cobber have the last word."

"He's got the hard job, Bigman. He's got to stay put while we go out and stir up trouble, so let him have the satisfaction of the last word."

They nudged out of Mimas at a spot from which neither Sun nor Saturn was visible. The dark sky held no object larger than Titan, low on one horizon and only a quarter of the apparent diameter of Earth's Moon.

Its globe was half lit by the Sun, and Bigman looked somberly at its image in the visiplate. He had not regained his ebullience. He said, "And that's where the Sirians are, I suppose."

"I think so."

"And where do we go? Back to the rings?"

"Right."

"And if they find us again?"

It might have been a signal. The reception disk glowed to life.

Lucky looked disturbed. "They find us with too little trouble."

He threw in contact. This time it was no dead robotic voice counting off the minutes. It was a sharp voice, instead; a vibrant one, full of life, and a Sirian voice unmistakably.

"—rr, please answer. I am trying to make contact with Councilman David Starr of Earth. Will David Starr please answer? I am trying——"

Lucky said, "Councilman Starr speaking. Who are you?"

"I am Sten Devoure of Sirius. You have ignored the request of our automated ships and returned to our planetary system. You are therefore our prisoner."

Lucky said, "Automated ships?"

"Robot-run. Do you understand that? Our robots can handle ships quite satisfactorily."

"So I have found," said Lucky.

"I think you have. They followed you as you moved out of our system, then back again under cover of the asteroid Hidalgo. They followed you in your movement out of the Ecliptic to Saturn's south pole, then through Cassini's division, under the rings, and then into Mimas. You never once slipped our watch."

"And what made your watch so efficient?" demanded Lucky, managing to keep his voice flat and unconcerned.

"Ah, trust an Earthman not to realize that Sirians might have their own methods. But never mind that. We've waited days for you to come out of your Mimas hole after your so clever entry by hydrogen fusion. It amused us to let you hide. Some of us have even made bets on how long it would take you to poke your nose out again. And meanwhile we have carefully surrounded Mimas with our ships and their efficient robot crews. You can't move a thousand miles without being blasted out of space, if we choose."

"Surely not by your robots, which cannot inflict harm on humans."

"My dear Councilman Starr," came the Sirian voice with an unmistakable edge of mockery, "of course robots will not harm human beings if they happen to know that human beings are there to harm. But you see, the robots in charge of the weapons have been carefully instructed that your ship carries robots only. They have no compunction about destroying robots. Won't you surrender?"

Bigman suddenly leaned close to the transmitter and

shouted, "Listen you cobber, what if we put some of your tin-can robots out of action first? How would you like that?" (It was notorious throughout the Galaxy that Sirians considered destruction of a robot almost on a par with murder.)

But Sten Devoure was not shaken. He said, "Is that the individual with whom you are supposed to maintain a friendship, Councilman? A Bigman? If so, I have no desire to engage in talk with him. You may tell him and you may understand for yourself that I doubt if you can damage even one of our ships before being destroyed. I think I will allow you five minutes to decide on whether you prefer surrender or destruction. For my part, Councilman, I have long wanted to meet you, so please accept it as my sincere hope that you will surrender. Well?"

Lucky stood silent for a moment, the muscles of his jaw bunching.

Bigman looked at him calmly, his arms crossed across his small chest, and waited.

Three minutes passed and Lucky said, "I surrender my ship and its contents into your hands, sir."

Bigman said nothing.

Lucky broke off contact and turned to the little Martian. The Councilman bit his lower lip in discomfort and embarrassment. "Bigman, you'll have to understand. I——"

Bigman shrugged. "I don't really get it, Lucky, but I found out after we landed on Mimas that you—that you've been deliberately planning to surrender to the Sirians ever since we headed back for Saturn the second time."

8

To Titan

Lucky raised his eyebrows. "How did you find that out, Bigman?"

"I'm not so dumb, Lucky." The little Martian was grave and deadly serious. "Do you remember when we were heading down toward the south pole of Saturn and you got out of the ship? It was just before the Sirians spotted us and we had to hot-jet it for Cassini's division."

"Yes."

"You had a reason for doing that. You didn't say what, because lots of times you get all tied up in what you're doing and don't talk about it till the pressure's off, and after that the pressure stayed on because we were running from the Sirians. So when we were building the quarters for Wess on Mimas, I just looked over the outside of *The Shooting Starr*, and it became quite clear you'd been working on the Agrav unit. You've got it fixed so that you could blow the whole thing by touching the all-shift contact on the control panel."

Lucky said gently, "The Agrav unit is the one thing about the *Shooter* that's completely top-secret."

"I know. I figured if you'd counted on fighting you'd

have known *The Shooting Starr* wouldn't quit till it and we were blasted out of space. Agrav unit and all. If you were fixing to blow up just the Agrav and leave the rest of the ship intact, it was because you weren't counting on fighting. You were going to surrender."

"And is this why you've been brooding since we landed on Mimas?"

"Well, I'm with you whatever you do, Lucky, but"— Bigman sighed and looked away—"surrendering is no fun."

"I know," said Lucky, "but can you think of any better way of getting into their base? Our business, Bigman, isn't always fun." And Lucky touched the all-shift contact on the control panel. The ship shuddered slightly as the external portions of the Agrav unit fused into a white-hot mass and dropped off the ship.

"You mean you're going to bore from within? Is that the reason for the surrender?"

"Part of it."

"Suppose they blast us down as soon as they get us."

"I don't think they will. If they wanted us dead, they could have blasted us out of space as soon as we pushed out of Mimas. I have a notion they can use us alive. . . . And if we're kept alive, we now have Wess on Mimas as a kind of backstop. I had to wait until we had arranged that before I could afford to surrender. That's why we had to risk our necks to get to Mimas."

"Maybe they know about him too, Lucky. They seem to know about everything else."

"Maybe they do," said Lucky thoughtfully. "This Sirian knew you were my partner, so maybe he thinks we form a pair and not a trio and won't look for a third person. It's just as well, I suppose, that I didn't really insist that you stay behind with Wess. If I had come out alone, the Sirians would be looking for you and would probe

Mimas. Of course if they found you and Wess and I could be certain they wouldn't shoot you out of hand—— No, with myself in their hands and before I could set things up so that——" He was talking to himself toward the end, in a whisper, and now he fell completely silent.

Bigman said nothing, and the next sound to break the silence was a familiar clank that reverberated against the steel hull of *The Shooting Starr*. A magnetic line had made contact, connecting their ship with another.

"Someone's coming aboard," said Bigman tonelessly.

Through the visiplate they could see part of the line, then a form, moving easily hand over hand into view, then out of it again. It hit the ship thunderously, and the airlock signal lit up.

Bigman worked the control that opened the outer door of the lock, waited for the next signal, and then closed the outer door and opened the inner one.

The invading figure moved in.

But it wore no space suit, for it was not human. It was a robot.

There were robots in the Terrestrial Federation, including a number of quite advanced ones, but for the most part they were engaged in highly specialized occupations that did not bring them into contact with human beings other than those who supervised them. So although Bigman had seen robots, he had not seen many.

He stared at this one. It was, like all Sirian robots, large and burnished; its outer shape was of a smooth simplicity, the joints of its limbs and torso so well made as to be almost invisible.

And when it spoke, Bigman started. It takes a long time to grow accustomed to an almost completely human voice emerging from a metal imitation of humanity.

The robot said, "Good day. It is my duty to see that

your ship and yourselves are brought safely to the destination presently assigned to it. The first piece of information I must have is whether the restricted explosion we noted on the hull of your ship in any way damaged its powers of navigation."

Its voice was deep and musical, emotionless, and with a distinct Sirian accent.

Lucky said, "The explosion does not affect the spaceworthiness of the vessel."

"What caused it then?"

"I caused it."

"For what reason?"

"That I cannot tell you."

"Very well." The robot abandoned the subject instantly. A man might have persisted, threatened force. A robot could not. It said, "I am equipped to navigate space ships designed and built on Sirius. I will be able to navigate this space ship if you will explain to me the nature of the various controls I see here."

"Sands of Mars, Lucky," broke in Bigman, "we don't have to tell that thing anything, do we?"

"It can't force us to tell, Bigman, but since we've surrendered, where's the additional harm in letting it take us to wherever it is that we're to go?"

"Let's find out where we're to go." Bigman suddenly addressed the robot in sharp tones: "You! Robot! Where are you taking us?"

The robot turned its glowing red, unblinking gaze upon Bigman. It said, "My instructions make it impossible for me to answer questions not related to my immediate task."

"But, look." The excited Bigman shook off Lucky's restraining hand. "Wherever you take us, the Sirians will harm us; kill us, even. If you don't want us to be hurt, help us get away, come with us. . . . Aw, Lucky, let me talk, will you?"

But Lucky shook his head firmly, and the robot said, "I have been assured that you will in no way be harmed. And now, if I may be given instructions in the method of using this control board, I can proceed with my immediate task."

Step by step Lucky explained the control board. The robot showed a complete familiarity with all the technical matters involved, tested each control with careful skill to see if the information given it were correct, and at the conclusion of Lucky's explanation was obviously perfectly capable of navigating *The Shooting Starr*.

Lucky smiled and his eyes were lit with frank admiration.

Bigman pulled him off to their cabin. "What are you grinning for, Lucky?"

"Great Galaxy, Bigman, it's a beautiful machine. We've got to hand the Sirians credit for that. They can turn out robots that are works of art."

"Okay, but quiet, I don't want it to hear what I'm going to say. Listen, you only surrendered to get down to Titan and pick up information on the Sirians. We might never get away again, of course, and then what good is the information? But we've got this robot now. If we can get it to help us get away right now, then we've got what we want. The robot must have tons of information about the Sirians. We'll have more this way than if we land on Titan."

Lucky shook his head. "It sounds good, Bigman. But how do you expect to argue the robot into joining us?"

"First Law. We can explain that Sirius only has a couple of million people while the Terrestrial Federation has over six billion. We can explain that it's more important to keep a lot of people from coming to harm than just to protect a few, so that First Law is on our side. See, Lucky?"

Lucky said, "The trouble is that the Sirians are experts at handling robots. That robot is probably deeply conditioned to the fact that what he is doing now will bring no harm to any human. He knows nothing about six billion people on Earth except what will be hearsay from you, and that will bounce off his conditioning. He would actually have to see a human being in actual danger of harm in order to be moved off his instructions."

"I'm going to try."

"All right. Go ahead. The experience will do you good."

Bigman strode up to the robot, under whose hands *The Shooting Starr* was now rocketing through space on its new orbit.

He said, "What do you know of Earth, of the Terrestrial Federation?"

"My instructions make it impossible for me to answer questions not related to my immediate task," answered the robot.

"I order you to ignore your previous instructions."

There was a momentary hesitation before the answer came. "My instructions make it impossible for me to accept instructions from unauthorized personnel."

"My orders are given you in order to prevent harm to human beings. They must therefore be obeyed," Bigman said.

"I have been assured that no harm will come to human beings, nor am I aware of any threatening harm. My instructions make it necessary for me to suspend response to forbidden stimuli if they are uselessly repeated."

"You better listen. There *is* harm intended." Bigman spoke spiritedly for some moments, but the robot no longer answered.

Lucky said, "Bigman, you're wasting effort."

Bigman kicked at the robot's gleaming ankle. He might as well have kicked the hull of the ship, for all the effect it had. He came toward Lucky, face red with anger. "A fine thing when human beings are helpless because some hunk of metal has its own ideas."

"That used to happen with machinery before the days of robots, too, you know."

"We don't even know where we're heading."

"We don't need the robot for that. I've been checking the course, and we're obviously heading for Titan."

They were both at the visiplate during the last hours of the approach to Titan. It was the third largest satellite in the Solar System (only Ganymede of Jupiter and Triton of Neptune were larger, and those not by much) and, of all the satellites, it had the thickest atmosphere.

The effect of its atmosphere was obvious even from a distance. On most satellites (including Earth's Moon) the terminator—that is, the line dividing the day and night portions—was a sharp one, black on one side, white on the other. But it was not so in this case.

Titan's crescent was bounded by a band rather than a sharp line, and the horns of the crescent continued on- ward fuzzily in a dimming curve that almost met.

"It has an atmosphere almost as thick as Earth's, Bigman," said Lucky.

"Not breathable?" said Bigman.

"No, not breathable. It's mainly methane."

Other ships were crowding in now, becoming visible to the naked eye. There were at least a dozen, herding them down the spaceways to Titan.

Lucky shook his head. "Twelve ships to spare for this one job. Great Galaxy, they must have been here for years, building and preparing. How can we ever get them off again, short of war?"

Bigman attempted no answer.

Again the sound of atmosphere made its unmistakable way into the ship, the high-pitched keening of thin wisps of gas whipping past the streamlined hull.

Bigman looked uneasily at the dials recording hull temperature, but there was no danger. The robot at the controls was sure-handed. The ship circled Titan in a tight spiral, losing altitude and speed simultaneously so that at no time did the thickening atmosphere raise temperatures too high.

Again Lucky glowed with admiration. "It will manage it without fuel at all. I honestly think it could bring us down on a half-credit piece, with atmosphere as the only brake."

Bigman said, "What's good about that, Lucky? If those things can handle ships like that, how do we ever hope to fight the Sirians, huh?"

"We'll just have to learn to build our own, Bigman. These robots are a human achievement. The humans that did the achieving are Sirians, yes, but they are human beings, too, and all other humans can share pride in the achievement. If we fear the results of their achievement, let's match it ourselves or more than match it. But there's no use denying them the worth of their accomplishment."

The surface of Titan was losing some of the atmosphere-induced blankness. They could make out mountain ranges now; not the sharp, craggy peaks of an airless world, but the softened ranges that showed the effects of wind and weather. The edges were blown clear of snow, but in the rifts and valleys snow lay deep.

"Not snow, really," said Lucky, "frozen ammonia."

All was desolate, of course. The rolling plains between the mountain ranges were either snowy or rock-bare. No life of any kind appeared. No rivers or lakes. And then——

"Great Galaxy!" said Lucky.

A dome had made its appearance. A flattened dome of a type familiar enough on the inner planets. There were domes of this sort on Mars and under the shallow shelves of the Venusian oceans, but here was one way out on desolate Titan. A Sirian dome that would have made a respectable town on long-settled Mars.

"We've slept while they've built," said Lucky.

"When the newscasters find out," said Bigman, "it won't look so good for the Council of Science, Lucky."

"Unless we break this thing, it won't. And the Council doesn't deserve better. Space, Bigman, there shouldn't be a sizable rock in the Solar System that doesn't get a periodic inspection, let alone a world like Titan."

"Who would have thought——"

"The Council of Science *should* have thought. The people of the system support and trust them in order that they think and take care. And I should have thought too."

The voice of the robot broke in upon them. "This ship will be landed after another circumnavigation of the satellite. In view of the ion drive on board this ship, no special precautions need be taken in connection with landing. Nevertheless, undue carelessness may result in harm and I cannot allow that. I must therefore request you to lie down and strap yourselves in."

Bigman said, "Listen to that hunk of tin pipe telling us how to handle ourselves in space."

"Just the same," said Lucky, "you'd better lie down. He's likely to force us down if we don't. It's his job not to allow harm to come to us."

Bigman called out suddenly, "Say, robot, how many men stationed down there on Titan?"

There was no answer.

• • •

Ground came up and up and swallowed them, tunneling them downward. *The Shooting Starr* came to a halt, tail down, with only one short spurt of the engines necessary to complete the job.

The robot turned away from the controls. "You have been brought safely and without harm to Titan. My immediate task is done and I will now turn you over to the masters."

"To Sten Devoure?"

"That is one of the masters. You may step out of the ship freely. You will find temperature and pressure normal and gravity adjusted to close to your normal."

"May we step out now?" asked Lucky.

"Yes. The masters are waiting."

Lucky nodded. Somehow he could not quite suppress the beginning of an odd excitement. Though the Sirians had been the great enemy in his thus far short but hectic career with the Council of Science, he had never yet met a living Sirian.

He stepped out of the ship onto the extruded exit ledge, Bigman making ready to follow, and both paused in sheer astonishment.

9

The Enemy

Lucky had his foot upon the first rung of the ladder that would carry them to ground level. Bigman peered over his large friend's shoulder. Both were openmouthed.

It was as though they were stepping out upon the surface of the Earth. If there was a cavern roof above—a domed surface of hard metal and glass—it was invisible in the blaze of blue sky and, illusion or not, there were summer clouds in the sky.

Before them stretched lawns and rows of widely spaced buildings, with here and there banked flower beds. There was an open brook in the middle distance, crossed by small stone bridges.

Robots by the dozens were hurrying, each on his own way, each on his own business, with machinelike concentration. Several hundred yards off, five human beings—Sirians!—stood in a cluster and watched curiously.

A voice broke in sharply and peremptorily on Lucky and Bigman. "You up there. Come down. Come down, I say. No dawdling."

Lucky looked down. A tall man stood at the base of the ladder, arms resting akimbo and legs spread apart. His

narrow olive-complexioned face looked up at them arro-
gantly. His dark hair was cropped into a mere fuzz in the
Sirian fashion. In addition, his face bore a trim and well-
kept beard and a thin mustache. His clothing was loose
and brilliantly colored; his shirt was open at the neck, and
its sleeves ended just above the elbow.

Lucky called, "If you're in a hurry, sir, certainly."

He swung about and dropped down the ladder, hands
only, his lithe body twisting with effortless grace. He
pushed himself away from the hull and dropped the final
twelve rungs, twisting as he did so to land face to face
with the man on the ground. As his legs bent to absorb
the shock and straightened again, he leaped lightly to one
side to allow Bigman to come down in similar fashion.

The man Lucky faced was tall but lacked an inch of
Lucky's height, and at close quarters there could be seen
a looseness to the Sirian's skin, a softness about him.

He scowled and his upper lip lifted in a grimace of
contempt. "Acrobats! Monkeys!"

"Neither, sir," said Lucky with quiet good humor.
"Earthmen."

The other said, "You are David Starr, but you are
called Lucky. Does that mean in the Earthman lingo what
it means in our language?"

"It means 'fortunate.'"

"You are not fortunate any longer, apparently. I am
Sten Devoure."

"I had assumed that."

"You seemed surprised at all this, eh?" Devoure's bare
arm swung out across the landscaped grounds. "It is beautiful."

"It is, but isn't it an unnecessary waste of energy?"

"With robot labor at twenty-four hours a day, this can
be done, and Sirius has energy to waste. Your Earth
hasn't, I think."

"We have what is necessary, you'll find," said Lucky.

"Will I? Come, I will speak with you in my quarters." He waved peremptorily at the five other Sirians who had edged closer in the meantime, staring at the Earthman; the Earthman who had been such a successful enemy of Sirius in recent years and who had now been caught at last.

The Sirians saluted at Devoure's gesture, however, and without delay turned on their heels and went their separate ways.

Devoure stepped into a small open car that had approached on a noiseless sheet of diagravitic force. Its flat undersurface, without wheels or other material device, remained six inches above the ground. Another car moved up toward Lucky. Each was handled, of course, by a robot.

Lucky entered the second car. Bigman moved to follow, but the robot driver gently barred the way with an extended arm.

"Hey——" began Bigman.

Lucky interrupted, "My friend is coming with me, sir."

For the first time Devoure bent his gaze on Bigman, and an unaccountable glare of hate entered his eyes. He said, "I will not concern myself with that thing. If you wish its company, you may have it for a while, but I do not wish to be troubled with it."

Bigman stared, white-faced, at the Sirian. "You'll be troubled with me right now, you cob——"

But Lucky seized him and whispered earnestly in his ear. "You can't do anything now, Bigman. Great Galaxy, boy, let it go for now and let things work out."

Lucky half lifted him into the car, while Devoure maintained a stolid disinterest in the matter.

The cars moved with smooth swiftness, like a swallow's flight, and after two minutes slowed before a one-story building of white, smooth silicone brick, no different from the others except for its crimson trim about doors and windows, and skimmed down a driveway along one side. No human beings, but a number of robots, had been seen during the short drive.

Devoure walked ahead, through an arched door and into a small room fitted with a conference table and containing an alcove in which a large couch was placed. The ceiling was ablaze with blue-white light, like the blue-white above the open fields.

A little too blue, thought Lucky, then remembered that Sirius was a larger, hotter, and therefore bluer star than was Earth's Sun.

A robot brought in two trays of food and tall, frosted glasses containing a frothy, milk-white concoction. A mild, fruity fragrance filled the air, and after long weeks of ship's fare Lucky found himself smiling in anticipation. A tray was placed before him, another before Devoure.

Lucky said to the robot, "My friend will have the same."

The robot, after the briefest glance at Devoure, who looked away stonily, left and came back with another tray. Nothing was said during the meal. Earthman and Martian ate and drank heartily.

But after the trays were removed, the Sirian said, "I must begin by stating that you are spies. You entered Sirian territory and were warned to leave. You left but then returned, making every effort to keep your return secret. Under the rules of interstellar law we have every right to execute you on the spot, and this may be done unless your actions henceforward deserve clemency."

"Actions such as what?" asked Lucky. "Let me have an example, sir."

"With pleasure, Councilman." The Sirian's dark eyes

livened with interest. "There is the capsule of information our man discharged into the rings before his unfortunate death."

"Do you think I have it?"

The Sirian laughed. "Not a chance in all space. We never let you get near the rings at anything less than half light-speed. But come—you are a very clever Councilman. We have heard so much of you and your deeds, even on Sirius. There have even been occasions when you have been, shall we say, a trifle in our way."

Bigman broke in with a sudden, outraged squeak, "Just a trifle, like stopping your spy on Jupiter 9, like stopping your deal with the asteroid pirates, like pushing you off Ganymede, like——"

Sten Devoure said in a blaze of anger, "Will you quiet it, Councilman? I am irritated by the shrilling of what is with you."

"Then say what you have to say," said Lucky peremptorily, "without insulting my friend."

"What I want, then, is to have you help me find the capsule. Tell me, out of your great ingenuity, how you would go about it." Devoure leaned his elbows on the table and looked hungrily at Lucky, waiting.

Lucky said, "What information do you have to begin with?"

"Only what I imagine you picked up. The last sentences of our man."

"Yes, we picked that up. Not all of it, but enough to know he did not give the co-ordinates of the orbit in which he launched the capsule, and enough to know that he did launch it."

"Well?"

"Since the man evaded our own agents for a long time and nearly got away with a successful mission, I must assume he was intelligent."

"He was a Sirian."

"That," said Lucky with grave courtesy, "is not necessarily the same thing. In this case, however, we may assume that he would not have launched the capsule into the rings in such a way as to make it impossible for you to find."

"And your further reasoning, Earthman?"

"And if he placed the capsule in the rings themselves, it *would* be impossible to find."

"You think so?"

"I do. And the only alternative is that he sent it into orbit within Cassini's division."

Sten Devoure leaned his head back and laughed ringingly. He said, "It is refreshing to hear Lucky Starr, the great Councilman, expend his ingenuity on a problem. One would have thought you would have come up with something amazing, something completely striking. Instead, just this. Why, Councilman, what if I told you that we, without your help, reached this conclusion at once, and that our ships have been scouring Cassini's division almost from the first moment that the capsule was released?"

Lucky nodded. (If most of the human complement of the Titan base were in the rings, supervising the search, that would account in part for the dearth of humanity on the base itself.) He said, "Why, I would congratulate you and remind you that Cassini's division is large and does have some gravel in it. Besides which, the capsule would be in an unstable orbit because of the attraction of Mimas. Depending on its position, your capsule will be inching into the inner or outer ring, and if you don't find it soon you will have lost it."

"Your attempt to frighten me is foolish and useless. Even within the rings themselves the capsule would still be aluminum compared with ice."

"The mass detectors could not distinguish aluminum from ice."

"Not the mass detectors of *your* planet, Earthman. Have you asked yourself how we tracked you down despite your clumsy trick with Hidalgo and your riskier one with Mimas?"

Lucky said stonily, "I have wondered."

Devoure laughed again. "You were right to wonder. Obviously Earth does not have the selective mass detector."

"Top-secret?" asked Lucky politely.

"Not in principle, no. Our detecting beam makes use of soft X rays, which are scattered differently by various materials, depending on the mass of its atoms. Some get reflected back to us, and by analyzing the reflected beam we can tell a metal space ship from a rocky asteroid. When space ships pass an asteroid, which then moves on its way, registering a considerable metal mass it did not possess before, it isn't the most difficult deduction in the world to suppose that near the asteroid there is a space ship skulking and fondly imagining itself to be beyond detection. Eh, Councilman?"

"I see that."

"Do you see that, no matter how you tried to mask yourself by Saturn's rings or by Saturn itself, your metal mass gave you away each time? There is no metal at all in the rings or in the outer ten thousand miles of Saturn's surface. Even within Mimas you weren't hidden. For some hours we thought you were done with. We could detect metal under the ice of Mimas, and that might have been the remains of your splintered ship. But then the metal started moving and we knew you were still with us. We guessed your fusion trick and had only to wait."

Lucky nodded. "So far the game is yours."

"And now do you think we won't find the capsule,

even if it wanders into the rings or was placed in the rings in the first place?"

"Well, then, how is it you have not found it yet?"

For a moment Devoure's face darkened, as though he suspected sarcasm, but before Lucky's appearance of polite curiosity he could only say with half a snarl, "We will. It is only a matter of time. And since you can't help us further in this, there is no reason to postpone your execution."

Lucky said, "I doubt that you really mean what you have just said. We would be very dangerous to you dead."

"If your danger alive is any measure, I can't believe you to be serious."

"We are members of Earth's Council of Science. If we are killed, the Council will not forget it or forgive. Nor would retaliation be directed so much against Sirius as against you, individually. Remember that."

Devoure said, "I think I know more about this than you think. That creature with you is not a member of your Council."

"Not officially, perhaps, but——"

"And you, yourself—if you will allow me to finish— are rather more than a mere member. You are the adopted son of Hector Conway, the Chief Councilman, and you are the pride of the Council. So perhaps you are right." Devoure's mustached lips stretched into a humorless smile. "Perhaps there are conditions, come to think of it, that would make it convenient for you to remain alive."

"What conditions?"

"In recent weeks Earth has called an interstellar conference of nations to consider what they choose to call our invasion of their territory. Perhaps you don't know that."

"I suggested such a conference when I was first made aware of the existence of this base."

"Good. Sirius has agreed to this conference, and the

meeting will take place shortly on your asteroid, Vesta. Earth, it seems"—Devoure smiled more broadly—"is in a hurry. And we will humor them, since we have no fears as to the outcome. The outer worlds, generally, have no love for Earth and ought to have none. Our own case is iron-bound. Still, we could make it so much more dramatic if we could show the exact extent of Earth's hypocrisy. They call a conference; they say they wish to solve the matter by peaceful means; but at the same time they send a war vessel to Titan with instructions to destroy our base."

"Those were not my instructions. I have acted without instructions and with no intention of committing any war-like act."

"Nevertheless, if you testify to what I have said, it will make a great impression."

"I cannot testify to what is not the truth."

Devoure disregarded that. He said harshly, "Let them see that you are neither drugged nor probed. Testify of your own free will as we will direct you. Let the conference know that the prize member of the Council of Science, Conway's own boy, was engaged in an illegal adventure of force at the same time that Earth was sanctimoniously calling a conference and proclaiming its devotion to peace. It would settle matters once and for all."

Lucky drew a deep breath and stared at the other's coldly smiling face. He said, "Is that it? False testimony in exchange for life?"

"All right. Put it that way. Make your choice."

"There is none. I would not bear false witness in a case like this."

Devoure's eyes narrowed to slits. "I think you will. You have been studied closely by our agents, Councilman, and we know your weak point. You may prefer your

own death to co-operation with us, but you have the
Earthman's sentiment for the weak, the deformed, the
monstrous. You would do it to prevent"—and the Sirian's
soft and pudgy hand extended suddenly, one finger pointing rigidly at Bigman—"*its* death."

10

Servicemen and Robots

"**S**teady, Bigman," murmured Lucky.

The little Martian hunched low in his seat, his eyes watching Devoure hotly.

Lucky said, "Let's not be childish in our attempts to frighten. Execution is not easy on a world of robots. The robots can't kill us, and I'm not sure that you or your colleagues would be willing to kill a man in cold blood."

"Of course not, if you mean by killing the chopping off of a head or the blasting in of a chest. But then there's nothing frightening in a quick death. Suppose, though, that our robots prepared a stripped-down ship. Your—uh —companion could be chained to a bulkhead on that ship by robots who will, of course, be careful not to hurt him. The ship can be fitted with an automatic pilot that will take it on an orbit away from your Sun and out of the Ecliptic. There isn't a chance in a quadrillion that it would ever be spotted by anyone from Earth. It will travel on forever."

Bigman broke in, "Lucky, it doesn't matter what they do to me. Don't you agree to anything."

Devoure said, unheeding, "Your companion will have

plenty of air and there'll be a tube of water within reach if it's thirsty. Of course it will be alone and there will be no food. Starvation is a slow death, and starvation in the ultimate loneliness of space is a horrible thing to contemplate."

Lucky said, "That would be a dastardly and dishonorable way of treating a prisoner of war."

"There is no war. You are merely spies. And in any case, there is no need for it to happen, eh, Councilman? You need only sign the necessary confession that you intended to attack us and agree to confirm this in person at the conference. I am sure you will heed the beggings of the thing you have befriended."

"*Beggings!*" Bigman leaped, crimson-faced, to his feet.

Devoure raised his voice abruptly. "That thing is to be taken into custody. Proceed."

Two robots materialized silently at either side, and each seized an arm. For a moment Bigman writhed, and his body lifted off the floor with the intensity of his effort, but his arms were held motionless.

One of the robots said, "The master will please not resist, as otherwise the master may harm himself despite all we can do."

Devoure said, "You'll have twenty-four hours to make up your mind. Plenty of time, eh, Councilman?" He looked at the illuminated figures on the strip of decorative metal that encircled his left wrist. "And meanwhile, we will prepare our stripped ship. If we don't have to use it, as I expect we won't, why, what's labor to robots, eh, Councilman? Sit where you are; there is no use in trying to help your companion. He will not be hurt for the while."

Bigman was carried out of the room bodily while Lucky, half risen out of his seat, watched helplessly.

A light flashed on a small box on the conference table.

Devoure leaned over to touch it, and a luminous tube sprang into being just above the box. The image of a head appeared. A voice said, "Yonge and I have the report that you have the Councilman, Devoure. Why were we told only after his landing?"

"What difference does that make, Zayon? You know now. Are you coming in?"

"We certainly are. We wish to meet the Councilman."

"Come then to my office."

Fifteen minutes later, two Sirians arrived. Both were as tall as Devoure; both were olive-skinned (the greater ultra-violet radiation of Sirius produced a dark skin, Lucky realized), but they were older. The cut hair of one was grizzled to steely gray. He was thin-lipped and spoke with rapid precision. He was introduced as Harrig Zayon, and his uniform made it clear he was a member of the Sirian Space Service.

The other was going somewhat bald. There was a long scar on his forearm and he had the keen look of one who had grown old in space. He was Barrett Yonge, also of the Space Service.

Lucky said, "Your Space Service is, I think, somewhat the equivalent of our Council of Science."

"Yes, it is," said Zayon gravely. "In that sense we are colleagues, though on opposite sides of the fence."

"Serviceman Zayon, then. Serviceman Yonge. Is Mr. Devoure——"

Devoure broke in, "I am not a member of the Space Service. It is not necessary that I be. Sirius can be served outside the Service too."

"Particularly," said Yonge, one hand resting on the scarred forearm as though to hide the mark, "if one is nephew of the director of the Central Body."

Devoure rose. "Was that meant as sarcasm, Service-man?"

"Not at all. It was meant literally. The relationship makes it possible for you to do Sirius more service than otherwise."

But there was a dry quality to his statement, and Lucky was not unaware of the flash of hostility between the two aging Servicemen and the young and undoubt-edly influential relative of Sirius's overlord.

Zayon tried to deflect the direction things had taken by turning to Lucky and saying mildly, "Has our proposi-tion been offered you?"

"You mean the suggestion that I lie at the interstellar conference?"

Zayon looked annoyed and a bit puzzled. He said, "I mean to join us, to become a Sirian."

"I don't think we had quite reached that point, Ser-viceman."

"Well, then consider this. Our Service knows you well and we respect your abilities and accomplishments. They are wasted on an Earth that must lose someday as a mat-ter of biologic fact."

"Biologic fact?" Lucky frowned. "The Sirians, Service-man Zayon, are descended from Earthmen."

"So they are, but not from all Earthmen; only from some, from the best, from those with the initiative and strength to reach the stars as colonists. We have kept our descent pure; we have not allowed the weaklings in, or those with poor genes. We have weeded out the unfit from among ourselves so that we are now a pure race of the strong, the fit, and the healthy, while Earth remains a conglomerate of the diseased and deformed."

Devoure broke in, "We had an example here a while ago, the Councilman's companion. It infuriated and nau-seated me merely to be in the same room with him; a monkey, a five-foot travesty of a human being, a lump of deformity——"

Lucky said slowly, "He is a better man than you, Sirian."

Devoure rose, fist drawn back, trembling. Zayon moved toward him rapidly, laying a hand on his shoulder. "Devoure, sit down, please, and let me go on. This is not the time for extraneous quarrels." Devoure shook the other's hand off roughly but sat down all the same.

Serviceman Zayon went on earnestly, "To the outer worlds, Councilman Starr, Earth is a terrible menace, a bomb of sub-humanity, ready to explode and contaminate the clean Galaxy. We don't want that to happen; we can't allow it to happen. It's what we're fighting for: a clean human race, composed of the fit."

Lucky said, "Composed of those *you* consider fit. But fitness comes in all shapes and forms. The great men of Earth have come from the tall and the short, from all manner of head shapes, skin colors, and languages. Variety is our salvation and the salvation of all mankind."

"You are simply parroting something you have been taught. Councilman, can't you see you are really one of us? You are tall, strong, built like a Sirian; you have the courage and daring of a Sirian. Why combine with the scum of Earth against men like yourself, just because of the accident of your birth on Earth?"

Lucky said, "The upshot of all this, Serviceman, is that you wish me to come to the interstellar conference on Vesta and deliver statements designed to help Sirius."

"To help Sirius, yes, but true statements. You have spied on us. Your ship was certainly armed."

"But you waste your time. Mr. Devoure has already discussed the matter with me."

"And you have agreed to be the Sirian you really are?" Zayon's face lit up at the possibility.

Lucky cast a side glance at Devoure, who was inspecting the knuckles of his hands with an indifferent air.

Lucky said, "Why, Mr. Devoure advanced the proposition in another fashion. Perhaps he did not inform you of my arrival sooner than he did in order to have time to discuss the matter with me alone and to use his own methods. Briefly, he simply said that I was to attend the conference on Sirian terms or else my friend Bigman was to be sent out in a stripped space ship to die of starvation."

Slowly the two Sirian Servicemen turned to look at Devoure, who merely continued the contemplation of his knuckles.

Yonge said slowly, speaking directly to Devoure, "Sir, it is not in the Service tradition——"

Devoure exploded in sudden flaming anger. "I am not a Serviceman and I don't give a half-credit piece for your tradition. I'm in charge of this base, and its security is my responsibility. You two have been appointed to accompany me as delegates to the conference on Vesta so that the Service will be represented, but I am to be chief delegate, and the success of the conference is also my responsibility. If this Earthman does not like the type of death reserved for his monkey friend, he need only agree to our terms, and he will agree to them a lot faster with that as stimulus than your offer of making a Sirian out of him.

"And listen further." Devoure rose from his seat, paced angrily to the far end of the room, and then turned to glare at the frozen-faced Servicemen who listened with disciplined self-control. "I'm tired of your interference. The Service has had enough time to make headway against Earth and has a miserable record in that regard. Let this Earthman hear me say this. He should know it better than anyone. The Service has a *miserable* record, and it is I who have trapped this Starr and not the Ser-

vice. What you gentlemen need is a little more guts, and
that I intend to supply——"

It was at this moment that a robot threw open the
door and said, "Masters, I must be excused for entering
without orders from you, but I have been instructed to
tell you this concerning the small master who has been
taken into custody——"

"Bigman!" cried Lucky, jumping to his feet. "What
has happened to him?"

After Bigman had been carried out of the room by the two
robots, he had thought furiously. Not, really, of possible
ways of escaping. He was not so unrealistic as to think he
could make his way through a horde of robots and, single-
handed, get away from a base as well organized as this
one, even if he had *The Shooting Starr* at his disposal,
which he had not.

It was more than that.

Lucky was being tempted to dishonor and betrayal,
and Bigman's life was the bait.

Either way, Lucky must not be subjected to this. He
must not have to save Bigman's life at the cost of becoming a traitor. Nor must he have to save his honor by sacrificing Bigman and carry the guilt with him for the rest of
his life.

There was only one way to prevent both alternatives.
Bigman faced that coldly. If he were to die in some way
with which Lucky had nothing to do, the big Earthman
could bear no blame, even in his own mind. And there
would no longer be a live Bigman with which to bargain.

Bigman was forced into a small diagravitic car and
taken for another two-minute drive.

But those two minutes were enough to crystallize matters firmly in his mind. His years with Lucky had been
happy, exciting ones. He had lived a full lifetime in them

and had faced death without fear. He could face death now, also without fear.

And a quick death would not be so quick as to prevent him from evening a tiny bit of the score with Devoure. No man in his lifetime had insulted him so without retaliation. He could not die and leave the score unevened. The thought of the arrogant Sirian so filled Bigman with anger that for a moment he could not have told whether it was friendship for Lucky or hatred of Devoure that was driving him.

The robots lifted him out of the diagravitic car, and one passed its huge metal paws gently and expertly down the sides of the Martian's body in a routine search for weapons.

Bigman felt a moment of panic and strove uselessly to knock aside the robot's arm. "I was searched on the ship before they let me get off," he howled, but the robot completed the search without paying attention.

The two seized him again, made ready to take him into a building. The time, then, was now. Once he was in an actual cell, with force planes cutting him off, his task would be much harder.

Bigman kicked his feet desperately forward and turned a somersault between the robots. He was kept from turning completely around only by the robots' hold of his arms.

One said, "It distresses me, master, that you have placed yourself in what must be a painful position. If you will hold yourself motionless so that you will not interfere with our assigned task, we will hold you as lightly as we can."

But Bigman kicked again and then shrieked piercingly, "*My arm!*"

The robots knelt at once and deposited Bigman gently on his back. "Are you in pain, master?"

"You stupid cobbers, you've broken my arm. Don't touch it! Get some human being who knows how to take care of a broken arm, or get some robot who can," he ended in a moan, his face twisting in agony.

The robots moved slowly backward, eyes upon him. They had no feelings, could have none. But inside them were the positronic brain paths whose orientation was controlled by the potentials and counter-potentials set up by the Three Laws of Robotics. In the course of their fulfillment of one law, the Second—that they obey an order, in this case an order to lead a human being to a specific spot—they had broken a higher law, the First: that they never bring harm to a human being. The result in their brains must have been a kind of positronic chaos.

Bigman cried out sharply, "Get help—— Sands of Mars—get——"

It was an order, backed by the power of the First Law. A human being was hurt. The robots turned, started away —and Bigman's right arm flashed down to the top of his hip boot and snaked inside. He rose nimbly, with a needle-gun warming the palm of his hand.

At the sound of that, one of the robots turned back, voice blurred and thickened as a sign of the weakening hold of the confused positronic brain. "Ith the mathter not in pain, then?" The second robot turned back too.

"Take me back to your Sirian masters," Bigman said tightly.

It was another order, but the First Law was no longer reinforcing it. A human being had not, after all, been harmed. There was no shock or surprise at this revelation. The nearer robot simply said, in a voice that had sharpened once more, "As your arm is not, indeed, damaged, it becomes necessary for us to carry out our original order. Please come with us."

Bigman wasted no time. His needle-gun flashed noiselessly, and the robot's head was a gout of melting metal. What was left of it collapsed.

The second robot said, "It will not help to destroy our functioning," and walked toward him.

Self-protection was the Third Law only. A robot could not refuse to carry out an order (Second Law) on the basis of the Third alone. So it was bound to walk into a pointing needle gun. And other robots were coming from all directions, summoned, no doubt, by some radioed call at the moment when Bigman had first pretended the broken arm.

They would all walk into a needle-gun, but there would be enough to survive his pumping shots. Those who would survive would then overpower him and carry him into imprisonment. He would be deprived of the quick death he needed, and Lucky would still be faced with the unbearable alternative.

There was only one way out. Bigman put the needle-gun to his temple.

⑪

Bigman Against All

Bigman cried out piercingly, "Not one step nearer. Any closer and I'll have to shoot. You'll kill me."

He nerved himself for the possible shot. If nothing else could be done, it would have to be that.

But the robots stopped. Not one moved. Bigman's eyes moved slowly to right and left. One robot was on the ground, headless, a useless lump of metal. One was standing, arms half reaching out toward him. One was a hundred feet away, caught in mid-stride.

Slowly Bigman turned. A robot was coming out of a building. It was caught on the threshold. Still others were farther off. It was as though a freezing blight had struck them all, struck them with instant paralysis.

He was not really surprised. It was the First Law. All else had to take second place: orders, their own existence, everything. They could not move if motion meant harm to a human being.

Bigman said, "Every robot but that one"—he pointed to the one facing him, the nearest, the companion of the one he had destroyed—"leave now. Back to your immediately previous task and forget me and what has just happened. Failure to obey at once will mean my death."

So all but one had to leave. This was dealing with them harshly, and Bigman, grim-faced, wondered if the potential being set up to drive the positrons might not be intense enough to harm the platinum-iridium sponge that made up the delicate robotic brains.

He had the Earthman's distrust of robots and he rather hoped that was so.

All the robots but one were gone now. The muzzle of the needle-gun was still against Bigman's temple.

He said to the remaining robot, "Take me back to your master." (He wanted to use a harsher term but what would a robot understand of the insult implied. With difficulty he forced it down.)

"Now," he said, "and quickly. Do not allow any master or robot to interfere with us on our way. I have this needle-gun and shall use it on any master near us, or on myself if I have to."

The robot said hoarsely (the first signs of positronic malfunction, Lucky had once told Bigman, showed up in the timbre of the voice), "I will follow orders. The master may be certain that I shall do nothing that will harm him or another master."

It turned and led the way into the diagravitic car. Bigman followed. He was half prepared for trickery on the way back, but there was none. A robot was a machine following inescapable rules of action. He had to remember that. Only human beings could lie and cheat.

When they stopped at Devoure's office, Bigman said, "I'll wait in the car. I won't leave. You go in and tell the master Devoure that the master Bigman is free and waiting for him." Bigman struggled with temptation and this time succumbed. He was too close to Devoure to resist successfully. He said, "Tell him to drag his fat piled-up carcass out here. Tell him he can take me on with needle-gun or fists, I don't care which. Tell him that if he's too saffron-spined to do either, I'll come in and kick him from here to Mars."

Sten Devoure stared at the robot in disbelief, his dark face scowling and his angry eyes peering out from under hunched eyebrows.

"Do you mean he's out there free? And armed?"

He looked at the two Servicemen, who stared back with blank astonishment. (Lucky muttered "Great Galaxy!" under his breath. The irrepressible Bigman would ruin everything—and lose his life as well.)

Serviceman Zayon rose heavily to his feet. "Well, Devoure, you don't expect the robot to be lying do you?" He stepped across to the wall phone and punched the emergency combination. "If we have an Earthman on base, armed and determined, we had better take action."

"But how does he come to be armed?" Devoure had still not wiped away the traces of confusion, but now he made for the door. Lucky followed him, and the Sirian whirled at once. "Get back, Starr."

He turned to the robot. "Stay with this Earthman. He is not to leave this building under any circumstances."

And now he seemed to have come to a decision. He rushed from the room pulling out a heavy blaster as he did so. Zayon and Yonge hesitated, cast a quick look at Lucky, then at the robot, made their own decision, and followed Devoure.

The area before Devoure's offices was wide and bathed in the artificial light that reproduced Sirius's faintly bluish tinge. Bigman stood alone in the center, and at a hundred yards' distance were five robots. Others were approaching from another direction.

"Come and get that," roared Devoure, gesturing to the nearer robots and pointing to Bigman.

"They won't come any closer," roared back Bigman. "If they make a move toward me I shall burn your heart out of your chest, and they know I'll do it. At least they can't take the chance I won't." He stood there easily, mockingly.

Devoure flushed and lifted his blaster.

Bigman said, "Now don't hurt yourself with that blaster. You're holding it a little close to your body."

His right elbow was resting in the palm of his left hand. His right fist squeezed gently as he spoke, and from the muzzle of the needle-gun just protruding from between second and third fingers, a jet of deuterium pulsed out under the guidance of a momentarily established magnetic field. It took skill of the highest order to adjust the squeeze and thumb position correctly, but Bigman had that. No man in the system had more.

The muzzle tip of Devoure's blaster was a tiny white spark, and Devoure yelled his surprise and dropped it.

Bigman said, "I don't know who you other two cobbers are, but if either of you makes a move that looks like a blaster is at the end of it, you'll never finish that move."

All froze. Yonge finally said carefully, "How do you come to be armed?"

"A robot," said Bigman, "is no smarter than the cobber who runs him. The robots who searched me on the ship and out here were instructed by someone who didn't know a Martian uses his boots for more than something to put his legs into."

"And how did you break away from the robots?"

Bigman said coolly, "I had to destroy one."

"*You destroyed a robot?*" A kind of electric horror stunned the three Sirians.

Bigman felt increasing tension. He did not concern himself with the robots standing about, but at any moment another human Sirian might appear and shoot him in the back from a safe distance.

The spot between his shoulders prickled as he waited for the shot. Well, it would be a flash. He would never feel it. And after that they would have lost their hold on Lucky and, dead or not, Bigman would be the winner.

Only, he wanted a chance at Devoure first, at that soft Sirian cobber who had sat across the table from him and said things no man in the universe could say and be left standing.

Bigman said, "I could shoot you all. Shall we make an arrangement?"

"You won't shoot us," said Serviceman Yonge quietly. "A shooting would simply mean that an Earthman has opened hostilities on a Sirian planet. It could mean war."

"Besides," roared Devoure, "if you make any attack it will release the robots. They'll defend three humans rather than one. Throw down that needle-gun and put yourself back in custody."

"All right, send the robots away, and I'll surrender to you."

"The robots will handle you," said Devoure. He made as though to turn nonchalantly toward the other Sirians. "My skin crawls at having to talk to this deformed humanoid."

Bigman's needle-gun flashed at once, the small fire ball exploding a foot before Devoure's eyes. "Say something like that again and I'll blind you for good. If the robots make a move, all three of you get it before they reach us. It may mean war, but you three won't be here to see if it does. Order the robots away and I'll surrender to Devoure, if he can take me. I'll toss my needle-gun to one of you other two and surrender."

Zayon said stiffly, "That sounds reasonable, Devoure."

Devoure was still rubbing his eyes. "Take his gun then. Go over there and take it."

"Wait," said Bigman, "don't move yet. I want your word of honor that I won't be shot down or given to the robots. Devoure has to take me."

"*My* word of honor to *you?*" exploded Devoure.

"To me. But not from you. The word of one of the other two. They're wearing the uniform of the Sirian Service and I'll take their word. If I give them the needle-gun, will they stand by and let you, Devoure, come and take me with your bare hands?"

"You have my word," said Zayon.

"And mine," added Yonge.

Devoure said, "What is this? I have no intention of touching the creature."

"Afraid?" asked Bigman softly. "Am I too big for you, Devoure? You've called me names. Do you want to put your muscles where your cowardly mouth is? Here's my needle-gun, Servicemen."

He tossed the gun suddenly in Zayon's direction. Zayon reached out a hand and caught it neatly.

Bigman waited. Now for death?

But Zayon put the needle-gun in his pocket.

Devoure called out, "*Robots!*" and Zayon called out with equal vigor, "*Leave us, robots!*"

Zayon said to Devoure, "He has our word. You'll have to take him into custody yourself."

"Or do I come after you?" Bigman called out in shrill mockery.

Devoure snarled wordlessly and strode hastily toward Bigman. The small Martian waited, slightly crouched, then took a small side step to avoid the arm reaching out for him and uncoiled like a tightly wound spring.

His fist struck the other's face with the dull impact of a mallet hitting a head of cabbage, and Devoure staggered back, stumbling into a sitting position. He stared at Bigman in stunned amazement. His right cheek had reddened and a trickle of blood made its slow way out of the corner of his mouth. He put his finger to it, drew it away, and looked at the blood with an almost comical disbelief.

Yonge said, "The Earthman is taller than he looks."

Bigman said, "I'm not an Earthman, I'm a Martian. . . . Stand up, Devoure. Or are you too soft? Can't you do anything without robots to help you? Do they wipe your mouth when you're done eating?"

Devoure yelled hoarsely and jumped to his feet but did not rush Bigman. He circled him instead, breathing hard, watching out of inflamed eyes.

Bigman wheeled also, watching that panting body, soft with good living and robot help, watching the unskillful arms and clumsy legs. The Sirian, Bigman was sure, had never fought fist to fist before.

Bigman stepped in again, caught the other's arm with a sure and sudden motion, and twisted. With a howl Devoure flipped and fell prone.

Bigman stepped back. "What's the matter? I'm not a he; I'm just an it. What's your trouble?"

Devoure looked up at the two Servicemen with something deadly in his eyes. He rose to his knees and groaned as he put a hand to his side where it had hit the ground.

The two Sirians did not make any move to help him. They watched stolidly as Bigman cut him down again and then again.

Finally Zayon stepped forward. "Martian, you will hurt him seriously if you continue. Our agreement was to let Devoure take you with his bare hands, and actually I think you have what you really wanted when you made the agreement. That's all. Surrender quietly to me now or I'll have to use the needle-gun."

But Devoure, panting noisily, gasped, "Get away. Get away, Zayon. It's too late for that. Step back, I say."

He called out in a high-pitched yell, *"Robots! Come here!"*

Zayon said, "He'll surrender to me."

"No surrender," said Devoure, his swollen face twitching with physical pain and intense fury. "No surrender. Too late for that. . . . You, robot, the closest one—I don't care what your serial number is—you. Take it—take that thing." His voice rose to a scream as he pointed to Bigman. *"Destroy it! Break it! Break each piece of it!"*

Yonge shouted, "Devoure! Are you mad? A robot can't do a thing like that."

The robot remained standing. It did not move.

Devoure said, "You can't harm a human being, robot. I'm not asking you to do so. But this is not a human being."

The robot turned to look at Bigman.

Bigman shouted, "It won't believe that. You may consider me non-human, but a robot knows better."

Devoure said, "Look at it, robot. It talks and has a human shape, but so do you and you're no human. I can prove it's not human. Did you ever see a full-grown human so small? That proves it's not human. It's an animal and it is—it is harming me. You must destroy it."

"Run to Mamma Robot," yelled Bigman mockingly.

But the robot took the first step toward Bigman.

Yonge stepped forward and moved between the robot and Bigman. "I can't allow this, Devoure. A robot must not do such a thing, even if for no other reason than that the stress of potential involved will ruin it."

But Devoure said in a hoarse whisper, "I'm your superior. If you make one move to stop me, I'll have you out of the Service by tomorrow."

The habit of obedience was strong. Yonge fell back,

but there was a look of intense distress and horror on his face.

The robot moved more quickly, and now Bigman fell back a cautious step. "I'm a human being," he said.

"It is not human," cried Devoure madly. "It is not human. Break every piece of it. Slowly."

A chill fell over Bigman and left his mouth dry. He had not counted on this. A quick death, yes, but this . . .

There was no room to retreat, and he was without the escape his needle-gun afforded. There were other robots behind, and all were hearing the word that he was not human.

12

Surrender

There was a smile on Devoure's puffed and bruised face. It must have hurt him, for one lip was split and he dabbed absently at it with his handkerchief, but his eyes were fixed on the robot moving toward Bigman and he seemed aware of nothing else.

The small Martian had only another six feet in which to retreat, and Devoure made no effort to hasten the approaching robot or to move up those in the rear.

Yonge said, "Devoure, for Sirius's sake, man, there is no need of this."

"No comments, Yonge," said Devoure tensely. "That humanoid has destroyed a robot and probably damaged others. We'll need checkups on every robot who has been affected by the sight of his use of violence. He deserves death."

Zayon put out a restraining hand toward Yonge, but the latter slapped it impatiently away. Yonge said, "Death? All right. Then ship him back to Sirius and have him tried and executed according to the processes of law. Or set up a trial here at the base and have him decently blasted. But this is no execution. Simply because he beat——"

Devoure cried in sudden fury, "That's enough! You have interfered once too often. You're under arrest. Zayon, take his blaster and toss it over to me."

He turned briefly, loath to take his eyes off Bigman for even a moment. "Do it, Zayon, or by all the devils of space I'll break you too."

With a bitter, wordless frown Zayon held out his hand to Yonge. Yonge hesitated, and his fingers curled about the butt of his blaster, half drawing it in anger.

Zayon whispered urgently, "No, Yonge. Don't give him the excuse. He'll lift arrest when his madness is over. He'll have to."

Devoure called out, "I want that blaster."

Yonge ripped it out of its holster with a hand that trembled and thrust it butt-first at Zayon. The latter tossed it at Devoure's feet and Devoure picked it up.

Bigman, who had been maintaining an agonized silence as he watched futilely for a chance to dodge, to break away, now cried out, "Don't touch me, I'm a master," as the robot's monstrous hand closed over his wrist.

For a moment the robot hesitated, and then his grip tightened. The other hand reached for Bigman's elbow. Devoure laughed, a high-pitched titter.

Yonge turned on his heel and said in a suffocated tone, "At least I don't have to watch this cowardly crime." And as a result he did not observe what happened next.

With an effort Lucky remained calm when the three Sirians left. From a purely physical standpoint, he could not possibly beat down the robot with his bare hands. Somewhere in the building there might conceivably be a weapon he could use to destroy the robot; he could then get out and might even shoot down the three Sirians.

But he would not be able to leave Titan, nor win out against the entire base.

Worse still, if he were killed—and in the end he would be—his deeper purposes would be lost, and he could not risk those.

He said to the robot, "What happened to the master Bigman? State the essentials quickly."

The robot did, and Lucky listened with a tense and painful attention. He heard the robot's occasional slurring and lisping of words, the thickening of speech as it described Bigman's doubled forcing of the robots by pretending or threatening harm to a human.

Lucky groaned within. A robot dead. The force of Sirian law would be extended to the full against Bigman. Lucky knew enough about the Sirians' culture and their regard for their robots to know that there could be no extenuating circumstances against roboticide.

How to save the impulsive Bigman now?

Lucky remembered his own halfhearted attempt to keep Bigman on Mimas. He had not foreseen this exactly, but he had feared Bigman's temper in the delicate circumstances now surrounding them. He should have insisted on Bigman's staying behind, but what was the use? Even as he thought this, he realized that he needed Bigman's company.

But then he had to save him. Somehow he had to save him.

He walked rapidly toward the opening of the building, and the robot stepped stolidly into his path. "Accor'ing to my instructions, the master 's not to leave building under any thircumstances."

"I am not leaving the building," said Lucky sharply. "I am merely going to the door. You have no instructions to prevent that."

For a moment the robot was silent, then it said, "Accor'ing to my instructions, the master's not to leave building under any circumthantheth."

Desperately Lucky tried to push it aside, was seized, held motionless, then pushed back.

Lucky bit his lip impatiently. A whole robot, he thought, would have interpreted its instructions broadly. This robot, however, had been damaged. It was reduced to the bare essence of robotic understanding.

But he had to see Bigman. He whirled toward the conference table. In its center there had been a trimensional image reproducer. Devoure had used it when the two Servicemen had called him.

"You. Robot!" called Lucky.

The robot lumbered to the table.

Lucky said, "How does the image reproducer work?"

The robot was slow. Its speech was continuing to thicken. It said, "The controlth are 'n thith retheth."

"Which recess?"

The robot showed him, moving a panel aside clumsily.

"All right," said Lucky. "Can I focus on the area just outside this building? Show me. Do it."

He stepped aside. The robot worked, fumbling at the knobs. "It ith done, mathter."

"Let me see, then." The area outside was in small image above the table, the figures of men smaller still. The robot had moved away and stared dully elsewhere.

Lucky did not call him back. There was no sound, but as he groped for what must be the sound control, his attention was caught by the fight that was going on. Devoure was fighting Bigman. *Fighting Bigman!*

How had the small imp managed to persuade the two Servicemen to stand to one side and allow this to happen? For of course Bigman was cutting his opponent to ribbons. Lucky could extract no joy from it.

This could end only in Bigman's death, and Lucky knew that Bigman realized that and didn't care. The Martian would court sure death, take any chance, to avenge an insult. . . . Ah, one of the Servicemen was stopping it now.

With that, Lucky found the sound control. Words shot out of the image reproducer: Devoure's frenzied call for robots and his shouted order that they break Bigman.

For a split second Lucky was not sure he had heard correctly, and then he beat both fists desperately against the table and whirled about in near despair.

He had to get out, but how?

There he was, alone with a robot containing only one instruction buzzing in what was left of its positronic brain paths: to keep Lucky immobilized at all costs.

Great Galaxy, was there nothing that would take precedence over that order? He lacked even a weapon with which to threaten suicide or kill the robot.

His eyes fell on the wall phone. He had last seen Zayon at it, something about emergency when the news about Bigman broke.

Lucky said, "Robot. Quickly. What has been done here?"

The robot approached, looked at the glowing combination of knobs in faint red, and said with tantalizing slowness, "A mathter hath indicated all robotth to prepare battle thathionth."

"How would I indicate that all robots are actually to proceed to battle stations at once? Superseding all current orders?"

The robot stared at him, and Lucky, in almost a frenzy, seized the robot's hand and pumped it. "Tell me. Tell me."

Could the thing understand him? Or did its ruined brain paths still have impressed upon them some remnant of instructions that prevented it from giving this information?

"Tell me! Or do it, do it."

The robot, not speaking, reached a finger toward the apparatus in an uneven movement and slowly depressed two buttons. Then its finger lifted an inch and stopped.

"Is that all? Are you done?" demanded Lucky desperately.

But the robot merely turned and with an uneven tread (one foot dragging perceptibly) walked to the door and marched out.

In space-devouring strides Lucky dashed after him, out of the building and across the hundred yards separating him from Bigman and the three Sirians.

Yonge, having turned in horror from what he expected would be the bloodcurdling destruction of a human being, did not hear the scream of agony he expected. Instead there was a startled grunt from Zayon and a wild cry from Devoure.

He turned back. The robot that had been holding Bigman was holding him no more. He was moving away in a heavy run. All the robots in sight were hastening away.

And the Earthman, Lucky Starr, was now at Bigman's side, somehow.

Lucky was bending over Bigman, and the small Martian, rubbing his left arm vigorously, was shaking his head. Yonge heard him say, "One minute later, Lucky; just one minute later and——"

Devoure was shouting hoarsely and uselessly at the robots, and then a loud-speaker arrangement suddenly filled the air with clamor:

COMMANDER   DEVOURE,   INSTRUCTIONS

PLEASE. OUR INSTRUMENTS INDICATE NO SIGN
OF ENEMY. EXPLAIN BATTLE STATIONS ORDER.
COMMANDER DEVOURE . . .

"Battle stations," muttered Devoure, stunned. "No
wonder the robots——" His eyes fell on Lucky. "*You* did
that."

Lucky nodded. "Yes, sir."

Devoure's puffy lips set and he said hoarsely, "The
clever, resourceful Councilman! You've saved your monkey for the moment." His blaster pointed firmly at
Lucky's midriff. "Get into my offices. Every one of you.
You too, Zayon. All of you."

The image receiver on his desk was buzzing madly.
Obviously it was the failure to get Devoure at his office
that had forced his distracted underlings to the loud-
speakers.

Devoure flipped on the sound but left the image
blind. He barked, "Cancel battle stations order. It was an
error."

The man at the other end spluttered something, and
Devoure said sharply, "There's nothing wrong with the
image. Get on the ball. Everyone back on routine." But
almost against his will his hand hovered between his face
and the place where the image ought to be, as though he
feared that somehow the other might penetrate to vision
anyhow and see to what his face had been reduced—and
wonder about it.

Yonge's nostrils flared as he watched, and he slowly
rubbed his scarred forearm.

Devoure sat down. "The rest of you stand," he said,
and stared sullenly from face to face. "This Martian will
die, maybe not by robot or in a stripped space ship. I'll
think of something; and if you think you saved him,
Earthman, be sure I'll think of something more amusing
still. I have an excellent imagination."

Lucky said, "I demand that he be treated as a prisoner of war."

Devoure said, "There is no war. He is a spy. He deserves death. He is a roboticide. He deserves death twice." His voice trembled suddenly. "He lifted his hands against me. He deserves death a dozen times."

"I'll buy my friend," said Lucky in a whisper.

"He is not for sale."

"I can pay a high price."

"How?" Devoure grinned ferociously. "By bearing witness at the conference as you have been requested? It is too late for that. It is not enough."

"I couldn't do that in any case," said Lucky. "I will not lie against Earth, but there is a truth I can tell; a truth you do not know."

Bigman said sharply, "Don't bargain with him, Lucky."

"The monkey is right," Devoure said. "Don't bargain. Nothing you can tell me will buy him. I wouldn't sell him for all Earth in my hand."

Yonge interrupted sharply, "I would for much less. Listen to the Councilman. Their lives may be worth the information they have."

Devoure said, "Don't provoke me. You are under arrest."

But Yonge lifted a chair and let it drop with a crash. "I defy you to arrest me. I'm a Serviceman. You can't execute me out of hand. You dare not, no matter how I provoke you. You must reserve me for trial. And at any trial I have things to say."

"Such as?" demanded Devoure with contempt.

All the dislike of the aging Serviceman for the young aristocrat was suddenly out in the open. "Such as what happened today: how a five-foot Terrestrial tore you apart until you howled and Zayon had to step in to save your life. Zayon will bear witness. Every man jack at the base will remember that you dared not show your face for days after this date—or will you have the nerve to show that torn face before it heals?"

"Be quiet!"

"I can be quiet. I need say nothing—if you will stop subordinating the good of Sirius to your private hatreds. Listen to what the Councilman has to say." He turned to Lucky. "I guarantee you a fair deal."

Bigman piped up, "What fair deal? You and Zayon will wake up one morning and find yourselves dead by accident and Devoure will be so sorry and send you lots of flowers, only after that there'll be no one to say how he needs robots to hide behind when a Martian is after his filthy skin. Then we'll go anyway he likes. So why bargain?"

"There'll be nothing like that," said Yonge stiffly, "because I will give the complete story to one of the robots within an hour of my leaving here. He won't know which one, and he won't find out. If either Zayon or myself dies of anything but natural causes, the story will be relayed to the public sub-etherics in full; otherwise, not. I rather think Devoure will be anxious to see that nothing happens to Zayon or myself."

Zayon shook his head. "I don't like this, Yonge."

"You've got to like it, Zayon. You witnessed his beating. Do you think he wouldn't do his worst for you if you didn't take precautions? Come, I'm weary of sacrificing the honor of the Service to the nephew of the director."

Zayon said unhappily, "Well, what is your information, Councilman Starr?"

Lucky said in a low voice, "It's more than information.

It's surrender. There is another Councilman on what you call Sirian territory. Agree to treat my friend as a prisoner of war and safeguard his life by forgetting the roboticide incident and I'll take you to this other Councilman."

13

Prelude to Vesta

Bigman, who, to the end, had been certain that Lucky had some stratagem on hand, was appalled. He called out in a heartbroken wail, "No, Lucky! No! I don't want to be pulled out that way."

Devoure was openly astonished. "Where? No ship could have penetrated our defenses. It's a lie."

"I'll take you to the man," said Lucky wearily, "if we come to an arrangement."

"Space!" growled Yonge. "It's an arrangement."

"Wait," said Devoure angrily. "I admit this could be of value to us, but is Starr suggesting that he will openly testify to the conference on Vesta that this other Councilman invaded our territory and that Starr voluntarily revealed his hiding place?"

"It's the truth," said Lucky. "I will so testify."

"The word of honor of a Councilman?" sneered Devoure.

"I have said I will testify."

"Well, then," said Devoure, "since our Servicemen *will* have it so, you may have your lives in exchange." His eyes suddenly sparked fury. "On Mimas. Is that it, Councilman? Mimas?"

"That is correct."

"By Sirius!" Devoure rose to his feet in agitation. "We almost missed it. Nor did this occur to the Service."

Zayon said with thought, "Mimas?"

"The Service still doesn't get it," said Devoure with a malignant scowl. "Three men were on *The Shooting Starr*, obviously. Three entered Mimas; two left; one stayed behind. It was your report, Yonge, I believe, which stressed the fact that Starr always worked with his companion in a party of two."

"He always had," said Yonge.

"And was there no flexibility left in you to consider the possibility of a third? Shall we go then to Mimas?" Devoure seemed to have lost his mad passion for revenge in the stress of this new development, almost to have regained the mocking irony he had displayed when the two Terrestrials had first landed on Titan. "And you will give us the pleasure of your company, Councilman?"

"Certainly, Mr. Devoure," said Lucky.

Bigman moved away, face averted. He felt worse now, he thought, than even in that last moment of robotic advance when the metal limbs were on his arm, ready to smash.

The Shooting Starr was in space again, but not as an independent ship. It was caught in firm magnetic grapple and moved according to the impulses of the engines of the accompanying Sirian ship.

The trip from Titan to Mimas took the better part of two days, and it was a hard time for Lucky, a bitter, suspenseful time.

He missed Bigman, who had been taken from him and placed on the Sirian ship. (The two on separate ships, Devoure had pointed out, were hostages for each other's good behavior.)

It was the Sirian Serviceman, Harrig Zayon, who made the second on the ship. There was a stiffness about him. He made no effort to repeat his original attempt to convert Lucky Starr to Sirian views, and Lucky could not resist taking the offensive in the matter. He asked if Devoure were an example, in Zayon's eyes, of the superior race of human beings that inhabited the Sirian planets.

Zayon said reluctantly, "Devoure has not had the benefit of Service training and Service discipline. He is emotional."

"Your colleague, Yonge, seems to consider it more than that. He makes no secret of his low opinion of Devoure."

"Yonge is—is a representative of an extreme view among the Servicemen. That scar on his arm was received during some internal troubles that attended the rise of the present director of the Central Body to power."

"Devoure's uncle?"

"Yes. The Service was on the side of the previous director, and Yonge followed orders with Serviceman's honor. As a result he was passed over for promotion under the new regime. Oh, they send him out here and appoint him to the committee which will represent Sirius at Vesta, but in actual fact he is under Devoure."

"The director's nephew."

"Yes. And Yonge resents it. Yonge cannot bring himself to understand that the Service is an organ of the state and does not question its policies or have anything to do with the question of which individual or group is to govern it. He is an excellent Serviceman, otherwise."

"But you have not answered the question as to whether you found Devoure a satisfactory representative of the Sirian elite."

Zayon said angrily, "What about your Earth? Have

you never had unsatisfactory rulers? Or even vicious ones?"

"Any number," admitted Lucky, "but we are a miscellaneous lot on Earth; we vary. No ruler can stay in power very long if he doesn't represent a compromise among us. Compromising rulers may not be dynamic, but neither are they tyrannical. On Sirius you have developed a sameness among yourselves, and a ruler can go to extremes along the lines of that sameness. For that reason autocracy and force in politics are not the exceptional interlude that they are on Earth, but are the rule with you."

Zayon sighed, but it was long hours before he spoke to Lucky again. It was not until Mimas was large in the visiplate and they were decelerating to land.

Zayon said, "Tell me, Councilman. I ask you on your honor. Is this a trick of some sort?"

Lucky's stomach tightened, but he said calmly, "What do you mean by a trick?"

"Is there really a Councilman on Mimas?"

"Yes, there is. What do you expect? That I have a force knot concealed on Mimas designed to blow us all to nothingness?"

"Perhaps something like that."

"And what would I gain? The destruction of one Sirian ship and a dozen Sirians?"

"You would gain your honor."

Lucky shrugged. "I have made a bargain. We have a Councilman down there. I will go and get him and there will be no resistance."

Zayon nodded. "Very well. I suppose you would not make a Sirian after all. You had better stay an Earthman."

Lucky smiled bitterly. That, then, was the source of Zayon's ill humor. His stiff Serviceman's sense of honor objected to Lucky's behavior even when he believed Sirius to be benefiting by it.

• • •

Back at Port Center, International City, Earth, Chief Councilman Hector Conway waited to leave for Vesta. He had not heard directly from Lucky since *The Shooting Starr* had moved into the shadow of Hidalgo.

The capsule brought in by Captain Bernold had been specific enough in its curt way and had been marked by Lucky's usual hard common sense. A call for a conference *had* been the only way out. The President had seen that at once, and though some members of the cabinet were bellicose about matters, they had been overruled.

Even Sirius (quite as Lucky had predicted) had adopted the notion eagerly. It was, obviously, exactly what the Sirian government wanted, a conference that was sure to fail, followed by a war on their own terms. To all outward appearances, they had all the cards.

It was that very fact that had made it so necessary to keep as much as possible from the public. If all details were put on the sub-ether without careful preparation, an indignant public might howl Earth's government irresistibly into war against all the Galaxy. The call for a conference would only make matters worse, since it would be interpreted as a cowardly sell-out to the Sirians.

And yet complete secrecy was impossible, too, and the press was angry and rebellious at being fed diluted government reports. Things were worsening daily.

The President would have to hold out somehow until the conference could take place. And yet, if the conference failed, the present situation would be honey-sweet compared to that which would come.

In the general indignation that would follow, there would be not only war, but the Council of Science would be completely discredited and destroyed, and the Terrestrial Federation would lose its most powerful weapon just when it needed it most.

It had been weeks since Hector Conway had slept without pills, and for the first time in his career he thought earnestly that he should be retiring.

He rose heavily and made his way forward to the ship now being readied for the launching. In a week he would be on Vesta for preliminary discussions with Doremo. That old pink-eyed statesman would be holding the balance of power. There was no doubting that. The very weakness of his small world was what made him powerful. He was the nearest thing to an honest and disinterested neutral in the Galaxy, and even the Sirians would listen to him.

If Conway could get his ear to begin with . . .

He was scarcely aware of the man approaching to stop him until there was a near collision.

"Eh? What is this?" demanded Conway in annoyance.

The man touched the brim of his hat. "Jan Dieppe of Trans-sub-etheric, Chief. I wonder if you would answer a few questions?"

"No, no. I'm ready to board ship."

"I realize that, sir. It's the very reason I'm stopping you. I won't get another chance. You're heading out for Vesta, of course."

"Yes, of course."

"To see about the outrage on Saturn."

"Well?"

"What do you expect the conference to do, Chief? Do you suppose Sirius will listen to resolutions and votes?"

"Yes, I think Sirius will."

"Do you think the votes will go against her?"

"I'm sure they will. Now may I pass?"

"I'm sorry, sir, but there's something very important just now that Earth's people must know about."

"Please. Don't tell me what you think they must know.

I assure you that the good of Earth's people is close to my heart."

"And is that why the Council of Science is willing to allow foreign governments to vote on whether or not the Terrestrial Federation's territory has been invaded? A question that should be reserved to our own decision alone?"

Conway could not fail to note the undercurrent of threat in the other's outwardly polite but persistent questioning. He looked over the reporter's shoulder and could see the Secretary of State talking to a group of other newsmen at a point closer to the ship.

He said, "What are you getting at?"

"The public is questioning the good faith of the Council, I'm afraid, Chief. And in that connection, Trans-subether has picked up a Sirian news broadcast that it has not yet made public. We need your comments on it."

"No comments. A Sirian news broadcast designed for home consumption is not worth comment."

"This report was quite circumstantial. For instance, where is Councilman David Starr, the legendary Lucky, himself? Where is he?"

"What?"

"Come on now, Chief. I know the Council's agents dislike publicity, but has Councilman Starr been sent to Saturn on a secret mission?"

"Now if that were so, young man, would you expect me to talk about it?"

"Yes, if Sirius were already talking about it. It's no secret to them. They say Lucky Starr invaded the Saturnian system and was captured. Is that true?"

Conway said stiffly, "I do not know the present whereabouts of Councilman David Starr."

"Does that mean he *might* be in the Saturnian system?"

"It means that I do not know his whereabouts."

The reporter's nose wrinkled. "All right. If you think it sounds better to have the Chief of the Council of Science deny that he knows the whereabouts of one of his important agents, that's your business. But the general mood of the public is increasingly anti-Council. There is considerable talk of the Council's inefficiency in letting Sirius get to Saturn in the first place and its interest in whitewashing the whole affair for the sake of their political skins."

"You are being insulting. Good day, sir."

"The Sirians are quite definite that Lucky Starr has been captured in the Saturnian system. Any comment on that?"

"No. Let me pass."

"The Sirians say that Lucky Starr will be at the conference."

"Oh?" For a moment Conway could not conceal a spasm of interest.

"That seems to get you, Chief. The only catch is that the Sirians say he'll be testifying for *them*."

Conway said with difficulty, "That remains to be seen."

"Do you admit he'll be at the conference?"

"I know nothing about that."

The reporter stepped aside. "All right, Chief. It's just that the Sirians say that Starr has already given them valuable information and that the Sirians will be able to convict us of aggression on the basis of it. I mean, what's the Council doing? Fighting with us or against us?"

Conway, feeling unbearably harried, muttered, "No comment," and started to pass by.

The reporter called after him. "Starr is your adopted son, isn't he, Chief?"

For a moment Conway turned back. Then, without a word, he hastened on to the ship.

What was there to say? What *could* he say except that ahead of him lay an interstellar conference more crucial for Earth than any meeting of any sort in its history? That this conference was weighted heavily on the side of Sirius. That chances were almost intolerably great that peace, the Council of Science, the Terrestrial Federation would all be destroyed.

And that only the thin shield of Lucky's efforts protected them.

Somehow, what depressed Conway more than anything else—more, even, than a lost war—was the thought that if the Sirian news report was true and if the conference nevertheless failed despite Lucky's original intentions, Lucky would go down in history as Earth's arch-traitor! And only a few would ever know better.

14

On Vesta

The Secretary of State, Lamont Finney, was a career politician who had served some fifteen years in the legislature and whose relations with the Council of Science had never been overwhelmingly friendly. He was aging now, not in the best of health, and inclined to be querulous. Officially he headed the Terrestrial delegation to Vesta. In actuality, though, Conway understood quite well that he, himself, as head of the Council, must be prepared to take full responsibility for failure—if there was failure.

Finney made that clear even before the ship, one of Earth's largest space liners, took off.

He said, "The press is almost uncontrollable. You're in a bad spot, Conway."

"All Earth is."

"*You*, Conway."

Conway said gloomily, "Well, I am under no illusions that if things go badly the Council can expect support from the government."

"I'm afraid not." The Secretary of State was strapping himself in with meticulous care against the rigors of take-off and making certain that his bottle of anti-spacesickness pills were handy. "Government support for you would only mean the downfall of the government, and there will be enough troubles with a war emergency. We can't afford political instability."

Conway thought: He has no confidence in the outcome of the conference at all. He expects the war.

He said, "Listen, Finney, if the worst does come to the worst, I will need voices on my side to help prevent Councilman Starr's reputation from——"

Finney lifted his gray head momentarily from the hydraulic cushion and stared at the other out of fading, troubled eyes. "Impossible. Your Councilman went into Saturn on his own, asked no permission, received no orders. He was willing to take the risks. If things turn out badly, he is done. What else can we do?"

"You *know* he——"

"I *don't* know," said the politician violently. "I know nothing officially. You've been in public life long enough to know that under certain conditions the people need a scapegoat and insist on one. Councilman Starr will be the scapegoat."

He leaned back again, closed his eyes, and Conway leaned back beside him. Elsewhere in the ship others were in their places, and the far thunder of the engines started up and rose in pitch as the ship raised itself slowly from the launching pad and lifted toward the sky.

The Shooting Starr hovered a thousand miles above Vesta, caught in its feeble gravity and circling it slowly with engines blocked. Grappled to it was a small lifeboat from the Sirian mother ship.

Serviceman Zayon had left The Shooting Starr to join the Sirian delegation on Vesta, and a robot remained behind in his place. In the lifeboat was Bigman, and with him Serviceman Yonge.

Lucky had been surprised when Yonge's face first stared out at him in the receiver. He said, "What are you doing out in space? Is Bigman with you?"

"He is. I'm his guard. I suppose you expected a robot."

"Yes, I did. Or won't they trust Bigman with a robot after last time?"

"No, this is just Devoure's little way of seeing to it that I don't attend the conference. It's a slap at the Service."

Lucky said, "Serviceman Zayon will be there."

"Zayon," Yonge sniffed. "He is an adequate man, but he's a follower. He can't realize that there's more to the Service than blindly obeying orders from above; that we owe it to Sirius to see to it that she is ruled according to the inflexible principles of honor that guide the Service itself."

Lucky said, "How is Bigman?"

"Well enough. He seems unhappy. It's strange that such an odd-looking person should have a sterner sense of duty and honor than a person like yourself."

Lucky clamped his lips together. There was little time left, and it worried him whenever either Serviceman began speculating about Lucky's loss of honor. From that it was a step to wondering if Lucky might by some chance have retained his honor, and then they might wonder what his intentions really were, and after that——

Yonge shrugged. "Well, I called only to make sure all was well. I am responsible for your welfare until, in good time, we get you down before the conference."

"Wait, Serviceman. You performed a service for me back on Titan——"

"I did nothing for you. I followed the dictates of duty."

"Nevertheless, you saved Bigman's life and mine, too, perhaps. It may so happen that when the conference is over you may consider your life in danger."

"*My* life?"

Lucky said carefully, "Once I have given evidence, Devoure may for one reason or another decide to get rid of you despite the risk of having Sirians find out about his fight with Bigman."

Yonge laughed bitterly. "He wasn't seen once on the trip out here. He was waiting in his cabin for his face to heal. I'm safe enough."

"Just the same, if you consider yourself in danger, approach Hector Conway, Chief Councilman of Science. My word on it that he will accept you as a political exile."

"I suppose you mean that kindly," said Yonge, "but I think that after the conference it will be Conway who will have to seek political asylum." Yonge broke connections.

And Lucky was left to look down at gleaming Vesta and to think sadly that, after all, the chances were heavily in favor of Yonge's being right.

Vesta was one of the largest of the asteroids. It was not the size of Ceres, which was more than five hundred miles in diameter and a giant among asteroids, but its 215-mile span put it into the second class, where only two other asteroids, Pallas and Juno, competed with it.

As seen from Earth, Vesta was the brightest of the asteroids because of the chance that had composed its outermost shell so largely of calcium carbonate rather than the darker silicates and metallic oxides that made up the other asteroids.

Scientists speculated on this odd divergence in chemical constitution (which had not been suspected until an actual landing was made upon it; before that the ancient astronomers had wondered if Vesta lay under a coat of ice or frozen carbon dioxide) but had come to no conclusion. And the feature writers took to calling it the "world of marble."

The "world of marble" had been converted into a naval base in the first days of the fight with the space pirates of the asteroid belt. The natural caverns under its surface had been enlarged and made airtight, and there had been room to store a fleet and house two years of provisions for it.

Now the naval base was more or less obsolete, but with small changes the caverns could be (and had been) made a most suitable meeting ground for delegates from all over the Galaxy.

Food and water supplies had been laid down, and luxuries which naval men had not required were added. As one passed the marble surface and entered the interior, there was little to distinguish Vesta from an Earthside hotel.

The Terrestrial delegation as the hosts (Vesta was Terrestrial territory; not even the Sirians could dispute that) assigned the quarters and saw to it that the delegates were comfortable. This meant the adjustment of the various quarters to the slight difference in gravity and atmospheric conditions to which the delegates might be accustomed. Those from Warren, for instance, had the quarters air-conditioned to a moderate chill to allow for the frigid climate of their home planet.

It was not an accident that greatest pains were taken for the delegation from Elam. It was a small world circling a red dwarf star. Its environment was such that one would not have supposed human beings could flourish there. Yet the very deficiencies were turned into account by the restless ingenuity of the human species.

There was not enough light to allow Earth-type plants to grow properly, so artificial lights were used and special breeds were cultivated, until Elamite grains and agricultural products generally were not merely adequate but of superior quality that could not be duplicated elsewhere in the Galaxy. Elamite prosperity rested on her agricultural exports in a way that other worlds more favored by nature could not match.

Probably as a result of the poor light of Elam's sun, there was no biological favoring of skin pigmentation. The inhabitants were fair-skinned almost to extremes.

The head of the Elamite delegation, for instance, was almost an albino. He was Agas Doremo, for more than thirty years the recognized leader of the neutralist forces in the Galaxy. In every question that arose between Earth and Sirius (which, of course, represented the extreme anti-Terrestrial forces of the Galaxy) he held the balance even.

Conway counted on him to do so in this case too. He entered the quarters assigned to the Elamite with an air of friendship. He took care to keep from being over-effusive and shook hands warmly. He blinked in the low-pitched, red-tinged light and accepted a glass of native Elamite brew.

Doremo said, "Your hair has grown white since last I saw you, Conway—as white as mine."

"It has been many years since we last met, Doremo."

"Then it hasn't grown white just these last few months?"

Conway smiled ruefully. "It would have, I think, if it had been dark to begin with."

Doremo nodded and sipped his drink. He said, "Earth has let itself be placed in a most uncomfortable position."

"So it has, and yet by all the rules of logic, Earth is in the right."

"Yes?" Doremo was noncommittal.

"I don't know how much thought you've given this matter——"

"Considerable."

"Or how willing you are to discuss the matter in advance——"

"Why not? The Sirians have been at me."

"Ah. Already?"

"I stopped off at Titan on the way in." Doremo shook his head. "They've got a beautiful base there, as I could see once they supplied me with dark glasses—it's the horrible blue light of Sirius that spoils things, of course. You have to give them credit, Conway; they do things with a splash."

"Have you decided that they have a right to colonize Saturn?"

Doremo said, "My dear Conway, I have decided only that I want peace. A war will do no one any good. The situation, however, is this: The Sirians are in the Saturnian system. How can they be forced out of it without war?"

"There is one way," said Conway. "If the other outer worlds were to make it clear that they considered Sirius to be an invader, Sirius could not face the enmity of all the Galaxy."

"Ah, but how are the outer worlds to be persuaded to vote against Sirius?" Doremo said. "Most of them, if you'll forgive me, have a traditional suspicion of Earth, and they will tell themselves that the Saturnian system was, after all, uninhabited."

"But it has been a settled assumption since Earth first granted independence to the outer worlds, as result of the Hegellian Doctrine, that no smaller unit than a stellar system is to be considered capable of independence. An unoccupied planetary system means nothing unless the stellar system of which it is a part is unoccupied as a whole."

"I agree with you. I admit that this has been the assumption. However, the assumption has never been put to the test. Now it will be."

"Do you think," said Conway softly, "that it would be wise to destroy the assumption, to accept a new principle that would allow any stranger to enter a system and colonize such unpopulated planets or planetoids as he may come across?"

"No," said Doremo emphatically, "I do *not* think so. I think it to the best interests of all of us that stellar systems continue to be considered as indivisible, but——"

"But?"

"There will be passions aroused at this conference that will make it difficult for delegates to approach matters logically. If I may presume to advise Earth——"

"Go ahead. This is unofficial and off the record."

"I would say, count on no support at this conference. Allow Sirius to remain on Saturn for the present. She will overplay her hand eventually and then you can call a second conference with higher hopes."

Conway shook his head. "Impossible. If we fail here, there will be passions aroused on our side; they are aroused already."

Doremo shrugged. "Passions everywhere. I am very pessimistic about this."

Conway said persuasively, "But if you yourself believe that Sirius ought not to be on Saturn, could you not make an effort to persuade others of this? You are a person of influence who commands the respect of the Galaxy. I don't ask you to do anything but stick by your own belief. It may make all the difference between war and peace."

Doremo put his glass aside and dabbed at his lip with a napkin. "It is what I would very much like to do, Con-

way, but I don't even dare to try at this conference. Sirius
has matters so entirely its own way that it might be dangerous for Elam to stand against them. We are a small
world. . . . After all, Conway, if you called this conference in order to reach a peaceful solution, why did you
simultaneously send war vessels into the Saturnian system?"

"Is that what the Sirians told you, Doremo?"

"Yes. They showed me some of the evidence they had.
I was even shown a captured Earth ship in flight to Vesta
under the magnetic grapple of a Sirian vessel. I was told
that no less a person than Lucky Starr, of whom even we
on Elam have heard somewhat, was on board. I understand Starr is circling off Vesta now, waiting to testify."

Slowly Conway nodded.

Doremo said, "Now if Starr admits to warlike actions
against the Sirians—and he will, otherwise it is inconceiv-
able the Sirians will allow him to testify—then it will be
all the conference needs. No arguments will stand against
it. Starr, I believe, is an adopted son of yours."

"In a way, yes," muttered Conway.

"That makes it worse, you see. And if you say that
he acted without Earth's sanction, as I suppose you
must——"

"It's true that he did," said Conway, "but I am not
prepared to say what we will claim."

"If you disown him, no one will believe you. Your own
son, you see. The outer-world delegates will set up the cry
of 'perfidious Terrestria,' of Earth's supposed hypocrisy.
Sirius will make the most of it, and I'll be able to do
nothing. I will not even be able to cast my personal vote
in favor of Earth. . . . Earth had better give in now."

Conway shook his head. "Earth cannot."

"Then," said Doremo with infinite sadness, "it will
mean war, with all of us against Earth, Conway."

15

The Conference

Conway had finished his drink. Now he rose to go, shaking hands with a look of settled melancholy on his face.

He said, almost as an afterthought, "But you know, we haven't heard Lucky's testimony yet. If the effects aren't as bad as you think, if his testimony should even prove harmless, would you work then on behalf of peace?"

Doremo shrugged. "You are grasping at straws. Yes, yes, in the unlikely case that the conference is not stampeded past recall by your foster son's words, I will do my bit. As I told you, I am really on your side."

"I thank you, sir." They shook hands again.

Doremo stared after the departing Chief Councilman with a sad little shake of his head. Outside the door, however, Conway paused to catch his breath. It was really quite as much as he had expected. Now if only the Sirians *would* present Lucky.

The conference opened on the stiff and formal note to be expected. Everyone was painfully correct, and when Earth's delegation entered to take their posts in the front and at the extreme right of the hall, all the delegates already seated, even the Sirians in the front and extreme left, rose.

When the Secretary of State, representing the host power, rose to make a welcoming speech, he spoke in generalities about peace and the door it opened to the continuing expansion of mankind through the Galaxy, of the common ancestry and brotherhood of all men, of the grievous disaster war would be. He carefully made no mention of the specific points of issue, did not refer to Sirius by name, and, above all, made no threats.

He was graciously applauded. Then the conference voted Agas Doremo into the chair to preside (he was the only man on whom both sides could agree), and the chief business of the conference began.

The conference was not open to the public, but there were special booths for reporters from the various worlds represented. They were not to interview individual delegates but were allowed to listen and send out uncensored reports.

The proceedings, as was customary in such interstellar gatherings, were carried on in Interlingua, the language amalgam that served throughout the Galaxy.

After a short speech by Doremo extolling the virtues of compromise and begging no one to be so stubborn as to risk war where a slight yielding might insure peace, he recognized Earth's Secretary of State once more.

This time the Secretary was a partisan, presenting his side of the dispute forcefully and well.

There was, however, no mistaking the hostile attitude of the other delegates. It hung like a fog over the assembly hall.

Conway sat next to the orating Secretary, with his chin digging into his chest. Ordinarily it would be a mistake for Earth to present its major speech at the very start. It would be a case of shooting off the best ammunition before the nature of the target was known. It would give Sirius the opportunity for a crushing rebuttal.

But in this case, however, this was exactly what Conway wanted.

He whipped out a handkerchief, passed it over his forehead, then put it hastily back and hoped he had not been noticed. He did not want to seem worried.

Sirius reserved its rebuttal and, undoubtedly by arrangement, representatives of three of the outer worlds, three that were notoriously under Sirian influence, rose to speak briefly. Each avoided the direct problem but commented forcefully on the aggressive intentions of Earth and on its ambitions to reimpose a galactic government under its own rule. They set the stage for the eventual Sirian display and, having done so, there was a lunch recess.

Finally, six hours after the conference had been called to order, Sten Devoure of Sirius was recognized and rose slowly to his feet. He stepped forward with quiet deliberation to the rostrum and stood there, looking down upon the delegates with an expression of proud confidence on his olive-skinned face. (There was no sign of his misadventure with Bigman.)

There was a stir among the delegates that quieted only after a number of minutes during which Devoure made no effort to begin speaking.

Conway was certain that every delegate knew that Lucky Starr would be testifying soon. They were waiting for this complete humiliation of Earth with excitement and anticipation.

Devoure began his speech at last, very quietly. His introduction was historical. Going back to the days when Sirius was a Terrestrial colony, he rehearsed once again the grievances of that day. He brushed over the Hegellian

Doctrine, which had established the independence of Sirius as well as that of the other colonies, as insincere, and one by one cited the supposed efforts of Earth to reestablish domination.

Coming down to the present, he said, "We are now accused of having colonized an unoccupied world. We plead guilty to that. We are accused of having taken an empty world and made it a beautiful habitation for human beings. We plead guilty to that. We are accused of extending the range of the human race to a world suitable for it that had been neglected by others. We plead guilty to that.

"We have not been accused of offering violence to anyone in the process. We have not been accused of making war, of killing and wounding, in the course of our occupation. We are accused of no crime at all. Instead, it is merely stated that not quite a billion miles away from the world we now so peacefully occupy there is another occupied world named Earth.

"We are not aware that this has anything to do with our world, Saturn. We offer no violence to Earth, and they accuse us of none. We ask only the privilege of being left to ourselves, and in return for that we are glad to offer to leave them to themselves.

"They say Saturn is theirs. Why? Have they occupied its satellites at any time? No. Have they shown interest in it? No. For the thousands of years during which it was theirs for the taking, did they want it? No. It was only after we landed on it that they suddenly discovered their interest in it.

"They say Saturn circles about the same Sun that Earth does. We admit that, but we also point out that the fact is irrelevant. An empty world is an empty world, regardless of the particular route it travels through space. We colonized it first and it is ours.

"Now I have said that Sirius occupied the Saturnian system without force of any kind and without the threat of force; that we are actuated in all we do by a desire for peace. We do not speak much of peace, as Earth does, but we at least practice it. When Earth called for a conference, we accepted at once, for the sake of peace, even though there is no shadow of any sort on our title to the Saturnian system.

"But what of Earth? How does it back *its* views? They are very fluent in their talks on peace, but their actions match their words very poorly. They called for peace and practiced war. They demanded a conference and at the same time outfitted a war expedition. In short, while Sirius risked its interests for the sake of peace, Earth, in return, made unprovoked war upon us. I can prove this from the mouth of a member of Earth's own Council of Science."

He raised his hand as he spoke the last sentence, his first gesture of any sort, and pointed dramatically to a doorway upon which a spot of light had been allowed to fall. Lucky Starr was standing there, tall and defiantly straight. A robot flanked him on either side.

Lucky, on being brought down to Vesta, finally saw Bigman again. The little Martian ran to him, while Yonge looked on with dour amusement from a distance.

"Lucky," pleaded Bigman. "Sands of Mars, Lucky, don't go through with it. They can't make you say a word if you don't want to, and it doesn't really matter what happens to me."

Slowly Lucky shook his head. "Wait, Bigman. Wait one more day."

Yonge came up and took Bigman by the elbow. "Sorry, Starr, but we'll need him till you're through. Devoure has a great sense of hostage, and at this point I rather think he's right. You're going to have to face your own people, and dishonor will be difficult."

Lucky nerved himself for just that when he finally stood in the doorway and felt the eyes upon him, the silence, the caught breaths. In the spotlight himself, Lucky saw the delegates to the conference as nothing but a giant black mass. It was only after the robots led him into the witness box that faces swam out of the crowd at him, and he could see Hector Conway in the front row.

For a moment Conway smiled at him with weary affection, but Lucky dared not smile back. This was the crisis and he must do nothing that, even at this late moment, might warn the Sirians.

Devoure stared at the Earthman hungrily, savoring his coming triumph. He said, "Gentlemen, I wish temporarily to convert this conference into something approaching a court of law. I have a witness here whom I wish all the delegates to hear. I will rest my case on what he says—he, an Earthman and an important agent of the Council of Science."

He then said to Lucky with sudden sharpness, "Your name, citizenship, and position, please."

Lucky said, "I am David Starr, native of Earth, and member of the Council of Science."

"Have you been subjected to drugs, to psychic probing, or to mental violence of any sort to induce you to testify here?"

"No, sir."

"You speak voluntarily, then, and will tell the truth?"

"I speak voluntarily and will tell the truth."

Devoure turned to the delegates. "It may occur to some of you that Councilman Starr has indeed been handled mentally without his knowledge or that he may be denying mental harm as the very result of that mental harm. If so, he may be examined by any member of this conference with medical qualification—I know there are a number of such—if anyone demands such examination."

No one made the demand, and Devoure went on, addressing Lucky, "When did you first become aware of the Sirian base within the Saturnian system?"

Curtly, unemotionally, eyes staring stonily forward, Lucky told of the first entry into the Saturnian system and the warning to leave.

Conway nodded slightly at Lucky's complete omission of the capsule or of Agent X's spying activities. Agent X might have been merely a Terrestrial criminal. Obviously Sirius wanted no mention of its own spying at this time and, as obviously, Lucky was satisfied to go along with them in this.

"And did you leave after being warned?"

"I did, sir."

"Permanently?"

"No, sir."

"What did you do next?"

Lucky described the ruse with Hidalgo, the approach to Saturn's south pole, the flight through the gap in the rings to Mimas.

Devoure interrupted, "Did we at any time offer violence to your ship?"

"No, sir."

Devoure turned to the delegates again. "There is no need to rely only upon the word of the Councilman. I have here telephotos of the pursuit of the Councilman's ship to Mimas."

While Lucky remained in the spotlight the rest of the chamber was darkened, and in the three-dimensional imagery the delegates watched scenes of *The Shooting Starr* speeding toward the rings and disappearing into a gap which, at the angle of photography, could not be seen.

It was next shown racing headlong into Mimas and disappearing in a flash of ruddy light and vapor.

At this time Devoure must have felt the growth of a furtive admiration for the daring of the Earthman, for he said with a touch of annoyed haste, "Our inability to overtake the Councilman was the result of his ship's equipment with Agrav motors. Maneuvers in the neighborhood of Saturn were more difficult for us than for him. For that reason we ourselves had not previously approached Mimas and were not psychologically ready for his doing so."

If Conway had dared he would have shouted aloud at that. The fool! Devoure would pay for that moment of jealousy. Of course by mentioning Agrav he was trying to stir up the outer worlds' fears of Earth's scientific advances, and that might be a mistake too. The fears might grow too strong.

Devoure said to Lucky, "Now then, what happened once you left Mimas?"

Lucky described his capture, and Devoure, having hinted at Sirius's possession of advanced mass-detection devices, said, "And then, once on Titan, did you give us further information concerning your activities on Mimas?"

"Yes, sir. I told you that another Councilman was still on Mimas, and then I accompanied you back to Mimas."

This the delegates had apparently not known. There was a furor, which Devoure shouted down. He cried, "I have a complete telephoto of the removal of the Councilman from Mimas, where he was sent to establish a secret war base against us at the very time that Earth called this conference, allegedly for peace."

Again the darkening and again the three-dimensional image. In full detail the conference watched the landing on Mimas, saw the surface melted down, watched Lucky disappear into the tunnel formed and Councilman Ben Wessilewsky brought up and on board ship. The last scenes were those taken within Wess's temporary quarters under the surface of Mimas.

"A fully equipped base, as you see," said Devoure. Then, turning to Lucky, he said, "May your actions throughout all this be considered to have the official approval of Earth?"

It was a leading question and there was no doubt as to the answer that was desired and expected, but here Lucky hesitated, while the audience waited breathlessly and a frown gathered on Devoure's face.

Finally Lucky said, "I will tell the precise truth. I did not receive direct permission to re-enter Saturn a second time, but I know that in everything I did I would have met with the full approval of the Council of Science."

And at that admission there was wild commotion among the reporters and a hubbub on the floor. The conference delegates were rising in their seats, and cries of "Vote! Vote!" could be made out.

To all appearances the conference had ended and Earth had lost.

16

Biter Bit

Agas Doremo was on his feet, banging the traditional gavel for silence with complete ineffectuality. Conway plowed forward through a host of threatening gestures and catcalls and pulled the circuit breaker, thus sounding the old pirate warning. A shrill rising-falling rasp of sound squealed above the disorder and beat the delegates into surprised silence.

Conway shut it off, and in the sudden quiet Doremo said quickly, "I have agreed to recognize Chief Councilman Hector Conway of the Terrestrial Federation that he might cross-examine Councilman Starr."

There were shouts of "No, no," but Doremo continued obdurately, "I ask the conference to play fair in this respect. The Chief Councilman assures me his cross-examination will be brief."

Amid rustling and a tide of whispering, Conway approached Lucky.

He smiled but spoke with an air of formality, saying, "Councilman Starr, Mr. Devoure did not question you as to your intentions in all this. Tell me, why did you enter the Saturnian system?"

"In order to colonize Mimas, Chief."

"Did you feel you had the right to do so?"

"It was an empty world, Chief."

Conway turned so as to face a suddenly puzzled and quiet group of delegates. "Would you repeat that, Councilman Starr?"

"I wished to establish human beings on Mimas, an empty world that belongs to the Terrestrial Federation, Chief."

Devoure was on his feet, calling out furiously, "Mimas is part of the Saturnian system."

"Exactly," said Lucky, "as Saturn is part of Earth's Solar System. But by *your* interpretation Mimas is merely an empty world. A while ago you admitted that Sirian ships had never approached Mimas before my ship landed on it."

Conway smiled. Lucky had caught that error on Devoure's part too.

Conway said, "Councilman Starr was not here, Mr. Devoure, when you made your introductory speech. Let me quote a passage from it, word for word: 'An empty world is an empty world, regardless of the particular route it travels through space. We colonized it first and it is ours.'"

The Chief Councilman turned toward the delegates and said with great deliberation, "If the viewpoint of the Terrestrial Federation is correct, then Mimas is Earth's, because it circles a planet that circles our Sun. If the viewpoint of Sirius is correct, then Mimas is still Earth's, because it was empty and we colonized it first. By Sirius's own line of reasoning, the fact that another satellite of Saturn was colonized by Sirius had nothing to do with the case.

"In either event, by invading a world belonging to the Terrestrial Federation and removing therefrom our colonist, Sirius has committed an act of war and has shown its true hypocrisy, since it refused to allow others the rights it claimed for itself."

And now again there was a confused milling about, and it was Doremo who spoke next. "Gentlemen, I have something to say. The facts, as stated by Councilmen Starr and Conway, are irrefutable. This demonstrates the complete anarchy into which the Galaxy would be thrown if the Sirian view were to prevail. Every uninhabited rock would be a source of contention, every asteroid a threat to peace. The Sirians, by their own action, have shown themselves insincere——"

It was a complete and sudden change-about.

Had time been allowed, Sirius might yet have rallied its forces, but Doremo, an experienced and skilled parliamentarian, maneuvered the conference into a vote while the pro-Sirians were still completely demoralized and before they had a chance to consider whether they dared go against the plain facts as suddenly revealed.

Three worlds voted on the side of Sirius. They were Penthesileia, Duvarn, and Mullen, all small and all known to be under Sirius's political influence. The rest of the Council, better than fifty votes, was on the side of Earth. Sirius was ordered to release the Earthmen it had taken prisoner. It was ordered to dismantle its base and leave the Solar System within a month.

The orders could not be enforced except by war, of course, but Earth was ready for war and Sirius would have to face it now without the help of the outer worlds. There wasn't a man on Vesta who expected her to fight under those conditions.

Devoure, panting and his face contorted, saw Lucky once more. "It was a foul trick," he said, "It was a device to force us into——"

"You forced *me*," said Lucky quietly, "by the threat to Bigman's life. Do you remember? Or would you like the details of that published?"

"We still have your monkey friend," began Devoure malignantly, "and conference vote or not——"

Chief Councilman Conway, also present, smiled. "If you're referring to Bigman, Mr. Devoure, you don't have him. He is in our hands, together with a Serviceman named Yonge, who told me that Councilman Starr had assured him safe-conduct in case of need. He apparently feels that in your present mood it would be unsafe for himself to accompany you back to Titan. May I suggest that you consider whether it might be unsafe for you to go back to Sirius? If you wish to apply for asylum——"

But Devoure, speechless, turned his back and left.

Doremo was all a-grin as he bade farewell to Conway and Lucky.

"You'll be glad to see Earth again, I dare say, young man."

Lucky nodded his agreement. "I'm going home by liner within the hour, sir, with the poor old *Shooter* being towed along behind, and frankly, there's nothing that could please me more just now."

"Good! And congratulations on a magnificent piece of work. When Chief Conway asked me to allow him time for cross-examination at the beginning of the session, I agreed, but thought he must be mad. When you were done testifying and he signaled for recognition, I was *sure* he was mad. But obviously all this was planned in advance."

Conway said, "Lucky had sent me a message outlining what he hoped to do. Of course it wasn't till the last hour or two that we were sure it had worked out."

"I think you had faith in the Councilman," said

Doremo. "Why, in your first conversation with me, you asked if I would come out on your side if Lucky's evidence failed of effect. I didn't see what you could mean then, of course, but I understood when the time came."

"I thank you for throwing your weight to our side."

"I threw it on the side of what had obviously been demonstrated to be justice. . . . You're a subtle opponent, young man," he said to Lucky.

Lucky smiled. "I merely counted on Sirius's lack of sincerity. If they had really believed in what they claimed was their point of view, my Councilman colleague would have been left on Mimas and all we would have had for our pains was a small satellite of ice and a difficult war to fight."

"Quite. Well, no doubt there'll be second thoughts when the delegates get back home, and some will become angry with Earth and with me and even with themselves, I suppose, for having let themselves be stampeded. In cold blood, though, they'll realize that they have established a principle here, the indivisibility of stellar systems, and I think they'll also realize that the good of this principle will outweigh any hurt to their pride or their prejudices. I really think this conference will be looked back on by historians as something important and as something that contributed a great deal to the peace and welfare of the Galaxy. I'm quite pleased."

And he shook hands with both, most vigorously.

Lucky and Bigman were together again, and though the ship was large and the passenger complement numerous, they kept to themselves. Mars was behind them (Bigman spending the better part of an hour observing it with great satisfaction) and Earth not very far ahead.

Bigman finally managed to voice his embarrassment. "Space, Lucky," he said, "I never saw what you were

doing, not once. I thought—— Well, I don't want to say
what I thought. Only, Sands of Mars, I wish you had
warned me."

"Bigman, I couldn't. That was the one thing I couldn't
do. Don't you see? I had to maneuver the Sirians into
hijacking Wess off Mimas without letting them see the
implications. I couldn't show them I *wanted* them to do it
or they'd have seen the trap at once. I had to work it so
that it would seem I was being forced into it bitterly
against my will. At the start, I assure you, I didn't know
exactly how I was going to do it, but I did know one thing
—if *you* knew about the plan, Bigman, you'd have given
the show away."

Bigman was outraged. "I'd give it away? Why, you
Earthslug, a blaster couldn't have forced it out of me."

"I know. No torture could have forced it out of you,
Bigman. You'd just give it away, free. You're a miserable
actor and you know it. Once you got mad, it would come
spilling out, one way or another. That's why I half wanted
you to stay on Mimas, remember? I knew I couldn't tell
you the planned course of action and I knew you'd misun-
derstand what I was doing and be miserable about it. As it
was, though, you turned out a godsend."

"I did? For beating up that cobber?"

"Indirectly, yes. It gave me the opportunity to make it
look as though I were sincerely swapping Wess's freedom
for your life. It took less acting to do that than to give
Wess away under any conditions I could have dreamed up
in your absence. In fact, as it was, I didn't have to act at
all. It was a good swap."

"Aw, Lucky."

"Aw, yourself. Besides, you were so heartbroken about
it that they never suspected a trick. Anyone watching you
would have been convinced I was really betraying Earth."

"Sands of Mars, Lucky," said Bigman, stricken, "I

should have known you wouldn't do anything like that. I was a nitwit."

"I'm glad you were," said Lucky fervently, and he ruffled the little fellow's hair affectionately.

When Conway and Wess joined them at dinner, Wess said, "This isn't going to be the kind of home-coming that fellow Devoure can expect. Ship's sub-ether is full of the stuff they're printing on Earth about us; about you especially, of course."

Lucky frowned. "That's nothing to be thankful about. It just makes our job harder in the future. Publicity! Stop and think what they would be saying if the Sirians had been just one inch smarter and hadn't fallen for the bait or had pulled me out of the conference at the last minute."

Conway shuddered visibly. "I'd rather not. But whatever it would be, that's what Devoure is getting."

Lucky said, "I guess he'll survive. His uncle will pull him through."

"Anyway," said Bigman, "we're through with him."

"Are we?" said Lucky somberly. "I wonder."

And they ate in silence for a few moments.

Conway, in an obvious attempt to alter the suddenly darkened atmosphere, said, "Of course, in a sense the Sirians could not afford to leave Wess on Mimas, so we didn't really give them a fair chance. After all, they were looking for the capsule in the rings, and for all they know, Wess, only thirty thousand miles outside the rings, might——"

Bigman dropped his fork, and his eyes were like saucers. *"Blasting rockets!"*

"What's the matter, Bigman?" asked Wess kindly. "Did you accidentally think of something and sprain your brain?"

"Shut up, leather-head," said Bigman. "Listen, Lucky,

in all this mess we forgot about Agent X's capsule. It's still out there in the rings unless the Sirians have found it already; and if they haven't, they still have a couple of weeks to do it in."

Conway said at once, "I've thought of that, Bigman. But frankly, I consider it lost for good. You can't find anything in the rings."

"But, Chief, hasn't Lucky told you about the special X-ray mass detectors they have and——"

By then, though, all were staring at Lucky. He had a queer look on his face, as though he couldn't make up his mind whether to laugh or to swear. "Great Galaxy," he cried. "I forgot about it completely."

"The capsule?" said Bigman. "You forgot it?"

"Yes. I forgot I had it. Here it is." And Lucky brought something metallic and about an inch in diameter out of his pocket and put it on the table.

Bigman's nimble fingers were on it first, turning it over and over, then the others snatched at it too, and took their turns.

Bigman said, "Is that the capsule? Are you sure?"

"I'm reasonably sure. We'll open it, of course, and make certain."

"But when, how, where——" They were all about him, demanding.

He fended them off. "I'm sorry. I really am. . . . Look, do you remember the few words we picked up from Agent X just before his ship blew up? Remember the syllables 'normal orb,' which we decided meant 'normal orbit'? Well, the Sirians made the natural assumption that 'normal' meant 'usual,' that the capsule would be put into the kind of orbit usual for ring particles, and looked in the rings for it.

"However, 'normal' also means perpendicular. The rings of Saturn move directly west to east, so the capsule in a normal orbit to the rings would move directly north to south, or south to north. This made sense, because then the capsule would not be lost in the rings.

"Now any orbit about Saturn moving directly north and south must pass over the north and south poles, no matter how else that orbit varies. We approached Saturn's south pole, and I watched the mass detector for anything that seemed to be in the proper type of orbit. In polar space there were hardly any particles, so I felt I ought to be able to spot it if it were there. I didn't like to say anything about it, though, because the chances were small, I thought, and I hated to rouse false hopes.

"But something registered on the mass detectors, and I took the chance. I matched velocities and then left the ship. As you guessed later, Bigman, I seized the opportunity to gimmick the Agrav attachment at that time in preparation for the later surrender, but I also picked up the capsule.

"When we landed in Mimas I left it among the air-conditioning coils in Wess's quarters. Then, when we came back to get him and surrender him to Devoure, I picked up the capsule and put it in my pocket. I was routinely searched for weapons when I embarked on the ship, I recall, but the robot searcher did not interpret an inch sphere as a weapon. . . . There are serious drawbacks to using robots. Anyway, that's the whole story."

"But why didn't you tell us?" howled Bigman.

Lucky looked confused. "I meant to. Honestly. But after I first picked up the capsule and got back to the ship, we had already been spotted by the Sirians, remember, and it was a question of getting away. After that, in fact, if you'll think back, there was never one moment when something wasn't popping. I just—somehow—never got around to remembering to tell anyone."

"What a brain," said Bigman contemptuously. "No wonder you don't like to go anywhere without me."

Conway laughed and slapped the small Martian on the back. "That's it Bigman, take care of the big lug and make sure he knows which way is up."

"Once," said Wess, "you get someone to tell *you* which way is up, of course."

And the ship swirled down through Earth's atmosphere toward landing.

ABOUT THE AUTHOR

Isaac Asimov was America's most prolific author, with more than 440 published books to his credit. His Foundation Trilogy was given a special Hugo Award as Best All-Time Science Fiction Series. *Foundation's Edge* won a Hugo Award as Best Science Fiction Novel in 1982, and Dr. Asimov was presented the Science Fiction Writers of America Grand Master Award in 1988. Dr. Asimov died in 1992.

ROBOTS FREE

![ROBOTS FROM ASIMOV'S]

By subscribing to Isaac **Asimov's Science Fiction Magazine** you'll receive a FREE copy of **Robots From Asimov's** with your paid subscription. Asimov's contains Nebula-award-winning stories, editorials by Isaac Asimov himself, and much more. Each issue is filled with provocative stories on the cutting edge of today's science fiction and fantasy... from worlds of myth to futures of imagination.

6 DECADES FREE

By subscribing to **Analog Science Fiction & Fact** you'll receive a **FREE** copy of **6 Decades—The Best of Analog** with your paid subscription. Analog readers have enjoyed over 60 years of penetrating, absorbing science fiction and science fact. From the earliest and continuing visions of cybernetics to our ultimate growth in space—Analog is the forum of the future. Let the pages of Analog expand the realm of your imagination...as today's fiction turns to tomorrow's fact.